Curse of the Savoy

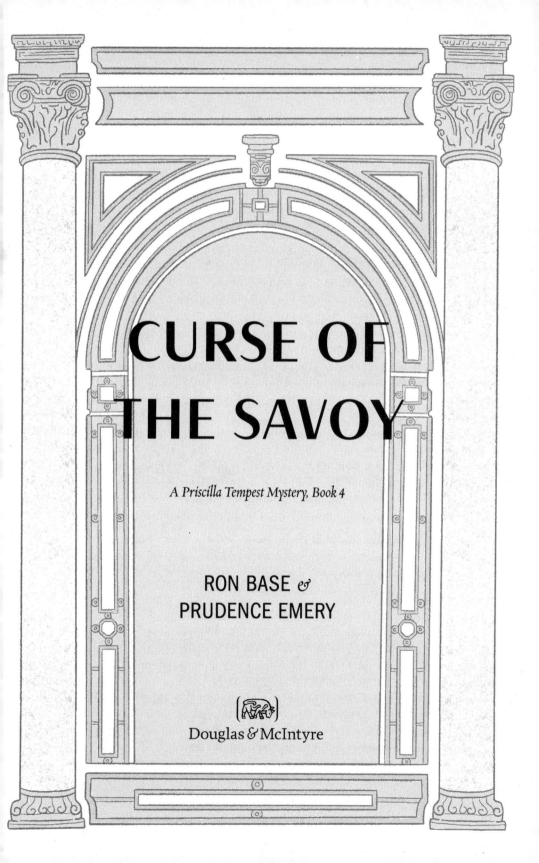

CURSE OF THE SAVOY

A Priscilla Tempest Mystery, Book 4

RON BASE *&* PRUDENCE EMERY

Douglas & McIntyre

1 2 3 4 5 — 29 28 27 26 25

Douglas and McIntyre (2013) Ltd.
P.O. Box 219, Madeira Park, BC, V0N 2H0
www.douglas-mcintyre.com

Edited by Pam Robertson
Cover © Maëlys Chay / Pekelo
Typeset by Ruth Ormiston
Printed and bound in Canada
Printed on 100% recycled paper

 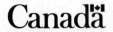

Canada Council
for the Arts

Conseil des Arts
du Canada

Canadä

BRITISH COLUMBIA
ARTS COUNCIL

BRITISH
COLUMBIA

Supported by the Province of British Columbia

Douglas and McIntyre acknowledges the support of the Canada Council for the Arts, the
Government of Canada, and the Province of British Columbia through the BC Arts Council.

Library and Archives Canada Cataloguing in Publication

Title: Curse of the Savoy / Ron Base & Prudence Emery.
Names: Base, Ron, author. | Emery, Prudence, 1936- author.
Series: Base, Ron. Priscilla Tempest mystery ; bk. 4.
Description: Series statement: A Priscilla Tempest mystery ; book 4
Identifiers: Canadiana (print) 20240501713 | Canadiana (ebook) 20240508165
ISBN 9781771624381 (softcover) | ISBN 9781771624398 (EPUB)
Subjects: LCGFT: Detective and mystery fiction. | LCGFT: Novels.
Classification: LCC PS8553.A784 C87 2025 | DDC C813/.54—dc23

For Pru

"I long ago came to the conclusion that nothing has ever definitely been proved about anything."

—*Madame Arcati, Noël Coward's* Blithe Spirit

Contents

CHAPTER ONE

The Dinner Party

The notorious dinner that triggered the curse was held in the Savoy Hotel's Pinafore Room. It was hosted by the legendary American filmmaker and actor Orson Welles, who was adamant that his guests enjoy the very best that the Savoy could offer.

A shame, then, that the curse overwhelmed everything. Or did it? There followed blackmail and murder, certainly, as well as a ruthless effort to cover up foul deeds. But was that because of the curse? Or was the series of terrible events that subsequently unfolded, and which nearly got Miss Priscilla Tempest killed, mere coincidence? In London's highest levels of society, among the very few in possession of at least part of the story, there was considerable debate.

And then there were the whispers about how the Queen of England became involved.

But we begin with that infamous dinner…

"In pursuit of the excellence Mr. Welles demands from us," noted Paolo Contarini, the Savoy's banquet manager, when he spoke with his usual great enthusiasm to the waitstaff minutes before the dinner, "we have all worked tirelessly to provide the sort of memorable occasion for which the Savoy is so famous. Everything is to perfection. The rhododendrons and azaleas have been flown in from the Riviera. The pink tablecloth is of the finest Irish linen, excellent for showing off the china. The Chablis Grand Cru comes directly from our cavernous wine cellars."

Contarini concluded with a despairing groan: "And still this man is not happy!"

The fourteen guests invited to dine that evening were impressive for their various levels of celebrity even within the hard-to-impress confines of the Savoy. In addition to Welles, they included the film director Alfred Hitchcock; his friend, the actor Cary Grant; the notorious London playgirl Miss Christine Keeler, whose affairs had helped bring down a government; and Lady Anne Harley, the grand old dowager who, when she wasn't resting at her Bermuda estate, was pretty much a permanent resident at the Savoy.

Jack Cogan, thirty-three, squat and muscular, was a man who worked out five days a week, blessed or cursed, depending on your point of view, with darkly cruel features that admiring women were said to find irresistible. Contrarily, those same features left men with the impression they were dealing with a ruthless pirate—which they were. Cogan, recently appointed to head his father's newspaper empire, was accompanied by his wife, Tiffany, the popular talk-show host he had married at the same time as he acquired control of his father's business. Already London's publishing pirate had earned himself the nickname "the Jackal."

Also present was the Lloyds banker Nick Quinn, short and rotund, with his equally short and rotund wife, Katherine; as well as the American novelist Norman Mailer, who had appeared to already be a sheet or two to the wind by the time he arrived. Mailer had written an American bestseller, but he was more famous—or infamous—for having stabbed his wife using a pen-knife. His wife refused to press charges.

Unshaven, his greying hair a mass of unruly curls, his shirt untucked, Mailer walked into the Pinafore Room and stared blearily at the nautical decor lifted directly from Gilbert and

Sullivan's fourth operetta. "What the hell is this?" he demanded of no one in particular.

"Good taste, Savoy style, old boy," said Welles, shaking Mailer's hand. "In case you missed the production of HMS *Pinafore*, here before you is the set reproduced—with a nice view of the Thames added."

"Jesus," breathed Mailer. "What am I doing here?"

"What are any of us doing here?" echoed Jack Cogan.

"Unless I miss my guess, I'm here because Mr. Welles is looking for money," said the banker Quinn.

"About the only reason we are anywhere," put in Katherine Quinn.

"My husband tells me you tried to kill your wife," Tiffany Cogan said to an attentive Mailer, obviously drawn to her long blond hair and short dress.

"I didn't try to kill her. I simply stabbed her," he replied mildly.

"Do you write about war?" Tiffany asked.

"How did you know?" Mailer looked impressed.

"That's all men write about," Tiffany sniffed.

"War and sex, baby," Mailer said. "After that, what is there?"

"Wives with knife wounds, apparently," observed Tiffany.

"A good meal," added the renowned British playwright and wit Noël Coward, who was accompanied by his friend Priscilla Tempest, reinstated recently as head of the Savoy's press office. Tonight, Priscilla dazzled in a chestnut-brown velvet party dress with matching tights that showed off long legs made all the more impressive by the silver Mary Jane pumps she had recently purchased. Her face was pale and pixieish, her short russet-blond hair restyled that afternoon in anticipation of the dinner.

A slim woman with auburn hair entered. "My goodness," whispered Noël to Priscilla. "It's Christine Keeler."

"I should know more about her," Priscilla said. "I've only vaguely heard about a scandal, but I was still back in Canada at the time."

"A scandal that shook the foundations of this country," said Noël *sotto voce*. "A few years ago, Miss Keeler was the world's most scandalous woman."

"It's a description, alas, with which I am all too familiar," said Priscilla. "Although I wouldn't claim world status—yet."

"Christine was discovered carrying on affairs simultaneously with the cabinet minister John Profumo and a Soviet naval officer attached to the Russian Embassy who was thought to be a spy," Noël continued. "The resulting scandal ruined Profumo's career and brought down the ruling Conservatives. Yet here she is tonight, slipping into the room all but unnoticed."

"But you have noticed, Noël," said Priscilla.

"Of course, my dear," Noël said with a sly smile. "I notice most things—and remember all things."

This evening Christine was in a sleeveless red sheath tailored to flatter her figure. A diamanté choker around her neck completed the chic ensemble. She frowned as soon as she spotted Jack Cogan with his wife and Mailer. "What's he doing here?" she asked with a jerk of her head in the newspaper mogul's direction as Welles walked up and greeted her.

"Ensuring good press while I'm in London," Welles said.

"I wouldn't count on it," Christine said. "Not if the way his father's papers have treated me these past few years is any indication. The Jackal runs things now, yet they still go after me."

"Serves you right for toppling a government," Welles said lightly.

"Don't underestimate yourself, Orson," Christine said with a catty smile. "If I can do it, you can too."

Alfred Hitchcock waddled into the Pinafore Room with Cary Grant, who looked every inch…Cary Grant, an impressed Priscilla quickly decided. Tall and debonair were the clichés that flashed through her mind before she could put a stop to them. Cary appeared a little greyer at the temples than he did on the screen, perhaps, but the lines on his face were either obscured by his deep tan or lightly etched in just the right places around his deep brown eyes, which now fixed on Priscilla.

"Are you an actress?" he inquired after introducing himself.

"Hardly," said Priscilla. "I work at the Savoy."

"Not changing the bedsheets, surely," said Cary.

"Not for now," Priscilla agreed. "I'm actually in charge of the press office."

"Good, please do your very best to keep the press away from me."

"Usually it's the other way around," Priscilla said. "The people I deal with crave attention."

"Not me. I'm far too old for craving."

"Cary Grant can never be too old." Did Priscilla sound breathless when she said this?

"Ah, but you see, I'm not Cary Grant."

"You're not?"

"I'm actually born and raised Archie Leach. People keep telling me I'm this strange character named Cary Grant. But I don't believe them."

They were interrupted by Hitchcock, his round porridge face set in an expression of impatience. "There you are, Hitch," Cary said, turning to the director. "I want you to meet my new friend, Priscilla. She works in the press office here at the Savoy."

"Enchanted," Hitchcock said in a disinterested voice.

"Hitch loves publicity—and blonds, although not necessarily in that order."

"Cary, I am most displeased with you," Hitchcock said in the slow, measured Essex drone that was his trademark.

"Oh? Why is that, Hitch?"

"Spending time with this young woman when you should be listening to me—as I convince you to star in *Topaz*, my next film."

"You see, Priscilla. No matter how hard I try, they simply won't let me retire."

"Why should you retire?" Priscilla asked.

"Because I'm far too old to be kissing young women like yourself on a big movie screen."

But what about off the big screen? Priscilla thought before she could stop herself.

"What do you think?" Cary asked Priscilla. "Should I do Hitch's movie?"

Priscilla was momentarily speechless, not sure what to say. Here was one of the most famous stars in the world, even though he had not made a movie in several years, still remarkably handsome, and he was asking her if he should make a movie with Alfred Hitchcock. She was about to blurt out "Of course you should" when Cary cut in.

"There you go," he said with a decisive nod at Hitchcock. "My new friend Priscilla doesn't want me to do it."

He squeezed Priscilla's arm gently and gave her a wink that weakened her knees. She was about to reply when Cary was distracted by the entrance of a tall, imposing man with a shock of white hair. "My goodness, it's Louis Mountbatten," Cary said enthusiastically. "A dear old friend. Haven't seen him for years." He made a beeline for Mountbatten.

Noël leaned over to speak into Priscilla's ear. "My goodness, this is a crowd. Now we have the former viceroy of India—the fellow, depending on your point of view, who either brought about the country's independence or sold the British Empire down the Ganges River. Who also happens to be an old acquaintance of mine."

Close by, Cary shook Mountbatten's hand. "Well, this is a pleasant surprise," Mountbatten said. "I didn't even know you were in town."

"A short visit," replied Cary. "How are you, Louis?"

"Oh, you know, soldiering on, I suppose," Mountbatten answered somewhat resignedly. "Putting out various fires along the way. What about you? Still making those films, are you?"

"I keep telling everyone I'm retired. No one seems to believe me—except perhaps for my new friend Priscilla." He guided Mountbatten over to Priscilla. "Have the two of you met?"

Mountbatten gave Priscilla a speculative look. "I don't believe we have." He took Priscilla's hand. His was clammy, she thought fleetingly.

"A pleasure to meet you, Lord Mountbatten." Was it? Gazing into Mountbatten's cold, expressionless eyes, Priscilla couldn't resist an involuntary shudder. What was that all about? she wondered.

"Miss Tempest is at the Savoy's press office," Cary explained. "She's sworn to protect me from the press."

"I wish someone could protect me from the damned press," Mountbatten said solemnly.

Welles came over. "Louis," he boomed, "delighted you made it. I was beginning to wonder."

"I'd love to tell you the affairs of state delayed me, Orson. But it was the bloody traffic."

"You've arrived just in time," Welles said. "We're about to get started."

"Ah, Noël, there you are," Mountbatten said as Noël joined them.. "I religiously scan the Queen's lists in search of your name and your ascension to a knighthood."

"A fruitless search thus far, I fear," replied Noël.

"Not long now, old boy, not long now."

"Have you met my friend Priscilla?" Noël asked, the excuse to change the subject.

Mountbatten trained those cold eyes on her. "Yes, everyone seems to want me to meet her. Why do you suppose that is, Miss Tempest?"

"I imagine it's part of my job, Lord Mountbatten. Meeting everyone, ensuring they are comfortable here at the Savoy."

"Hmm," was all Mountbatten said before he turned abruptly away.

"I don't think Lord Mountbatten likes me," Priscilla whispered to Noël as guests moved toward a dining table Priscilla was certain could land a small plane. Each guest's place was indicated by an elegant little name card positioned near the Henning Seidelin cutlery crafted especially for the Savoy.

"I don't believe Lord Mountbatten likes anyone these days," Noël opined. "The world has passed him by and he doesn't like it one bit. Also, if what I'm hearing is true, Louis is doing a lot of bed-hopping and that's potentially getting him into trouble."

"What does his wife think of his bed-hopping, as you call it?"

"She's doing a fair amount of hopping herself. That's a good deal of bed hopping," offered Priscilla.

"It's love among the upper classes," stated Noël. "If you're not sleeping with someone you shouldn't, you're not in fashion."

Noël was glancing around at the others as he spoke.

"Is something wrong?" Priscilla asked.

"No, no, it's fine, a silly little thing really," he said, fidgeting with his ever-present cigarette holder.

"Noël!" boomed Orson Welles from his position at the head of the table. He waved the cigar in his hand around to indicate Priscilla. "You have failed to introduce me to the lovely creature you are with."

"May I present Miss Priscilla Tempest," stated Noël with a wicked smile. "Miss Tempest keeps the champagne flowing in the Savoy's press office."

"It seems you make still more friends, Miss Tempest," Mountbatten observed from across the table.

"I hope I may add you to my list, Lord Mountbatten," Priscilla said.

A thin, unconvincing smile was Mountbatten's only response.

Orson rose to his feet, a majestic figure in a white dinner jacket. Like a great bearded whale, Priscilla thought. The twenty-five-year-old genius who'd made *Citizen Kane* had now grown old and gone grandly fat.

"I would now welcome you all to the Pinafore Room and express my delight that you are here—especially you, Louis. An honour."

"A pleasure, Orson," Mountbatten said. "Even if you are looking for money."

"Mr. Quinn, I don't want you getting the wrong idea," Orson called to the banker at the far end of the table.

"I understand, Mr. Welles," Quinn retorted cheerfully. "I'm always a very popular fellow at these affairs."

"Until he says no," added his wife.

Amid a rumble of laughter, Orson said, "No money talk tonight, though. Alas, we are missing the man in charge of finances, my producer, Harry Alan Towers, who had to cancel at the last minute."

"Excuse me, Orson," interrupted Noël, a note of concern in his voice, "but am I then to assume that there will be only thirteen guests for dinner tonight?"

"That is correct," Welles said, slightly perplexed at having surrendered to Noël his audience's undivided attention.

"There is the matter of the curse," said Noël. Priscilla shot him a quick look.

"Curse? What curse?" Welles's porcine face had settled into a frown.

"The curse of the Savoy, old chap," explained Noël calmly, as if this curse at the Savoy were a well-known fact.

As his guests traded puzzled glances, Welles arranged a look of amusement. "Do explain to us what the devil you are talking about."

Priscilla hoped Noël would back away at this point, but she failed to take into account his overweening ego—or perhaps it was the gravity of his subject that made him feel it was necessary to provide an explanation.

"In 1898—" Noël began.

"The year you checked into the Savoy," put in Hitchcock.

"I arrived a year or two later," Noël allowed. "But in that year, a South African millionaire named Woolf Joel hosted a dinner party in this very room. Two of Joel's guests cancelled at the last minute and thus there were thirteen for dinner. As the evening wore on, the conversation turned to various superstitions, including the unlucky number thirteen."

"A rather harmless notion," suggested Lady Anne Harley in her plummy rasp of a voice, finally making her presence known. Her late husband was Lord Desmond Harley. The Harleys traced their roots back to Sir Grenville Harley, who'd made his fortune in the slave trade.

"Not entirely true," Noël demurred. "The origin of the ill luck surrounding the number thirteen has been around forever. It is Judas, the thirteenth guest, who arrives at the Last Supper and betrays Jesus."

"But what has that to do with the Savoy?" asked Mountbatten.

"The reverse of the Last Supper, actually," Noël went on. "It is not the guest who arrives, but the one who leaves. That guest, the curse goes, will meet a terrible fate."

"That's so silly," scoffed Lady Anne, her heavily lidded eyes blazing with indignation. "Whoever heard of such a thing?"

Hitchcock appeared uncustomarily animated as he spoke up: "There is Norse lore that says the evil and chaos of the world was first introduced by the terrible god Loki when he attended another dinner party, this one in Valhalla. Loki happened to be the thirteenth guest."

"At the time, Mr. Joel, the South African host, dismissed any notion of a curse," Noël went on with his typical equanimity. "He proceeded to demonstrate its fallacy by leaving the dinner first—claimed he had to board a cruise ship and return to Johannesburg. However, soon after arriving home, Woolf Joel was shot dead."

The guests were silent. Welles puffed on his cigar. Across the table, Cary Grant cast a doubtful glance at Alfred Hitchcock.

Noël waved around his ivory cigarette holder as though revving up to continue. "It might have ended there, but it didn't. Within the year four other guests at that dinner, two from here in London, one from Istanbul and another from Lisbon, all ended up dead under mysterious circumstances. The news of a possible curse made the papers. The Savoy management at the time was understandably concerned that the superstition might actually be real. Or at least of concern for guests. Thus, for years afterwards, if thirteen guests were present in this room for a meal, a fourteenth person was added, often one of the waiters."

"Terribly awkward," observed a scornful Lady Anne. "Introducing a complete stranger into an intimate dinner—and a *waiter* at that. Goodness gracious."

"Precisely," Noël said. "Thus, the management devised a rather unique solution."

"And what solution was that?" asked Orson Welles, arranging to sound bored by Noël's hijacking of his dinner.

"A cat," Noël said with satisfaction.

CHAPTER TWO

Kaspar

"A cat?" The disappointment in Welles's voice was palpable. "Honestly, Noël, *a cat?*"

"Ah, but a very unusual cat," Noël said assuredly. "A cat named Kaspar. When there are thirteen guests in the Pinafore Room, as there are this evening, Kaspar is added. Thus there are fourteen, and thus the curse of the Savoy is averted."

"Poppycock," proclaimed Lady Anne with satisfaction, not immune to the pleasures of inspiring mild chuckling and the slow, measured shaking of heads. "Pure poppycock."

"I couldn't agree more," chimed in Welles, sitting back as though relaxing in the knowledge that with the curse amounting to no more than a cat, the great playwright and raconteur was quickly losing his audience.

"I for one tend to take curses seriously," Hitchcock said, putting an end to the murmuring. "The ancient Romans and Greeks originated them. You could go to a friendly magician and he would arrange a curse tablet against whomever had wronged you. So, curses have been around forever. I don't think they should be discounted." He looked at Noël. "Is it possible to meet this cat named Kaspar?"

"Given the circumstances, that is an excellent idea," answered Noël. "Let me speak to one of the waiters."

Dropping his cigarette holder onto the table, he stood—elegantly, Priscilla thought, the veteran actor on his stage—

and slipped from the room amid a babble of conversation. Priscilla watched Welles puff ferociously on his cigar. She noticed Christine Keeler leaning into Jack Cogan. He seemed to like that. His new wife didn't. Tiffany, in fact, looked quite miserable. Curious, thought Priscilla: the Jackal's newspapers had made life hell for Christine and yet here she was whispering rather sexily into his ear.

Mountbatten was deep in conversation with Cary Grant. "You must come," Priscilla overheard him saying to the actor. "I had no idea you were going to be in town, otherwise I would have sent you an invitation earlier." Further along, Norman Mailer was trying to explain to the banker Nick Quinn and his wife why he had called his first novel *The Naked and the Dead* when, Mrs. Quinn pointed out, sadly, she couldn't find anyone naked in the book.

Noël re-entered followed by a waiter carrying a three-foot-tall sculpture of a sleek black cat resting on its haunches. Noël took the sculpture from the waiter and placed it on the table in front of the unoccupied seat. "Ladies and gentlemen, may I present to you…*Kaspar!*"

Welles removed the cigar from his mouth and lifted himself up slightly in order to get a better view. The other guests all stared as though not quite sure what to make of the cat. Norman Mailer was shaking his curly head. "Jesus, that is the goddamn weirdest thing I've ever seen. The cat actually looks scary."

There *was* something creepy about Kaspar, Priscilla agreed. Noël ran an appreciative hand over Kaspar's sleek head as he explained, "The Savoy's Kaspar was carved in 1927 by the designer Basil Ionides. Why he chose a cat is lost to the mists of time. However, Kaspar has been a valued guest in the Pinafore Room ever since."

"With all due respect, old man," Welles said, "this is a bit of a novelty, no question—the equivalent, I suppose, of me distracting everyone with one of my magic tricks—but there is nothing more to it. Really, enough is enough."

He lumbered to his feet and, taking the bell that had been placed beside him, rang it a couple of times. As soon as he did, the doors flew open and a line of waiters in white jackets entered pushing gleaming silver carving trolleys with whole smoked salmon on platters.

"Saved by the hors d'oeuvres," Welles declared. He looked more relaxed having regained at least a modicum of command. "Scottish salmon if I'm not mistaken, Miss Tempest?" Once again Welles trained his eyes on Priscilla. The waiters set to carving the smoked salmon so thin the guests could see the blade of the knife through the flesh.

"That is correct, Mr. Welles," Priscilla hurried to assert, happy to aid in changing the subject away from cats and curses.

"From Craigellachie on the River Spey, home to the finest salmon," she continued, her Savoy cheering cap firmly in place. "The salmon is smoked here in London before coming to the Savoy—fresh as can be."

"And absolutely superb," Welles added while waiters presented the salmon to the guests. He frowned at Kaspar and then waved his cigar at one of the servers. "Take this, uh, cat, away, will you please?"

"Do you think that's a good idea, Orson?" asked Hitchcock as a waiter lifted Kaspar off the table.

"It's not even a very good sculpture, if you want my opinion," Welles said. "Away with it."

"Away, indeed," called Lady Anne. "I've had the finest meals in the world's finest restaurants, but let me tell you, nothing comes close to what I've experienced here at the Savoy. The food is very much a part of the reason I stay here while in London."

"Hear, hear," chimed in Priscilla, delighted by such a glowing report.

"Therefore," Lady Anne continued, "let us concentrate on what I'm sure will be an extraordinary meal."

"Besides," said Christine Keeler, "that cat gives me the willies."

"I agree," said Mailer gruffly. "There is something damned evil about that cat. One look at him, and I need a drink."

"It's obvious, you've been looking at him quite frequently," Noël offered.

There were more murmurs of agreement as Kaspar was whisked out the door. Priscilla watched Noël and Hitchcock exchange worried glances.

In the glow of the fine meal, *boeuf Wellington avec légumes verts,* Kaspar and the attendant curse appeared to have been forgotten. It surfaced again only when Lady Anne looked at her watch as a dessert, *mousse aux framboises,* was about to be served. She announced that she was so sorry but she had to leave. "I am meeting my son, James, for a quick drink in the American Bar before he departs for a diplomatic post in Moscow."

"Ah yes, James Harley, the young diplomat destined for greatness, or so I'm told," Noël said, rising to his feet along with everyone else.

"One of those damned progressive politicians," grumbled Cogan.

"I am, alas, only too familiar with the kind," chimed in Mountbatten.

"Now you leave my boy alone, Jack, and you as well, Lord Mountbatten," admonished Lady Anne, those hooded eyes reflecting defiance. "Else I will put a curse on the two of you."

"I'll keep that in mind," Cogan said mildly.

"Duly noted," added Mountbatten.

Lady Anne bussed Welles's cheek. "A superb meal, a wonderful evening. Thank you so much, Orson," she trilled.

"You realize, Lady Anne, you are the first to leave." The unmistakable warning drawl of Alfred Hitchcock.

"Oh, rubbish," Lady Anne said with a fluttery, dismissive wave of her hand. "There is no such thing as a curse." She turned to Priscilla. "Young lady, to prove what nonsense all of this is, I would like you to wake me up tomorrow morning at nine. I have an important appointment at ten thirty. Ordinarily, I would have the front desk do it, but since you are an employee here, I ask you."

"I would be only too pleased to," Priscilla said.

"And, Noël, that will put an end to your nonsense." She cast him a reproachful look.

"I'm sure you are right, Lady Anne," Noël spoke gravely. "And do say hello to your son for me. Unlike my very conservative friend here, I am an admirer of his."

"Careful, Noël," Cogan cautioned. "I may instruct the drama critics at my papers to give Harold Pinter a good review."

"My God, anything but that," bleated Mountbatten.

"You truly are a cad," Noël said.

Cogan gave a short laugh. "Yes, I am. I am very rich and I own a lot of newspapers. How could I be anything else?"

Lady Anne steamed off, a flagship of the fleet moving out of a safe harbour, leaving the others to struggle back into their seats as dessert was served.

"I suppose that is the end of that," Noël whispered to Priscilla out of the corner of his mouth.

"You are terrible," Priscilla said to him in a low voice.

"Not at all." Priscilla detected a malicious gleam in Noël's eye, the unrepentant gadfly in his element. "I believe the curse is, in fact, real and should at least have been brought to Orson's attention to avoid any mishap that might ruin this evening. Which for whatever reason is very important to him."

"On the other hand," Priscilla ventured, "one might suspect that you disliked Orson getting all the attention and decided to steal a bit for yourself."

Noël reacted in mock horror. "Perish the thought, Priscilla. Perish the thought! I am merely a humble scribbler and occasional thespian, content to exist in the shadow of the Great Orson." He paused for effect. "Well, mostly exist."

"Dear, dear Noël, did I hear you mention my name?" Welles was on his feet, cigar in hand, thick eyebrows curled over eyes like black marbles. His immense frame seemed to fill the room.

"Merely breathlessly describing you as the Great Orson, dear boy."

"And you, Noël, the magician who can steal the thunder faster than I can pull a rabbit out of my hat."

"Merely delivering a timely warning, old chap," argued Noël.

"But you don't believe that curse nonsense any more than anyone actually believes I have a rabbit in my hat," said Welles.

"I'm not so sure. After all, management does keep Kaspar on call." Noël gave a shrug. "Is it mere silly tradition? Or is the hotel covering its derrière—just in case? Hard to say. At any rate, I believe it is wise to at least consider the possibility of the curse."

"What about the second person to leave?" As the other guests finished their mousse, Christine Keeler started to her feet—a shimmering presence in red, Priscilla thought. It was possible, in that moment, to understand how prominent cabinet ministers and Russian spies might fall under Christine's spell.

"I believe you are safe," Welles said. "At least when it comes to curses."

"I hope so, because I too must be off." Priscilla was certain Christine darted a glance at Jack Cogan before she bussed both of Welles's cheeks. "But thank you for a lovely evening." She smiled at Noël. "And Noël, thank you for entertaining us with your cat. Such an evil cat, I would say."

"My pleasure," Noël replied.

She kissed Welles one more time before waving farewell to everyone and breezing out the door, taking care, it seemed to Priscilla, not to give Cogan a final look. Perhaps Priscilla was making too much of these exchanges—or lack of them. An uneasy and huffy Tiffany reignited her suspicions.

Christine's departure was the cue for everyone else to begin making their exits. Priscilla watched Nick Quinn and his wife, Katherine, slip away quietly and quickly. Not a good sign, she thought. A smiling Cary Grant drew her away from thoughts of disappearing bankers. "I wonder if you would like to join me for a drink in the American Bar."

Cary Grant inviting her for a drink? Be still my beating heart, Priscilla thought excitedly. How could she say no? She started to open her mouth when she heard Welles say, "I was just about to ask Miss Tempest the same question."

"There you go, Miss Tempest," Mountbatten noted tartly as he passed. "An excess of friends." He arched an eyebrow.

What was that raised brow supposed to mean? Priscilla worked up an uncertain smile as Mountbatten took Cary's arm. "Don't forget my dinner," he said.

Cary said, "I look forward to it," before Mountbatten went out the door.

The warning ghost of Peter, Count of Savoy, materialized to remind Priscilla that as an employee, she should not be accepting cocktail invitations from the guests no matter how sexy and hard to resist.

She took a deep reinforcing breath. "As much as I'd love to join you both," she said in her best diplomatic voice, "I'm afraid duty calls. I must be at work first thing in the morning."

"Most necessary," Noël agreed. "Come along, Priscilla. We can share a cab."

"Perhaps another time," Cary said, reaching out to shake her hand. "You are a very charming young lady."

Priscilla forced herself to keep her mouth firmly closed. If she opened it, she was all but certain she would tell Cary Grant that she would happily follow him to the ends of the earth.

"I should point out, Noël, that you live at the Savoy when you are in London," Priscilla said as their cab sped along the Strand, thronging with the crowds departing nearby theatres.

"That is an undeniable fact of my life," Noël agreed, shifting contentedly. "And what a pleasant habitation it is."

"Then how is it we are sharing a cab?"

"While, as you cleverly have deduced, I live at the Savoy," said Noël, slyly, "for certain rendezvous, I must travel elsewhere. Thus, the cab. Thus, you."

"I see."

"Besides, I wanted a quiet moment to bend your ear."

"Bend away," said Priscilla.

"Your thoughts on tonight's events."

"You were a bit of a beast with Orson Welles," Priscilla suggested.

"My assessment is that I let him down rather easily. I am a bit surprised that you, as a loyal Savoy employee, didn't know about the curse—or its antidote, Kaspar."

"Curses are not ordinarily a subject for discussion in the press office," Priscilla said. "After all, any thought that the hotel might be cursed is not exactly guaranteed to attract clientele."

"Not the entire hotel," amended Noël. "Only the Pinafore Room."

"Also, I thought Christine Keeler was right. There really is something quite creepy about Kaspar."

"I am practically part of the furniture at the Savoy, and over the years I have heard several stories involving strange goings-on not only in the Pinafore Room but in the hotel itself. A friend of mine—a seer of some repute, I might add—believes the Savoy is inhabited by unsettled spirits. Those spirits, according to her, *fuel* the curse of the Savoy."

"I hope you are wrong about all of this," Priscilla said, choosing her words diplomatically. "But I suppose I will find out in the morning."

"Yes, I suppose you will," Noël said. Disconcertingly noncommittal, Priscilla thought, shaking off a growing feeling of apprehension.

The cab pulled up to her flat at No. 37–39 Knightsbridge. Noël wouldn't allow her to pay and shooed her out. She fumbled for the latchkey in her bag as the cab pulled away. She'd found the key and was starting to cross the pavement when a black cat leapt into view. Priscilla let out a yelp of alarm as the cat arched its back, its eyes a ghastly yellow piercing the darkness. Then it was gone. Priscilla waited until her heart stopped beating so fast and mounted the stairs to the entrance.

A black cat! What next? She consoled herself with the thought that the bad luck of a black cat crossing one's path was no more a possibility than the curse of the Savoy.

Poppycock! as Lady Anne would say.

CHAPTER THREE

Doom, Impending

Priscilla spent a restless night. Her dreams were full of diabolical black cats, their yellow eyes like laser beams, their fangs bared as they made shrieking attacks on a helpless Priscilla, who was eventually rescued by Cary Grant.

In his movies, Cary Grant never took his clothes off. In her dream, he didn't have any on. He looked as good, Priscilla decided, without clothes as he did with them on.

She shouldn't be thinking like that about guests at the Savoy, she admonished herself as she struggled out of her warm bed. Better to concentrate on the obligation to check on Lady Anne Harley at 9 a.m. She should not be thinking of black cats and curses, either. There were so many things she mustn't think about, including the sad fact that lately she had been waking too many mornings alone in bed.

No wonder she was dreaming of being rescued by a naked Cary Grant.

Because she had been more or less on duty last night, she had behaved herself, hadn't drunk too much champagne, and therefore felt bright-eyed and bushy-tailed, as her father back home in Toronto would say. A shower wiped away lingering thoughts of black cats. The curse was all nonsense, she resolved as she emerged to study herself in the mirror, deciding at the same time that there were merits to being a good girl for at least one night.

In her bedroom—she would clean it up soon, she really, truly would—she chose a black Yves Saint Laurent pantsuit with a fuchsia scarf as the armour with which she would outfit herself in order to face the day. She looked at her watch and decided she had better get a move on. She was to knock on Lady Anne's door in half an hour.

It wasn't until she was in a cab on the way to the Savoy that it hit her: Supposing Noël was right and there really was a curse? And Lady Anne had died overnight? Despite her best efforts to ward off these thoughts, Priscilla felt an all-too-familiar stomach-tightening sensation as the cab turned off the Strand.

The Front Hall was unusually quiet this morning, the air scented with the fragrance from the huge flower arrangements prepared each day by the hotel's staff. She waved to the assistant reception manager, Vincent Tomberry, as she approached the reception desk. He returned with a snap of his head and a frosty look. Mr. Tomberry was one of the many male employees who believed women had no place at the Savoy other than to make the beds. Priscilla was determined to prove him wrong. So far, given his stony expression, she had failed.

"Good morning, Mr. Tomberry," Priscilla said cheerfully.

"Miss Tempest," in a voice as cold as yesterday's mackerel.

"Could you please give me the number of Lady Anne Harley's suite?"

"And why would you require that?" demanded Tomberry.

"Lady Anne asked me to wake her up this morning."

"An unusual request."

"We at the Savoy pride ourselves on fulfilling guests' requests, even the unusual ones," Priscilla retorted formally.

Tomberry seemed poised to say something that was probably nasty but then restrained himself. Instead, he made a production of studying the register before announcing: "Suite 615."

"Thank you, Mr. Tomberry."

"*Most* curious if you ask me, Miss Tempest."

As she stepped into the lift, Priscilla felt her stomach twist into an even tighter knot.

She got off the lift and went along the silent corridor to Lady Anne's suite. She paused at the door, listening for any movement from within. Was the elderly woman still asleep? Or dead? Priscilla swallowed hard and knocked.

No one answered.

Priscilla knocked again. Still nothing from inside.

Suddenly, the door opened. A sleepy Lady Anne, all but lost in a quilted robe, hair in big curlers swathed in a protective headscarf, said, "Goodness gracious. What are you doing here?"

Relief flooding through her, Priscilla replied, "My apologies, Lady Anne, but last night you asked me to wake you up this morning. You said you had an appointment."

"I said that? Are you sure?"

"I believe you also wanted to put the lie to what Mr. Coward told us about a curse at the Savoy."

"Ah, yes, yes. Now it's coming back." Lady Anne's tired eyes popped with recognition. "I'm so sorry, my dear. I was up half the night worrying about my son, James. I'm afraid I'm in a bit of a fog."

"I hope everything is all right," Priscilla said sympathetically.

"I'm not sure," said Lady Anne in a voice full of concern. "We were to meet for a drink last night, but he never arrived. He didn't board his flight to Moscow, either. I've been trying to contact him, but he's not answering his phone. I am terribly worried."

"If there's anything I can do…" Priscilla started to say.

"I'm sure there's a logical explanation. James can be some-what…elusive." She reached out and took Priscilla's arm. "But thank you so much for remembering an old lady. I might have slept right through if you hadn't knocked."

She pulled away with what Priscilla read as a desperate look, saying, "I know it's silly, and I did pooh-pooh the idea last night, quite loudly in fact."

"Understandable," Priscilla interjected tactfully.

"Still, given what's happened since I left that dinner, I cannot stop thinking about that curse."

"Well, you're very much alive."

"Yes, there is that," Lady Anne said with a quick, weak smile. "I am alive but—"

The screams coming from further along the hallway cut her off abruptly.

CHAPTER FOUR

A Right Bastard

A wild-eyed housekeeper shot out the door at Suite 621 as Priscilla approached. "I had no idea," she exclaimed. "No idea..."

The housekeeper stumbled off while Priscilla took a deep breath and pushed open the door. Inside, Jack Cogan sat on a straight-backed chair in the midst of the suite. A slim gold letter opener of the type available at the Savoy protruded from his shoulder. Blood trickled down the crisp white shirt he was wearing.

"Mr. Cogan!" exclaimed Priscilla. "Are you all right?"

"Obviously not," Cogan gasped between clenched teeth.

"I'll call for help—"

"Christ, no!" Cogan protested. "Pull the damned knife out of me."

"I don't—" Priscilla started.

"Do it!" snapped Cogan.

Priscilla advanced, tentatively reaching out to the dagger-like letter opener. She saw that it wasn't in very far. She closed her eyes, grasped the hilt and pulled. Cogan swore loudly as the blade came out. Priscilla fell back holding the letter opener as the door to the bathroom opened and Christine Keeler came out in the same red dress she had been wearing the night before. She looked angry—but her hair looked great, Priscilla thought. She stopped when she saw Priscilla.

"He's a right bastard," Christine announced, as if that explained the mystery of how one of Britain's most powerful media moguls might have ended up with a letter opener sticking out of him.

"What did he do to you? Are you all right?"

"He shags me and then says there's nothing he can do to keep me out of his papers." She turned and shook a fist at him. "Bastard! Bloody duplicitous bastard!"

"Get her out of here," Cogan shouted. Whatever pirate-like attractiveness he might have displayed the night before was lost in a rage of pain and anger. "Get her the hell out—now!"

Christine stormed over to Cogan and, before Priscilla could do anything to stop her, slapped him hard. Christine then swung around and strode out the door, slamming it behind her.

"Good riddance," Cogan said, holding the side of his face where she had struck him. He glared up at Priscilla. "You work for the hotel, don't you?"

"Priscilla Tempest. We met last night, Mr. Cogan."

That didn't seem to register. "Get me something that I can use to stop the bleeding," he ordered. "And be quick about it."

Priscilla dashed into the bathroom and came back with a hand towel. He grabbed it from her and pressed it against the wound in his shoulder. "Here's what I need you to do. Get on that phone over there and get me an operator. Once you do that, I'll give you the number."

"You need medical attention, sir."

"I need you to do what I tell you—and don't bloody argue."

Priscilla hurried over to a desk phone and rang the operator. Cogan mumbled the number and Priscilla conveyed it. He struggled out of the chair and, holding the towel against his bleeding shoulder with one hand, he took the receiver from her with the other. His call was answered almost immediately. "Yeah, it's me.

I need you at the Savoy. The Thames entrance. What the hell do you mean, when? Right away, damn you!"

He handed the receiver back to Priscilla. "I've a jacket over there on the sofa. Get it." Priscilla retrieved the jacket. "Now, drape it over my shoulders and then help me out of here."

"I'm not sure this is a good idea," Priscilla ventured.

"What would you like to do? Call an ambulance? Bring on the coppers along with the press? The next thing you know this is splashed all over the front pages of every paper I don't own. Not the sort of publicity the Savoy is looking for."

Priscilla thought about the circus that would erupt if any of this incident got out: Britain's most famous homewrecker stabbing one of Britain's best-known newspaper barons, a newly married man, in a suite at the Savoy. Priscilla didn't want to think about the magnitude of the possible scandal. "All right," she said wearily, "if you're up for it, we can go down the back stairs."

"Let's do that."

Making sure the coast was clear, Priscilla allowed Cogan to brace himself against her as they left his suite. They made their way slowly along the hallway to the stairwell. Cogan was breathing hard as they started down. "How much further?"

"Almost there," Priscilla said.

"Guess you never expected to be doing this first thing in the morning," Cogan said. Through his pain, he managed to sound almost amused.

"Not even the last thing at night," Priscilla replied.

"I would say I have a knack for bringing out the worst in women."

She did not disagree with him.

They reached the bottom of the stairwell without encountering anyone. Outside the Thames entrance, a black Rolls-Royce waited. A liveried chauffeur opened the back door quickly and then relieved Priscilla. Once Cogan was settled in the car, the chauffeur closed the door, nodded at Priscilla and slipped behind the wheel. A moment later the Rolls sped away.

No appreciation at all for saving if not Cogan's hide, then certainly his reputation. But that's what you did as an employee at the Savoy, Priscilla reminded herself as she re-entered the hotel. You served your guests' needs. No matter if the guest was, as Christine Keeler so accurately pointed out, a right bastard.

Priscilla was in the Front Hall before she noticed the spots of Jack Cogan's blood speckled on the cuff of her blouse. Not a hint of gratitude, *and* Cogan had bled on her. What's more, he had placed her in a difficult position. A stabbing incident had taken place in one of the hotel's suites. What was she supposed to do about reporting it? To whom should she report? This news was not something that would endear her to Clive Banville, the hotel's general manager. He had only recently returned her to the press office. The police? As the Jackal had pointed out, that would bring the press and scandal.

No, best to scrub off the blood and put the entire incident behind her, exercising the unparalleled discretion that the Savoy was known for.

But what about the housekeeper? Priscilla didn't know the woman's name, but she would find out who had been on duty and have a quiet talk with her.

In the meantime, she had better check on Lady Anne. Priscilla wanted to make sure she was all right, and also get an idea of what the dowager might have witnessed between Christine and Cogan.

Priscilla took the lift back to the sixth floor. Still fussing about her sleeve as she stepped into the hallway, Priscilla failed to see the open door at Lady Anne's suite until the hotel's head of security, a white-faced Major Jack O'Hara, appeared on the threshold.

"It's Lady Anne," he said grimly.

CHAPTER FIVE

Double, Double Toil and Trouble

Priscilla pushed past Major O'Hara and rushed into the suite. Lady Anne Harley lay on the bed, still in her quilted housecoat, her hair still in curlers. With her eyes closed, the dowager might have been in a peaceful sleep.

Except she wasn't.

Priscilla was dimly aware of Major O'Hara's voice behind her: "I received a call from the operator saying Lady Anne had been on the phone and appeared to be in some sort of distress before she was abruptly cut off. I came up to check on her, and when she didn't answer the door, I entered and found her like this. There was no pulse, I'm afraid."

Priscilla turned her eyes away. "I was just here," she said dully. "She wanted me to wake her up."

The Major gave Priscilla a puzzled look. "She wanted you to wake her? Why would she want you to do that?"

"She was worried about her son. He was to meet her last night and didn't. She said this morning he was scheduled to board a flight to Moscow—and didn't."

"I see," said O'Hara.

"Should we call the police?"

Major O'Hara frowned. "I believe she's had a heart attack. I don't suspect foul play. I'll get our doctor up here shortly. But for now, let's leave the police out of it."

"It's the curse," Priscilla said with an unexpected sob. Until now, she thought she had been doing a good job holding her emotions in check.

"What? What do you mean?" The Major's frown had turned to bewilderment.

"There was a dinner last night in the Pinafore Room." Priscilla's words came out in a rush as she choked back tears. "There were thirteen guests. We were warned about the curse of the Savoy. No one believed it. Now, this…"

"Curse? You don't mean that silly old myth that's been around here forever? No one actually believes it."

"Bad things are said to happen to the first person who leaves," Priscilla intoned. "Lady Anne left before anyone else."

"That's absurd." Major O'Hara was shaking his head. "There is no curse. An elderly woman, sadly, has succumbed to what in all likelihood is a heart attack. Perhaps brought on by worry concerning her son. No more to it than that. Any suggestion otherwise, Miss Tempest, will not reflect well on you or on this hotel."

Major O'Hara was right. Proclaiming that a curse had led to Lady Anne's death would only bring more trouble. And there was already far too much trouble this morning.

Trouble, she could not help thinking, that began last night— when Kaspar the cat was removed from the Pinafore Room.

One dinner guest stabbed, another dead.

No curse?

Double, double toil and trouble…

An hour later, Major O'Hara reported that he had not been able to reach Lady Anne's son, James. The doctor on call had arrived to officially pronounce Lady Anne dead. Attendants from Leverton & Sons, one of London's most prestigious funeral services, took the body into its care after it was decided that, her son's absence notwithstanding, it was best to remove Lady Anne from the suite.

In late morning, and still in shock, Priscilla arrived back in the press office at Room 205. There were two ways of looking at the press office and its blond-wood walls, its brown furniture worn down from years of use by reporters' bums, its wall of celebrity photographs to remind the famous that there were others just as famous, if not more so. One way, Priscilla mused, was to view it as a safe place in which to escape the Savoy's troubles and cares. The other way was to view it more threateningly: as the place where all those troubles and cares were born.

"Something's wrong," Susie Gore-Langton declared.

"What makes you say that?" Priscilla asked irritably.

"It's the look on your face. I know that look only too well."

Susie had recently come back to work at the Savoy following an unexpected hiatus. The time away had not dulled her antennae when it came to detecting a potential crisis. Susie was an English rose, her face delicate and flushed, but it was her youthful figure that was known to stop London traffic—and to draw the attention of the men in her life.

"There's been a death," Priscilla reported.

"A death? Someone's dead?" Susie's green eyes, as they often did in times of crisis, had grown to saucer-like proportions.

"Yes, Susie," Priscilla said in a patient voice. "Lady Anne Harley. They think it was a heart attack."

"My God," said Susie. "I know her."

"You do? How do you know her?"

"I wouldn't exactly say I *know* her, but I met her when I dated her son."

"You dated James Harley?"

"Me and half the women in London, I imagine," Susie said, giving her lovely mouth a nasty twist.

"Major O'Hara and the people at the funeral home have been trying to reach him, but so far, no luck."

"That sounds like James. He has a habit of either showing up late or not showing up at all."

"His mother said more or less the same thing about him. How long did the two of you date?"

"Not long. A couple of months. The mysterious James Harley," Susie said regretfully. "He was always flying off somewhere without saying anything. Highly undependable—like most of the men I seem to meet."

"He sounds like a real prize," ventured Priscilla.

"But I did like his mother," Susie added sadly. "I am sorry to hear of her death. She deserved a better son, that's for certain." Susie paused, reflecting. "Still, for a moment or so there, I suppose I might have been a little bit in love with James—fool that I so often am."

"You don't happen to remember where he lives, do you?"

"I know his place from when I was seeing him," Susie replied.

"Why did the two of you break up?"

"I wouldn't say we had enough of a relationship to actually 'break up.' Better to say he dumped me for someone else."

"Do you know who?"

"I found out later that it was that tramp Christine Keeler."

"I had no idea," Priscilla said, thinking that Miss Keeler certainly did get around.

"The way I heard it, Christine didn't last long, either. I understand they ended quite acrimoniously, perhaps when she realized what a prick he is."

The shrill ringing of the telephone interrupted their conversation. Susie picked up the receiver. She listened for a moment, the fear growing in her eyes. "Very well, I'll tell her."

Susie replaced the phone on its cradle.

"What now?" Priscilla demanded.

"Mr. Banville," blurted Susie.

"What about him?" As if Priscilla didn't know.

"He wants to see you."

"And that would be immediately, I suppose."

"An hour ago!"

CHAPTER SIX

Find James Harley!

Clive Banville was the Savoy's general manager. His unhappiness with Priscilla was as reliable as rain in London. Banville had recently demoted her, but the demotion hadn't lasted long. Priscilla had no idea who they belonged to, but powerful voices apparently had whispered in Banville's ear, persuading him to change his mind. Her job was safe. For now.

As she made her way up the steps and along the corridor to the general manager's office, Priscilla could not shake off the possibility that the curse of the Savoy could be working hard to get her fired—permanently this time.

Banville's assistant, the evil Sidney Stopford, known to all as El Sid, manned the guard post outside what Priscilla had come to call the Place of Execution. Sidney's little eyes gleamed malevolently behind gold-rimmed glasses. A scrawny red moustache hung above a twitchy mouth that turned into a scowl as soon as Priscilla appeared.

"*He* has been looking for you," announced El Sid, sounding like a magistrate at the Old Bailey pronouncing a death sentence.

"Well, Sidney, I am here now."

El Sid picked up the receiver, punched a button, then paused a moment before announcing: "Miss Tempest is here—*finally.*"

Sidney hung up—looking, in Priscilla's estimation, entirely too smug. "He's *waiting* for *you*," he said ominously.

Priscilla was having a hard time swallowing as she opened one of the double doors. But any time she had to enter Banville's office, trouble swallowing—and breathing too—was a given.

"There you are, Miss Tempest," Banville called from behind the massive desk he employed as a buffer between himself and troublesome employees such as Priscilla. Banville was the exact picture of the sort of establishment pillar who might be entrusted with the smooth running of one of the world's great hotels: perfectly tailored morning suit, perfectly cut hair shot through with just the right amount of silver, perfectly square jaw thrusting as Priscilla approached, his piercing blue eyes inspecting her. Looking at Clive Banville, one simply could not imagine anyone else occupying his position.

"Good afternoon, sir," Priscilla said, taking her usual place in front of Banville's desk, head slightly lowered, hands clasped in front of her, showing the combination of meekness and innocence she always hoped would elicit a dollop of sympathy from Banville.

Not that it ever worked—as it failed to work today.

"Miss Tempest," said Banville icily. "Once again, having called for you, I find no one can locate you."

"My apologies, sir," said Priscilla weakly.

"I will say again, as I have had to say so many times before, when I call, you must come immediately."

"As you know, sir," Priscilla began, mustering an explanation, although not exactly an accurate one, for why she had been unavailable, "we have had to deal with the unfortunate death of one of our guests this morning, Lady Anne Harley."

"Yes, I am told that you were with her just before she died."

"That is correct, sir. We have been trying to get in touch with her son, James. So far without success, I'm afraid."

"I should have been brought up to date before now," huffed Banville. "Lady Anne has been a valued guest at the Savoy for many years, and her son is one of our most distinguished diplomats."

"I understand, sir," Priscilla said, detecting a slight softening in Banville's tone. "But Major O'Hara was also present. I thought he would have kept you apprised of these events."

"Yes, well…" Banville appeared somewhat flummoxed by a weapon seldom launched from Priscilla's arsenal of excuses—logic. Not to be put off for long, he changed tack. "However, there is another troubling matter that I have not been kept informed about."

"Another matter, sir?" Desperately, she tried to anticipate what matter that could be. Had word somehow gotten back to Banville about the stabbing incident in Jack Cogan's suite? Had the housekeeper who was a witness talked?

"The dinner party hosted by Mr. Orson Welles the other night in the Pinafore Room. I believe you were present."

"Yes, I was," Priscilla said, pleased that for a change she could provide an honest answer.

"What is this I am hearing about a curse?"

Priscilla's stomach dropped. What was she supposed to say about that?

"I'm afraid I was unaware of any curse until Mr. Coward, who was also present, brought it up. He was concerned that there were thirteen guests, which would trigger a curse associated with the room."

"I understand he insisted on bringing out Kaspar."

Priscilla reacted with surprise. "You know about Kaspar?"

"Yes, yes, I know about him," Banville stated impatiently. "It is one of those creaky old superstitions that has been around forever. It has no place in a modern hotel."

"I would agree, sir, however—"

"However, what?" It was all too evident that Banville did not like the word *however*.

"The thirteenth guest was Lady Anne."

"And she left first?"

"I'm afraid she did, sir," Priscilla gulped.

"My God," said Banville with a palpable groan.

"But I'm certain it was nothing more than a terrible coincidence that she happened to succumb to a heart attack the following morning."

"Coincidence?" Banville sounded offended by this word as well.

"I would say, sir."

"You might well say, Miss Tempest. Unfortunately, others might not say the same thing. Others might be more inclined to believe this was the curse of the Savoy at work again after all these years. The spectre of that curse has been whispered about forever. The thing is, no one has paid it much attention—until now."

"While I remain convinced there is nothing to it, taking no chances I've been working to ensure that word of a curse does not reach the press." Not to mention the looming scandal surrounding a stabbing in one of the river suites, Priscilla thought.

"Very good," said Banville with an unusually appreciative nod. "Let us make sure that this entire incident is behind us as quickly as possible."

"I agree, sir," said Priscilla helpfully, beginning to hope against hope she might escape the Place of Execution unscathed.

"For now, we must reach James Harley so that he can resolve any lingering issues with his mother and this hotel."

"As I said, it is unfortunate that, thus far, Mr. Harley has been unavailable," reminded Priscilla.

"Have you attempted to contact him?" Banville asked.

"No sir, I haven't. I didn't think—"

"What you think, Miss Tempest, is of no interest at present," Banville interjected. "Your job is to protect this hotel. To that end, you will work to locate James Harley and ensure that he does not discuss publicly any nonsense about a curse surrounding the unfortunate death of his mother. Is that understood?"

"Completely, sir," gulped Priscilla.

"And let me know as soon as you have contacted him."

"Very good, sir." The good soldier obeying the order to go over the top into no man's land.

"And Miss Tempest…"

"Sir?"

"Mr. Cary Grant of Beverly Hills, California, is staying with us, yes?"

"I believe he is," confirmed Priscilla.

"I have it on good authority that Mr. Grant has taken an interest in you."

Priscilla, blindsided, fumbled for a denial. "I'm not sure where you heard such a thing, but that is hardly the case."

Well, perhaps it's a little bit the case, Priscilla amended to herself.

"Nonetheless, I remind you that it is the policy of the Savoy that employees are not to fraternize with guests. You are aware of that policy, are you not?"

"I am indeed, sir."

"Then I will depend on you to adhere to it." Banville made a dismissive gesture. "That will be all for now, Miss Tempest."

Escaping the Place of Execution, ignoring El Sid's sullen look as she scurried away, Priscilla broke into the corridor outside the office. She stopped to lean against the wall, taking deep, resuscitative breaths, considering the possibility that her boss could somehow read her rather salacious mind, at least when it came to Cary Grant. Whether he could or not, she resolved then and there to make sure that from now on she avoided Mr. Grant.

"Are you all right?"

She turned as Cary Grant reached out and touched her shoulder…that touch of mink, she thought distractedly.

The Cary Treatment

"You look ill," Cary Grant said solicitously.

"No, I'm fine," said a flustered Priscilla.

"Are you sure? You're quite pale, if you don't mind my saying."

She wanted to explain that she had just escaped from the Place of Execution, where she had been warned in no uncertain terms to stay away from Cary Grant—and now here he was. But she couldn't say that, so she was rendered speechless.

"Oh dear," Cary said with a shake of his head. "Whatever ails you has robbed you of the power of speech."

"Not…at all…" Fighting for words that might fit sensibly into a declarative sentence. "I…well…I…"

"Don't try to talk," Cary advised, his tanned face reflecting concern. "Would you like to sit down? Can I bring you some water?"

"I'm…well, I keep saying I'm fine, don't I?" Priscilla babbled on. "But I really am fine…really…"

"No idea where I would get water on short notice, but it does seem like the thing to say, doesn't it? In a crisis, one brings water. That's what you do in the movies."

"Is that what you did in *Charade*?" Priscilla had finally found her voice.

"I don't remember if anyone even drank water in *Charade*, to be honest," Cary said with a reflective frown.

"It's my favourite of your movies," Priscilla offered.

"I was far too old to be carrying on with Audrey, but she was very forgiving." Cary regarded her with narrowed eyes. "I'm not very helpful, am I?"

"I'm fine," Priscilla said.

"You do keep saying that."

The door to Banville's office opened and the impressively imposing figure of Clive Banville stepped out. He immediately spotted Priscilla with Cary Grant and stopped, as though not quite sure what he was seeing. "Miss Tempest."

Priscilla jumped in alarm, as though she had received an electric shock—which, in some ways, she had.

"Mr. Banville," said Priscilla, attempting a quick recovery. "You have met Mr. Cary Grant?"

Banville's unforgiving expression quickly softened. "Yes, I previously had the honour of welcoming Mr. Grant to the Savoy."

"Good to see you again, uh—" It was Cary's turn to be at a loss for words.

"This is Mr. Banville," Priscilla put in hurriedly.

"Banville," said Cary, shaking the general manager's hand. "Such a pleasure."

"I am a great fan," Banville said, not quite obsequiously but close enough that it caught Priscilla by surprise.

"I must tell you, I am most impressed with your staff," Cary said, oozing charm from every pore. "I'm particularly impressed with your Miss Tempest. I was just telling her how much I appreciate her efforts to keep the press away."

Banville seemed confused by Cary's praise. "Yes, well…" he said. "Miss Tempest is—"

"Spectacular, wouldn't you say?" Cary interjected.

"Just so," Banville stated formally. He cleared his throat loudly. "Yes, well, I must be off."

"I'm sure you're extremely busy, running an establishment like the Savoy," Cary said.

"It is never-ending," Banville said. This time he shook Cary's hand. "Let me know if there is anything we can do to make you happy during your time with us."

"I feel I am in good hands with Miss Tempest," Cary said.

It was all Priscilla could do to stifle a groan of despair. That was the last thing she wanted Banville to hear. Whatever he thought of Cary's declaration, he hid it behind a watery smile and a "very good" before parading away.

"There you are," said Cary as soon as Banville was out of earshot. "The general manager himself has entrusted you with my happiness during my stay at the Savoy."

"I doubt very much that is what he was getting at," Priscilla responded.

"Nonsense." Cary was still smiling but the smile was a trifle more insistent. "A drink, or I'm afraid I shall have to report to Mr. Banville that you have failed to do what the Savoy has sworn to do, which is to make me happy."

"Mr. Grant—"

"I will be in touch." He gave Priscilla the same dazzling smile he must have used to melt Audrey Hepburn in *Charade*. It had much the same effect this time.

Susie tensed as Priscilla arrived back at 205. "Well?"

"Well, what?"

"Do we still have a job?"

"You worry far too much about losing your job, Susie," Priscilla said impatiently.

"With very good reason."

"Today, you don't have to worry—not until I meet Cary Grant for a drink."

"Cary Grant? But he is a guest at the hotel, is he not?"

"He is."

"I thought it was against hotel policy for employees to do things like that."

"That is true," Priscilla acknowledged.

"Oh God," whined Susie.

"Perhaps I will run off with Cary Grant. That will solve all my problems."

"But he's so old," Susie said.

"He's not *that* old," Priscilla countered, heading into her office. "Anyway, I may not have any choice—that is, if he will even have me."

"As long as he doesn't find out about your dark, lascivious past," Susie called cattily.

"I don't have a dark, lascivious past," Priscilla countered.

"But you're working on it," retorted Susie.

Not nearly hard enough, Priscilla thought, given the reality of her life lately. Besides, a drink with Cary Grant would, in all likelihood, be no more than a drink. Meanwhile, the whereabouts of James Harley was the job at hand.

She called out to Susie. Immediately, Susie popped her head in the door. "Yes, my liege?"

"You said you had James Harley's address."

"I do, but—but I hope you're not going to ask me to go with you," Susie was saying as she jotted down the address on a notepad.

"Don't worry, I'll handle it," Priscilla said, taking the address.

"A word of advice," Susie added, her tone abruptly more serious.

"Yes?"

"The first thing he will do when he sees you is ask you for a date."

"Not necessarily."

"No, he will. Believe me. He asks everyone. But whatever you do, don't go out with him," Susie said vehemently. Then she reconsidered slightly. "Although, knowing you, you might be tempted."

"What's that supposed to mean?"

"It simply means you are easily seduced by charming men. And James, whatever his many shortcomings, is a charmer."

"His charm won't work on me," Priscilla said.

"It very well might."

"The only reason I'm looking for him is to tell him about his mother."

Susie just smiled knowingly. "I'm willing to wager that not even a dead mother will stop James."

A Murder of Quality

According to the names on the brass plate adjacent to the inter-com, there were six apartments in the fine old Kensington building where James Harley resided. Harley's was at the top.

Priscilla pressed the ivory-coloured button beside his name. The intercom stayed silent. She pressed again, fearing that in fact he might have moved. She rang again. Still nothing.

The front door burst open and a man in a trench coat, a fedora pulled over his eyes, emerged and hurried down the steps, then walked briskly away along the street. Priscilla grabbed at the door before it closed.

Far above the shadowed lobby, a rectangular skylight framed by an intricate stained-glass design reflected light colours across a spectacular winding mahogany staircase. Alfred Hitchcock should know about these stairs, she thought, as she started to climb. They were a perfect setting for one of his thrillers.

At the sixth-floor landing, she stopped to catch her breath. The faint light from the skylight was filled with swirling dust particles. As Priscilla approached Harley's flat, she saw that the door was ajar. She knocked. "Hello..." she called out. No one answered. She pushed the door open further. "Mr. Harley, are you here?" Mr. Harley wasn't answering.

Priscilla faced a wood-panelled hallway. Expensive luggage was stacked against the wall, evidence that Harley had been planning to catch the flight to Moscow he was supposed to be on. A light burned at the far end of the hall. She called out again, hearing only the muffled sounds of the traffic outside. She ventured along to a sitting room and took in the classic fireplace, the landscapes in gilded frames, the body on the sofa covered in blood.

Priscilla's hand shot involuntarily to her mouth, but not fast enough to stifle the loud gasp that sounded right out of a bad West End melodrama.

The dead man was shoeless, though his dark brown argyle socks went with his tweed trousers. In death, staring at the ceiling, his green eyes were wide and the pupils dilated. His skin had turned a ghostly white. His thick hair was a rich brown, and he possessed the kind of firm jaw usually reserved for handsome devils in clothing adverts. What Priscilla assumed was his suit jacket had been tossed across an upholstered occasional chair. She wasn't sure in retrospect what made her pick up the jacket, but that's when she saw the file folder on the chair beneath it. The folder contained six black-and-white photographs. In one of the photographs, Christine Keeler, naked, her hair in disarray, tumbling to her shoulders, stood with a young man. He was in shadow, but it was evident he too was nude.

Christine was not in the other photos. Instead, an older man was partially obscured by a thicket of trees in the English countryside. A slightly blurry quality made Priscilla think the pictures had been taken from a distance using a telephoto lens.

Why did the older man look so familiar? Was he one of the guests at the Orson Welles dinner? Lord Louis Mountbatten, the Queen's cousin? The more Priscilla studied the photos, the more certain she became that it *was* Mountbatten. He was kissing a younger man with wavy blond hair. A second and third photo showed the two of them tangled intimately together on the ground. Though they both remained clothed, these were not images His Lordship would want made public. She quickly gathered up all the photos and shoved them in her shoulder bag, trying not to think of the possible ramifications of what she was doing—removing evidence from a murder scene—or of how much trouble she could once again be wading into. She just needed to focus on keeping the Savoy's name clear. Simultaneously, her head filled with wild thoughts of curses and black cats. She must not allow herself to think like that. She had to clear her head.

She spotted a telephone on a writing desk in the corner. If she had any sense, she would just walk away, but she picked up the receiver and waited for the operator to come on the line so that she could be connected to the police.

"Given the evidence we have found, we have concluded the dead man is James Harley," stated Detective Chief Inspector Robert "Charger" Lightfoot. Priscilla was seated with the inspector in the claustrophobic confines of a police car parked outside the Kensington apartment house.

"Brilliant detective work, Inspector," Priscilla said acidly. Lightfoot rewarded her with a frosty glare.

Uniformed bobbies had arrived minutes after Priscilla called. They had whisked her down to street level, where she was held until Inspector Lightfoot arrived in a flurry of take-charge authority and moved her away from the growing mob of reporters gathering on the pavement. Priscilla was amazed at how quickly the press had arrived, as though they had a sixth sense about these things.

"A murder of quality, that's what draws these vermin," huffed Inspector Lightfoot. "Some poor working sod gets knifed in South London, and nobody shows up. Not a word in the papers.

But this is James Harley, Conservative Party boy wonder, and so they swarm."

The inspector looked world-weary. His face, deeply carved with lines and crevices, might have been chipped off the side of a cliff. His watery blue eyes had seen it all in his time as a copper and did not want to see more, thank you very much. Certainly, he disliked the view he had of Priscilla Tempest, a view he had encountered too many times before. She was an irksome young woman, as far as he was concerned, unreliable and prone to dishonesty in her answers.

"What is it, Miss Tempest?" Lightfoot asked, not very pleasantly. "Is Mr. Harley a friend of yours?"

"Not a friend at all," Priscilla corrected. "I never met him."

Lightfoot's bushy white eyebrows raised majestically above hard eyes clouding with suspicion. "If that's the case, Miss Tempest, remind me again how it is you happened to be in his flat."

"As I told you and informed the officers who initially questioned me, I have been trying to locate Mr. Harley, as his mother passed away this morning in her suite at the Savoy."

"This would be Lady Anne Harley," interjected Lightfoot, "an elderly woman who apparently died of natural causes."

"Yes," Priscilla said with a nod. "Finally I obtained his address and came around. When I arrived at his flat, the door was open. I went in and found him on the sofa, covered in blood."

"I'm afraid whoever did this used a knife on Mr. Harley's throat." Lightfoot paused and then asked, "What time did you arrive?"

"At about three thirty," Priscilla reported.

"And you're sure you don't know the deceased?"

"Why do you keep asking me that?" demanded Priscilla, annoyed but also growing increasingly concerned.

"Because, Miss Tempest," said Lightfoot pointedly, "you arrive at a flat and suddenly there is a dead man with his throat cut. No one else is present, only you." For good measure, he added an accusatory glance.

"What are you suggesting?" Priscilla asked, outraged. "That I murdered a man I've never met?" She had no problem demonstrating the combination of anger and disbelief she was feeling.

"No one is saying that," said Lightfoot.

"I told you about the man I saw leaving as I went in."

"Who might well have been a resident in this building."

"He might have been with Mr. Harley," Priscilla countered. Rather lamely, she thought.

"Is that all, Miss Tempest? Is there anything else you can add that might aid us in our investigation?"

The way the inspector was studying her, she was left with the uneasy feeling that he was eyeing his number one suspect. Ridiculous, she thought to herself. But then she became aware of the compromising photos in her shoulder bag. Given the inspector's already suspicious nature, she was beginning to regret the unthinking moment of haste that had caused her to snap them up. And there was one more thing. Something she had not dared mention to the police.

The curse of the Savoy.

Aloud she said, "There's nothing else, Inspector. If you don't mind, I must get back to work."

"Yes, I forgot, Miss Tempest," said Lightfoot acidly. "You do have a job that does not involve finding dead bodies."

CHAPTER NINE

Cleopatra in Gold and Feathers

"I can't believe he's *dead*," Susie kept saying in shock as soon as Priscilla told her the next morning about James Harley's death. "I simply can't believe it."

"You have my sympathies, Susie."

"I mean I *dated* him. I *hated* dating him, but now he's *dead* and I feel terrible. I mean I may have loved him. A little bit. Maybe. I can't believe it!"

"Susie…"

"And then you found him," Susie went on, near tears. "I can't believe *you* found him. It must have been awful."

"It was," Priscilla agreed.

She was saved from more of Susie's histrionics by a ringing telephone. Priscilla snapped up the receiver. "Savoy Press Office, Priscilla Tempest speaking."

"Miss Tempest," a soft girlish voice said, "this is Christine Keeler."

Priscilla's grip tightened on the receiver. "Miss Keeler."

"I thought I should give you a call." She paused. "You know, after what happened the other day."

"Yes, we need to talk," Priscilla said, thinking of the photos she had taken from Harley's flat. "But not over the phone."

"Let's meet at Murray's on Beak Street," Christine answered promptly. "When are you available?"

"We should meet today."

"I will see you there at two o'clock?"

"Two it is," agreed Priscilla.

As Priscilla came off the phone, Susie was collapsed in tears on the sofa.

"I can't believe it," Susie repeated yet again. She looked up at Priscilla with teary eyes. "I do believe I loved him, Priscilla, and now he's gone!"

The massive stone facade of Hardy House, the building on Beak Street where Murray's Club was housed, resembled a bank, an ironic disguise for one of London's most notorious establishments. Murray's was accessed through an arched entranceway. A flight of stairs led down to the basement where the club, founded in 1913, had been located since the late 1930s.

At two o'clock, Murray's was all but deserted, no sign of the topless dancers the club was famous—or infamous—for. The youthful hostess on the door wore a short polka dot dress with puffed sleeves and a plunging neckline. "This is the 'O-you-beautiful-gal' costume designed by the great Ronald Cobb, who created all the costumes for our dancers," the hostess explained.

"Are you one of the dancers?"

"Not a chance," said the hostess. "But I do get to wear Mr. Cobb's designs."

As soon as Priscilla gave her name, the hostess brightened. "Yes, Christine said you were coming. She's not here yet, but let me show you to her table."

Christine's table was at the back with a good view of the stage where the nightly floor show featured, according to the club's adverts, "thirty-six of England's loveliest showgirls."

One of those showgirls, once upon a time, had been Christine Keeler, which made Priscilla wonder what she was doing back here all these years later.

"I do wonder about that myself," said Christine, breathless, when she arrived fifteen minutes later and Priscilla asked the question. "All the trouble in my life started right here in this basement ten years ago." She grinned. "I didn't usually have this many clothes on. I was Cleopatra in gold and feathers with my boobs showing."

Not today, Priscilla thought. Today, Christine was the picture of the conservative British businesswoman, in a charcoal-grey suit with a demure knee-length skirt, a Hermès scarf at her throat. She might have been a bank employee on a lunch break. Except for her eyes. They were not the brown eyes of a bank clerk. They were old and knowing. They had seen all the angles and had taken into consideration all the tricks. Priscilla wondered if she too would have eyes like that in a few years—that is, if she didn't already have them.

"It was a strange underground fantasy life," Christine continued. "I didn't realize how strange until I emerged from it."

"But here you are back," Priscilla interjected.

"Murray's isn't at all what it once was," Christine offered. "People don't come here the way they used to. At this time of day, it's a good place to talk. I know the ears here, the eyes. The ears don't listen. The eyes don't see."

"You should see this." Priscilla lifted up her shoulder bag and extracted a photograph. She laid it in front of Christine.

"Where did you get this?" Christine asked in a whispery voice after she'd stared at the photo for a minute or so.

"It was in James Harley's apartment. I found the photos after I discovered his body. Someone had slit his throat."

"My God," Christine said, the colour draining from her face. "When?"

"His mother died of a heart attack in her suite at the Savoy this morning. I went to James's apartment to give him the news."

Christine dropped a napkin over the photograph as though she couldn't bear to look at it any longer. "What do the police say? Do they know who did it?"

"Right now, unless I miss my guess, they are viewing me as a possible suspect."

"You?" Christine reacted with consternation. "Why would you kill James?"

"The fact is, I wouldn't. I didn't even know the man. But you obviously did."

"Yes, unfortunately."

"That isn't him in the photograph?"

"A handsome young Scottish earl. I should have known better, I suppose. But then I should have known better about so many things. The earl must have had a hidden camera in his bedroom that he failed to tell me about. The next thing I knew, James was getting in touch. Somehow, he had obtained the photo. I'm not sure, but I think he's part of a group that extorts money from well-known people."

"What did James want?" Priscilla asked.

"Revenge, I suppose. I certainly didn't have any money myself. But he said certain people he was involved with could sell the pictures to Jack Cogan's newspapers. That was the business those people were in, James said. The world was full of rich people willing to pay money to save their reputations. That's why I was with Jack. He said he wouldn't buy the photo if I— well, you know how that turned out."

"After he slept with you, I suppose he said he still might buy it."

"He said he had no control over his editors. That's when I decided it might be a good idea to stab him."

The hostess approached wearing a cheery smile. "Can I get you girls anything?" she inquired.

Christine looked at Priscilla. "I'm fine."

"Make that a gimlet for me please, Charlotte. Vodka instead of gin."

As soon as the hostess turned away, Priscilla leaned forward and dropped her voice. "In Harley's flat there were also photographs of someone who looks an awful lot like Lord Mountbatten. He's in the woods with a young man."

Christine arched an ironic eyebrow. "If a picture like that were made public, it would be the end of Louis Mountbatten in the world in which he exists. He would do just about anything to keep photos such as you're describing out of the press."

"I took the photos that were in Harley's flat, but there could be more. If that's the case, you may receive a visit from the police."

"I thank you for the photo, but you've put yourself at a bit of a risk. Do you mind if I ask why?"

"For purely selfish reasons, if I'm being honest. Should the police have found the photographs then they would have questioned you. I worried it would then be only a matter of time before the news of your encounter with Jack Cogan leaked out. This way, I hope to avoid a scandal at the Savoy. I suppose I'm thinking much the same about Lord Mountbatten."

The hostess was back with Christine's gimlet. As soon as it was set down, Christine picked it up and drank half of it. Her eyes watered. "That's just what a gal needs when she's looking at a naked picture of herself. She lifted her glass to Priscilla. "Here's to you, Priscilla. I do think you must be a bit mad for what you've done, but you won't hear a peep out of me." She finished the gimlet and then dropped the photo into her handbag.

"Do you have any idea who might have murdered Harley?" Priscilla asked, wondering if she shouldn't have ordered a drink herself.

"It wasn't you or me, of that much I'm sure." She looked pensive for a moment before saying, "You know, in the midst of the Profumo thing, I was convinced the establishment was going to knock me off. Were it not for all the publicity, being hounded day and night by the press, they would have done just that."

"Do you think that's what's happening now?"

"All I know is if there are people out there blackmailing establishment blokes like Lord Mountbatten, there are other people bound to stop them by any means necessary."

"Even murder?"

"Just ask James Harley," Christine said pointedly. She thought for another minute or so. "There is one other thing to be considered, I suppose."

"What's that?"

"The curse," Christine said sombrely. "Maybe there really is a curse of the Savoy."

The Gossip's Bridle Club Meets

"Fiddlesticks, there is no such thing as a curse," said Laurence Olivier contemptuously over the warm din of early evening cocktail conversation in the Savoy's American Bar. Occupying their usual corner table, in addition to Olivier, were John Gielgud, Noël Coward and Priscilla, the members in good standing of the Gossip's Bridle Club. Discussions swirled around such vital issues of the day as whose play was a disaster, what film had bombed and, most importantly, who was sleeping with whom.

Priscilla brought her fellow members news of James Harley's murder. In the course of relating the events leading up to her discovery of the body, Priscilla had touched upon the subject of the curse. "The fact is, whether I like it or not, the curse may have affected both Lady Anne Harley and her son," Priscilla said ruefully. "Me, too, when it comes to that."

"How so?" inquired Gielgud.

"Because I found James murdered in his flat, the police seem to think I might somehow be responsible."

"Ridiculous," announced Olivier in a voice suggesting that should be the end of the matter.

"Nonetheless, I am having trouble shaking off the notion that the black cloud of the curse hangs over me," Priscilla said. She glanced at Noël. "Or am I going mad with paranoia?"

"Not at all," said Noël, focused on attaching a cigarette to his ivory cigarette holder. "I think you have every right to be worried."

"Such nonsense," chimed in Gielgud, looking around for a waiter who could replace his gin and tonic. "I hate to agree with Larry about anything, but I'm afraid he is right in this instance. There is no such thing as curses, except in bad plays— and Shakespeare."

"And to which bad play might you be referring?" asked Noël, watching Gielgud out of the corner of his eye.

"With all due respect, Noël, *Blithe Spirit* is not one of your better efforts. Terrible second act problems when the medium shows up. That part is nothing but an excuse for bad actresses to act worse."

"It is regarded as one of my many masterpieces," Noël stated mildly, before adding a bit more defensively: "I will have you know, curses play no part in what I call my improbable farce— save perhaps for the fact that it sometimes attracts actors who couldn't play comedy if their lives depended on it."

"If you happen to be referring to the time *I* took on the impossible part of Charles in your play," interjected Gielgud, a trifle miffed, "I made a Herculean effort to wring every possible laugh from it. Audiences loved my performance."

"Yes, but Johnny, I have to point out that you played Charles for troops starved for any sort of entertainment—during the war in Burma!"

"I do believe a youthfully beautiful leading man was more than capable of a touch of comic magic in *Private Lives*," Olivier said with a hint of smugness. "At least that's what the critics said of my performance as Victor."

"A master of comedy, what can I say?" stated Noël in a voice as dry as the martini Olivier was drinking.

"Yes, I should think that's an accurate description," Olivier replied with satisfaction.

Gielgud rolled his eyes.

"The fact is, Lady Anne died after attending the dinner," Priscilla interrupted, playing her usual role as referee, attempting, sometimes futilely, to keep the conversation on track. "And now her son is dead too—murdered. And whether I like it or not, I am a suspect. If that is not a curse at work, I don't know what is."

"I rest my case," said Noël benignly.

"That's not a curse," cautioned Gielgud. "That's a terrible coincidence."

"Call it what you will, dear boy, but the facts are what the facts are."

"There's something else, as well," Priscilla said.

Three pairs of eyes focused on her immediately.

"There may be another possible suspect," Priscilla said. She now had the undivided attention of the three men. "Yesterday morning, I went to wake up Lady Anne in her suite."

"Yes, at the dinner she asked you to do that as her way of demonstrating there is no such thing as a curse," Noël put in. "We now know how that turned out."

"No sooner had I awakened Lady Anne than I heard a scream from a suite further along the hall," Priscilla continued. "I found Jack Cogan with a letter opener sticking out of him."

"The Jackal," breathed Noël.

"A moment later, a woman appeared in the room. It was Christine Keeler."

"*The* Christine Keeler?" asked Olivier.

"If I'm remembering the tattling in *Spy* magazine correctly," joined in Gielgud, "Miss Keeler and Harley were once an item, were they not?"

"They were," Priscilla agreed.

"You told the police about this, I'm sure."

"I told Mr. Cogan I wouldn't say anything—the discretion of the Savoy, you understand."

"I don't understand at all," interjected Noël. "The fact remains, Miss Keeler used a knife-like object, and it was a knife that was employed to end the life of James Harley, was it not?"

"Christine broke up with him—quite a nasty breakup I'm told," Priscilla explained. "But was it bad enough that she would murder him?"

"There is another question that we should consider," offered Gielgud, breaking the silence that had ensued.

"And what would that be?" asked Noël.

"Setting aside the curse aspect, what was Orson Welles doing hosting that dinner in the first place?"

Noël was now busily attempting to light his cigarette, using his Ronson Maximus lighter with its distinctive snakeskin finish. "I'm not sure what you mean, dear boy," he said as soon as he had finally produced a flame and lit his cigarette.

"Consider the rather impressive guest list. Why would Orson bring such an eclectic group together? An aging film star—"

"We are all aging film stars, dear boy," interjected Olivier.

"Hitchcock—for whom I starred in *Secret Agent*, one of his most dazzling early achievements—"

"You had hair back then," interjected Noël. "Or was it one of your many hairpieces?"

"Let me finish, please," Gielgud said irritably. "As I started to say, Hitchcock and Cary Grant, thrown in with the woman who brought down the British government, a young newspaper tycoon, a wealthy dowager, and you, Noël, along with Priscilla. Am I leaving anyone out?"

"A Lloyds banker named Quinn and his wife," said Noël helpfully. "Also, the American novelist Norman Mailer."

"Mailer? What's he noted for?"

"Stabbing his wife with a penknife," answered Noël.

"A literary genius," pronounced Gielgud. "A strange crew to say the least. What was the reason for bringing all of you together?"

"To raise money for his next movie, at least that's what we all assumed," said Priscilla. "Cue the Lloyds banker and his wife."

"Let us not forget the unexpected presence of Louis Mountbatten, who is certainly not to be caught dead investing in a movie," Noël said, balancing his cigarette holder on an ashtray. "But Johnny does have a point. Why? With the exception perhaps of the banker, those present were in no position to finance another potential Orson disaster. After all, the poor man has left any number of unfinished masterpieces in film cans strewn across Europe. Who among us would dare take another chance on him—even if they had the funds? And further, did Orson finance the dinner? Such extravagance! I can't imagine, given what I've heard are his strained financial circumstances, how he could ever pay for it. And if he didn't, then who did?"

"What about the man he said was producing the picture?" Priscilla asked. "The fellow whose absence triggered all this talk about a curse."

"You mean Harry Alan Towers?" Noël waved his cigarette holder dismissively. "A scoundrel of the first order. I'd be dumbfounded if he paid for it. And I'd be dumbfounded if it turned out he could finance Orson's movie."

"If you knew what was behind that dinner," Gielgud said, "it might be easier to understand the events that have subsequently unfolded."

Noël placed his hand gently on Priscilla's arm. "This is where you come in, my dear. You must do what you have become very good at."

"What is that?" Priscilla asked.

"Getting to the bottom of things. Solving the mystery."

"I wish I was as certain about my abilities as you are, Noël."

"We're here to help in any way we can," chimed in Olivier eagerly.

"Oh my God," groaned Gielgud. "The poor woman doesn't stand a chance."

The Man Who Paid for Dinner

Back in 205, Priscilla mulled over Noël's assertion that she was very good when it came to getting to the bottom of things.

Solving the mystery, in other words. Perhaps not a bad idea, considering that she was already involved—and under suspicion.

Why had Orson Welles hosted the dinner that begat the curse? And could it possibly be connected with the murder of James Harley? That is, *if* she allowed herself to believe in curses. She was trying very hard not to.

It was becoming increasingly difficult.

She picked up one of the three phones on her desk and asked the operator to connect her to Paolo Contarini, the hotel's banquet manager.

A former head waiter, Paolo had transformed the Savoy's catering and banquet business since taking over as manager. He practically lived in a cramped office in the basement that overflowed with files containing the records of every banquet and private dinner, along with extensive notes about the preferences of regular clients. An assistant and two clerks helped manage a staff of sixty. But even so, Paolo ended up doing most of the planning and preparation himself. He would also know who paid the bill in the end.

"The pleasure of a phone call from the elusive Priscilla Tempest," Paolo said.

"Goodness me, Mr. Contarini, am I so elusive?"

"A refreshingly free spirit, I would say, amid all this conformity," replied Paolo merrily. "What may I do for you, Miss Tempest?"

"A favour, if you don't mind."

"Anything! What is it they say around here? We do the impossible? Miracles take a bit longer? No, no. I perform miracles every day, and I make certain they take no time at all."

"This doesn't require a miracle—at least I don't think it does. The Orson Welles private dinner in the Pinafore Room…"

"Ah, yes…that," said Paolo.

"Problems?"

"Let us say, many miracles were required in order to please Signor Welles. He is, shall we say, a…*demanding* client. But that's fine. All in a day's work."

"Who was charged for the dinner? Was it Mr. Welles?"

"Although he demanded nothing but the best from us, he definitely did not pay the bill. In fact, he refused to even look at it, insisting that it be sent on to…"

"Yes?"

"A minute please, Miss Tempest, while I check that account." There was silence for a time. Priscilla could hear Paolo rustling papers. He came back on the line: "Yes, here it is, that account was settled by a Mr. Kirk Strong."

Kirk Strong? The name meant nothing to her. There was no one by that name at the dinner.

"I have an address," Paolo was saying. "Would you like that?"

"Please."

"Swain's Lane. Number eleven. In North London, I believe."

"Is that where you sent the bill?"

"No, because of previous difficulties involving Signor Welles and the settling of his accounts, we asked Mr. Strong to come around and deal with payment in person, which he did—in cash, I might add."

"Did you handle it, Paolo?"

"I did. Mr. Strong is an American it turns out, quite a pleasant chap."

"Do you remember what he looked like?"

"Why would you ask, Miss Tempest?" For the first time, Paolo's voice carried a note of suspicion.

"Just curious," Priscilla said hastily. "I wondered if it might have been one of Mr. Welles's dinner guests. Apparently not. As far as I know, Mr. Strong did not actually attend the dinner. Odd."

"I would humbly suggest that Signor Welles is not a gentleman who should be hosting lavish dinners at a great hotel, given what I have been led to understand about the state of his finances," Paolo went on, his voice relaxing. "However, that was not a concern in this instance. As for Mr. Strong, unusually tall, but maybe not so unusual for an American. Early thirties, thick black hair. A certain presence about him. You do not miss Mr. Strong when he enters a room."

"You've been very helpful, Mr. Contarini. Thank you."

"The information I have given you, Miss Tempest, you understand it must remain strictly *entre nous*, as it were. I would not want anything to get back to Mr. Welles."

"Heavens no, Mr. Contarini. Thank you. You already know what a darling you are."

"Yes, but I like to be reminded by a pretty woman," Paolo said eagerly.

"Consider yourself reminded, Mr. Contarini."

As soon as Priscilla was off the phone, Susie stuck her head in the door. "Who is Orson Welles?" she asked in all innocence.

"You don't know who Orson Welles is?"

"Should I?"

"*Citizen Kane?*"

"Is Mr. Kane here with Mr. Welles?"

"Susie, for heaven's sake," Priscilla exploded in exasperation. "*Citizen Kane* is a *movie!* Welles was the director. It's a classic."

"I see." She added sullenly, "I can hardly be expected to know the identity of every guest at this hotel."

"No, Susie, I suppose you can't," Priscilla said resignedly. "Now that you are aware of Mr. Welles, what about him?"

"He just called. He asked to see you in his suite as soon as possible."

CHAPTER TWELVE

A Tub Full of Welles

Given her recent unhappy experiences with guests in their suites, Priscilla was nervous as she approached 525, the suite occupied by Orson Welles. Not that she had much choice. This was the great Orson Welles summoning her, even if Susie had no clue as to who he was. Besides, she thought as she knocked on the door, this could be a chance to find out more about the reasons behind Welles's dinner in the Pinafore Room and the tall, dark and mysterious American, Kirk Strong, who had paid the bill.

The door opened to reveal a short man in a navy-blue suit and a bright-yellow bow tie. His pink face emphasized eyes the size of headlights As the short man stared at her, unblinking, she had the uneasy feeling she was meeting a visitor from outer space disguised, quite effectively actually, as either a prime minister or a vicar.

"Can I help you?" he asked with an accent so cultivated that, coming from this alien-like fellow, it was quite disconcerting.

"Yes, I'm Miss Tempest," Priscilla announced.

"Harry Alan Towers," said the short man, holding out a pudgy hand. "I am Orson's producer. He's been expecting you. Won't you please come in."

Harry Alan Towers stepped aside, bowing slightly to admit Priscilla into a sitting room whose drapes were closed to shut out daylight. Desks and chairs were strewn with newspapers and piled with scripts, and the air was rich with the stench of cigar smoke. A voice boomed from behind a partially open door on the far side of the room: "Is that you, Priscilla?"

"Mr. Welles?" she called back.

"Come along through," Welles ordered.

"Please, go ahead," Towers urged. He held out his arm as though to direct her.

With concern mounting, Priscilla crossed to the door. "I'm here, Mr. Welles."

"Come in, come in," he urged from the other side of the door.

Priscilla stepped into a white-tiled bathroom thick with cigar smoke. Through the haze, Priscilla could make out Orson Welles facing her in a big porcelain bathtub—a great white Buddha immersed in soap bubbles. A half-smoked cigar was jammed in the corner of his mouth. A tray was attached to either side of the tub, upon which Welles held an open script in one hand, a pencil in the other.

"There you are, finally," Welles announced merrily. "I can't imagine you're the shy type, Priscilla. I'm not going to bite."

Given his girth, Priscilla was unsure as to how he would get out of the tub, let alone bite her.

"I don't think I should be in here, Mr. Welles."

"Where else should you be?" The deep rumble of Welles's voice echoed in the bathroom. "This is where I work. This is my office." He removed the cigar from his mouth and used it to point to the chair in the corner. "Take a seat. This won't take long."

Priscilla felt she had no choice but to sit where she had been told. Welles's voice rang out: "Harry! Get your ass in here."

Harry Alan Towers appeared in the doorway. "Right here, Orson," he said.

"Priscilla, you've already met my friend Harry. Harry is a veteran producer. Isn't that right, Harry?"

"That's true, Orson."

"Don't you get a kick out of Harry's accent?" Orson said to Priscilla. "You'd think he had attended Eton or some such college, but he's from a working-class family in—what?—Wandsworth. Is that it, Harry?"

"That's correct, Orson," Towers said agreeably. "An old mill town where the River Wandle meets the Thames."

"Harry was a child actor. I imagine that's where he learned to talk the way he does." Welles pointed his cigar at Towers. "That right, Harry, a child actor?"

"I'm flattered that you know those details of my early life," said Towers, lowering those headlight eyes slightly in a show of modesty.

"In fact, I played Moriarty in one of Harry's Sherlock Holmes radio productions."

"A brilliant performance," Towers confirmed.

"Tell Priscilla what we've got up our sleeves, will you, Harry?"

"Yes, I would like to hear that," Priscilla said with a supportive smile. "After all, Mr. Towers, I now hear you are the man responsible for organizing that impressive dinner Mr. Welles hosted. So many well-known people. Quite amazing."

"That was Orson," said Towers. "Everyone was there to celebrate him."

"Nonsense, Harry," Welles said, managing to look humble and at the same time pleased with himself, "you threw it all together."

"It's a shame that Mr. Kirk Strong couldn't have attended," said Priscilla, as though Strong's involvement in the dinner was a given.

Towers gawked at her. Welles looked confused. "Who is Kirk Strong?"

"I have no idea who you are talking about." Towers wasn't so much gawking now as glaring.

"I'm so sorry, I thought that's who the hotel staff was dealing with."

"Well, they weren't," snapped Towers. "They dealt with me—and with Orson, of course."

"Definitely me," agreed Welles, taking a puff on his cigar.

"You were going to tell me about Mr. Welles's latest project," said Priscilla, deciding, given the coolness suddenly in the air, to quickly change the subject.

"I would be happy to." Towers took a deep breath as though to shake off the thought of Kirk Strong. "We would like to hold a press conference to announce the start of production on Orson's next film masterpiece."

"You see why I like Harry, Priscilla? We haven't even made the movie and it's already a masterpiece."

"With you at the helm, Orson, what else could it be?"

"Well, it could be a goddamn disaster, but let's hope not," Welles said. He looked over at Priscilla. "You're bound to ask me what the film is about, aren't you, Priscilla?"

She wasn't, but she summoned an eager nod. "I'm sure you're going to tell me, Mr. Welles."

"A thriller. Titled *The Deep*. Jeanne Moreau will star. Isn't that right, Harry?"

"An international star of the first calibre," Towers once again confirmed. "With her in front of the camera and you behind, Orson, we can't possibly miss."

"Can't we?" This time Welles's smile was a touch more cynical. "Let's see about that."

"Very well," said Priscilla, "when would you like to hold the press conference?"

"What do you say, Harry? Next week sometime?"

"Good for me, Orson," Towers said.

"What about Monday, Priscilla? How's that?"

"If I may, Mr. Welles, I would suggest Thursday," Priscilla said. "That way we can make the weekend papers. However, before I make a final commitment, I would need to check our schedule."

"Thursday it is," said Welles. "But let's not hold it in the Pinafore Room. All this nonsense about Kaspar and a curse. I don't want a repeat of that."

"I understand," Priscilla said. "May I suggest the River Room? It comfortably accommodates one hundred. And the press tends to like it because of the lovely view of the Thames."

"I'd prefer the press concentrating on Harry and me rather than staring out the window, but I suppose it will do. Anything else you want to say, Harry?"

"The River Room is good for me, Orson. And no matter what the view, no one will be able to take their eyes off Orson Welles informing the world of our great partnership."

"There is one thing about Harry you should be aware of." Welles gave Priscilla a sly look. "That Sherlock Holmes radio show I was telling you about?"

"Yes, Mr. Welles?" Priscilla said.

"He never paid me."

Towers looked embarrassed. "I'm sure that wasn't the case, Orson."

"I'm afraid it is, old man. I'm afraid it is." Towers looked devastated. "But not to worry, old man," Welles added with a benevolent smile. "All will be forgiven on the first day of principal photography."

"That's a deal, Orson," said Towers with recovered enthusiasm. "First day it is."

"My bath is getting cold," Welles announced, throwing the remains of his cigar to one side. "Time to vacate the office." He started to rise, a great white whale adorned with soap.

Priscilla shot to her feet. "Mr. Welles!" she cried. That was all she needed, she thought, to get caught in a suite with a naked Orson Welles.

She heard his rumbling chortle as she escaped out the door.

CHAPTER THIRTEEN

Kaspar's New Home

Why would Harry Alan Towers lie about knowing this Kirk Strong individual? Priscilla asked herself as she crossed the Front Hall. Who was he anyway, and why would he pay for a dinner he didn't even attend? All she had on him was the address on Swain's Lane. Maybe it was nothing…

Or maybe it wasn't.

Entering 205, Priscilla came to an abrupt stop when she saw Susie glaring at the black cat sculpture of Kaspar.

"Where did that come from?"

"They say they don't know what else to do with it," said Susie gloomily. "It's a terribly scary thing, if you ask me."

"We're to take care of it?" Priscilla asked in dismay.

"Apparently." Susie's face scrunched into a look of disgust. "It's awful. I'm sure it's cursed."

"It's not cursed, for heaven's sake," Priscilla said. "It's supposed to ward off the curses."

"I know what they say, but look at him. He's evil. I don't want the thing here."

"Put it in my office," Priscilla said, "and let's be done with it."

Susie stood and picked up Kaspar gingerly. Holding him at arm's length, she carried him into Priscilla's office and mounted him on an end table beside the sofa. Kaspar stared at them—rather menacingly, Priscilla couldn't help but think.

"Look at him," Susie said in a hushed voice. "He's putting a curse on us at this very moment."

"Susie," said Priscilla impatiently. "Don't be so ridiculous."

"It's not ridiculous," Susie insisted. "Ask anyone who has been around this hotel. They all believe in Kaspar's curse, including Mr. Coward."

"That's enough," Priscilla ordered. "Back to work. Mr. Welles wants us to organize a press conference. Thursday in the River Room. Get on the phone and round up the usual suspects."

"Is that our friend Kaspar?" asked Cary Grant. Priscilla swung around to find him poised on the threshold. "I hope I'm not interrupting anything."

"No, certainly not," Priscilla said, gathering herself together. "I was wondering how you're doing."

"I'm doing just fine, thank you," Cary said, smiling. He nodded at the sculpture. "A new addition to the office?"

"I'm afraid so," said Priscilla.

Susie's eyes were darting quickly—far too knowingly as far as Priscilla was concerned—back and forth between the two of them.

"Now, Susie," Priscilla said, anxious to deflect attention away from Kaspar. "Surely you know who this is."

"Of course," she said, standing to offer her hand. "How could I not know the famous film star Mr. Stewart Granger?"

Priscilla regarded her assistant with exasperation. "Susie, this is *Cary Grant*."

Susie's face reddened in embarrassment. "I'm so sorry, Mr. Grant."

"It's all right, Susie," Cary said, smiling cheerfully as he took her hand. "It happens all the time."

"Would you care to step into my office, Mr. Grant?" Priscilla asked in a formal voice.

"I would be most pleased, Miss Tempest," Cary replied with equal formality.

Ignoring Susie's suspicious eyes, Priscilla ushered Cary into her office and closed the door.

"I thought I'd come by and see how *you* are doing," Cary said, dropping onto the sofa beside Kaspar, crossing his legs and adjusting the seam of his trousers so that he was the picture of elegant comfort.

"I've been concerned about you, Mr. Grant."

"Heavens, why would you be concerned about me?"

"As you know," Priscilla said with a smile, "I have been tasked with ensuring that you are happy during your stay with us."

"I've never been happier," he said. "Your assistant thinks I'm Stewart Granger, it's been days since anyone asked me to do a movie—and, best of all, I'm talking to a lovely young woman this morning. It does not get much better."

"That's very encouraging," Priscilla said.

"Yes, be sure to tell your boss. What's the chap's name again?"

"Banville. Mr. Banville."

"Make sure you tell Mr. Banville how happy that fellow Cary Grant is. Although, more and more, people don't seem to recognize him. Which is fine with me. Let them think I'm Stewart Granger."

"Well, I'm very happy to see you no matter who you're calling yourself," Priscilla said.

"Then let us have that drink we talked about."

"I suppose a drink can't hurt," Priscilla said. "After all, as you point out, it is the task of those of us at the Savoy to keep our guests happy."

"It must be the curse of Kaspar," Cary said eyeing the cat.

"What about it?" Priscilla was suddenly worried all over again.

"Looking at you, I have this strange sensation, as though we are in a movie. I should be kissing you passionately as it fades to the end."

"I'm not sure that sensation has anything to do with Kaspar," Priscilla said, willing herself not to even think about allowing Cary Grant to kiss her. "In any event, I don't think it's such a good idea."

"No, I suppose not," Cary said disappointedly. He gave Kaspar a sad look as he stood. "Sorry, Kaspar. It appears life trumps even cursed black cats."

"Real life trumps everything," Priscilla agreed, opening the door.

She followed him into the outer office. "Nevertheless, I will be telephoning you," Cary called over his shoulder. "There is no escape."

She wasn't sure she would even try.

"A pleasure to meet you, Mr. Grant." Susie placed the emphasis on his last name. Her eyes were agleam.

"Granger," Cary replied with a devilish grin. "Stewart Granger." He cast Priscilla a final look—a longing look? No, it couldn't be.

"That was a longing look if ever I saw one," Susie said as soon as Cary was out the door.

"Not another word," Priscilla said, escaping quickly into her office and shutting the door so that she would not have to look at Susie's knowing smirk.

She settled uneasily at her desk, keeping an eye on Kaspar in case he should come to life and spring on her. He'd only been resident in her office for a short time, yet already he was making her uneasy. She had to get out of the office, she decided, to escape Kaspar and walls that were closing in. She had to go somewhere else.

She knew just the place.

CHAPTER FOURTEEN

Ethel Lives Next Door

Swain's Lane, a leafy street flanked by two-storey stand-alone houses, stood quietly beneath an overcast late-afternoon sky. The curtains on the ground floor at No. 11 were drawn, as were the blinds in the upstairs windows. The home of the mysterious Kirk Strong? wondered Priscilla. It looked harmless enough. But then why should she be expecting anything else?

As Priscilla watched from her Morris Minor, a blue Renault chugged along the street and parked beside the house next door to No. 11. A tiny white-haired woman in a flowered dress struggled out and then waddled unsteadily to the rear of the car and opened what the British insist on calling the boot. She bent over to pull out a cloth grocery bag, lost her balance and had to grip the edge of the boot to keep from falling.

Priscilla got out of her car and hurried across to the woman. "Can I help you?" she called.

The woman turned as Priscilla approached. "Yes, yes, a little out of breath I'm afraid."

"Here, allow me," Priscilla said.

"Most kind," the woman said. "Most kind…"

Priscilla reached into the boot and pulled out the bag, which was filled with fresh vegetables. Holding the bag with one hand, Priscilla steadied the woman with the other.

"My name is Ethel, by the way," the woman said as they reached the door. "Ethel Cambridge."

"Ethel, I'm Priscilla Tempest. It's nice to meet you."

"Don't know what's wrong with me lately, lovey," Ethel said. "Not myself. Age might have something to do with it." Ethel fumbled with her handbag, searching for her house key. "Do you live around here?" she asked.

"No, I'm in the neighbourhood looking for something to rent."

"There's not much that goes on around here that I don't know about," Ethel said, continuing to rummage through her bag. "Johnny rents his place next door, but it's taken—although the tenants aren't there very often." Ethel issued a triumphant smile. "Here we go." She lifted the key up, the evidence of her find.

"Johnny?" Priscilla said as Ethel inserted the key into the lock.

"Johnny Edgecombe. He owns the house. I like Johnny, very helpful to me on occasion, but he's quite a character, let me tell you."

"How so?"

Ethel turned to Priscilla, dropping her voice to a conspiratorial level. "Well, he owns that *notorious* club, doesn't he?"

"Does he?" asked Priscilla, at a loss as to what club Ethel was referring to.

"It's called the Flamingo," Ethel reported confidentially. "If what I can understand from Johnny is correct, they play...*jazz* on the premises."

"You don't say?" Priscilla made her eyes widen in alarm.

"I *do* say, lovey."

"Have you been there?"

"No, no!" Ethel looked horrified. "I wouldn't be caught dead in such a place."

"No?"

"Goodness, no. I like Johnny, as I say. He's a charmer. I can see why the ladies are attracted to him. But I don't even want to think about what Johnny might be up to."

By now Ethel had the door open. "Are you sure you're going to be all right?" Priscilla asked.

"I'm fine now, feeling much better," she said taking the bag from Priscilla. "I probably need a cup of tea. Would you like to join me?"

"That's kind of you to offer," Priscilla said. "But if there's nothing available for rent in this neighbourhood, I should be getting back."

"Let me have your number, lovey, and if I hear of anything I can give you a ring."

"I would really appreciate that," Priscilla said, taking a note-pad and a pen out of her bag. "Particularly if you hear of any-thing next door."

"Yes, that fellow and his friends coming and going at all hours. Not very reliable, you ask me. Who knows how long they will last around here."

"You don't happen to know the renter's name by any chance?" Priscilla asked as she jotted her number on the notepad and then tore it out. "Maybe I could talk to him."

"Never spoken with him," Ethel said.

"You don't know if it's Kirk Strong, do you?"

"No idea." She gave Priscilla a look. "How would you know?"

"I know a friend of Kirk's. He said something about him liv-ing in this neighbourhood. I thought No. 11 might be the place."

"No idea, but then lots of mysterious people come and go at all hours. All quite secretive. They do keep me interested, I will say that for them."

"I can just imagine," Priscilla said.

And she certainly could.

Priscilla was dead tired by the time she arrived home, unsure whether she was any further ahead than she had been a few hours before. She had learned nothing that would give any credibility to Noël Coward's assertion that she could get to the bottom of things—things like the death of James Harley. She reached her fifth-floor flat. In the darkness she found her latchkey, and then realized she didn't need it. The door was unlocked. Had she forgotten to lock it?

Her sitting room was in darkness save for the table lamp illuminating Jack Cogan. The Jackal was slumped in an easy chair, in shirtsleeves, his tie askew, his suit jacket discarded on the sofa. The uncertain light deepened the lines of his face, adding to the aura of menace he exuded.

"My God, woman," he said. "Where have you been?"

Cogan issued a machine-gun burst of laughter—highly amused by his own wit, Priscilla supposed as she closed the door. Her stomach, always so predictable at tense times like this, was performing flips.

"How did you get in here?" Priscilla edged into the room, taking in the empty Scotch bottle on the table beside his chair.

"This place is a dump. Don't you ever clean it up?"

"I'm never home," she replied. "And you haven't answered my question."

"Also, there's nothing to drink. I had to bring my own Scotch."

"It looks as though you've done a good job with it."

Cogan gave the empty bottle a sideways glance. "Waiting around for you."

"Answer me, please, Mr. Cogan," Priscilla said irritably. "How did you get in, and *why* are you here?"

"How I got in." Cogan took his eyes off the Scotch to consider his answer. "I'd love to tell you that in my dark past I was a master burglar who could break in anywhere. But that's not the case. If I were you, I'd lock the door when you go out. Otherwise, blokes like me can easily get in."

"But then why would you even bother?"

"Simple enough. I wanted to talk to you."

"You could do that during business hours in my office at the Savoy," Priscilla pointed out.

Cogan waved away the thought. "Indeed, I could. Except I wanted to get you away from all that stuffy formality, the 'yes, Mr. Cogan, no Mr. Cogan' bullshit they demand of you."

"Well, Mr. Cogan, nothing changes. You are still Mr. Cogan. What can I do for you—Mr. Cogan?"

"You don't have anything else to drink, do you?"

"I'm afraid not," Priscilla said, deciding he didn't need the Stoli in her icebox.

Cogan kicked at the footstool in front of his chair. Priscilla became aware of the leather bag on top of it.

"Open it," Cogan ordered.

Priscilla hesitated, doubting there was anything good inside.

"Go on," Cogan urged.

She bent to unzip the bag. It was stuffed with bundles of bank notes. She closed her eyes for a couple of seconds, hoping she was seeing things. When she opened them again, the money was still there.

"Five thousand pounds," she heard Cogan say.

"What's it for?" She carefully rezipped the bag.

"For you, Priscilla," Cogan said with a chuckle. "A gift from me to you—encouragement, if you will."

"Encouragement for what?"

"Encouragement to keep quiet."

"Everyone wants me to be quiet," Priscilla said wearily.

"But I'm the one paying five thousand pounds for your silence."

"I don't want your money," Priscilla said resolutely. "I can't keep it."

"Sure, you can," Cogan said with an assured smirk.

"Besides," Priscilla added, "I have no idea what I'm supposed to keep quiet about."

"You know damned well," Cogan said.

"If that's the case, then you don't need to waste your money on me. I'm not going to say anything."

"Call it insurance," Cogan said.

"You don't need insurance," Priscilla countered.

"Then think of it as down payment."

"Down payment for what?"

"For your new job."

"I already have a job," Priscilla said, struggling to keep a reasonable tone.

"I'm giving you a better job. I've recently taken over my father's business. It's a lot to handle, and there are many critical eyes on me. You will run interference for me as my public relations vice-president, keeping my nose clean and reporting directly to me."

"Mr. Cogan, I believe you have had too much to drink."

"You're right about that, Priscilla—since I have just hired you, I can call you Priscilla."

"You have *not* hired me!" Priscilla said shrilly.

"Yes, I have." Proclaimed with the absolute certainty, thought Priscilla, of a mean, rich bastard who always gets his way. Cogan pulled himself to his feet. "You start in two weeks. That should give you time to tell those stuffed shirts you work for where to go." He looked at his watch, peering closely as though having trouble reading its face. "It's late. I'm drunk. Time to go."

"You shouldn't drive, Mr. Cogan."

"Are you kidding?" He shot Priscilla a disdainful look. "I *never* drive. There's a car waiting for me outside. Everything is taken care of. In my world, it's all good, whatever I want—and now I want you."

"Take your money, Mr. Cogan," Priscilla demanded as he lifted his jacket off the sofa. "You know as well as I do that I'm not going to work for you."

"You've got your hush money," Cogan said, going to the door and opening it. "I'm not taking it back. A deal's a deal. You're working for me."

"There is no deal, and I'm not—" Her words were cut off by the door slamming shut.

She crossed back to the leather bag on the footstool. She stared down at it.

Shit!

CHAPTER FIFTEEN

The Morning After

The next day the tabloids were full of the news that James Harley, the young darling of the diplomatic corps, on the eve of being posted to Moscow, had been murdered in his Kensington flat. The papers reported that Harley's throat had been cut. It was further reported that the body had been discovered by a Miss Priscilla Tempest, who had gone to Harley's flat after his mother, Lady Anne Harley, died of an apparent heart attack in her Savoy Hotel suite.

Going through the morning papers and seeing her name come up repeatedly made Priscilla groan with despair. Even the *Times* mentioned her. The arrival of the handsomely greying floor waiter Karl Steiner with morning coffee did little to dispel her misery. She had been outed, so to speak. The anonymous servant to the Savoy's rich and famous suddenly was no longer quite so anonymous. Her name was out there in the open, linked to discovering bodies in London flats.

"Well, you're *hardly* mentioned," offered Susie supportively. "I don't think most readers will pay the least attention."

"It's not *most* readers I'm worried about," said Priscilla. "It's a reader named Clive Banville."

The colour began to drain from Susie's face. "You don't think—" she began.

"Please don't go there, Susie," Priscilla ordered, cutting off more of Susie's moaning and groaning about possible job loss.

Priscilla's phone began to ring. Both women stared at it as though it might come alive and attack. "Who do you suppose it is?" asked Susie in a whispery voice.

"Possibly someone who wants to speak to us," said Priscilla. "It happens all the time."

"It could be Mr. Banville," Susie said with trepidation. "By now he must have seen the morning papers..."

Susie's phone began ringing in the other room. "You get that," Priscilla said. As Susie left to take the other call, Priscilla swallowed hard before picking up the receiver.

"Why didn't you tell me?" Percy Hoskins, ace reporter for the *Evening Standard*, was on the line. Today, the angry Percy Hoskins. On other days he might be mistaken for Priscilla's lover, except Priscilla bristled at the notion. Most days, she was ready to kill him. As she gathered the strength needed to confront him, she decided this might well be one of those days.

"Tell you what?" asked Priscilla, feigning ignorance.

"James Harley. If you love me as you do, you would have let me have the scoop about his murder."

"First of all, I don't love you," Priscilla countered quickly. "Secondly, I don't know what it is, but when I find a dead body, my first inclination, as mad as it seems, is not to phone Percy Hoskins with the news."

"You might have let me know," Percy replied sullenly. Then he added in a more conciliatory tone, "How are you doing?"

"Not good." For a lot of reasons Percy didn't have to know about, Priscilla thought.

"Also, what's this I hear about a dinner party, a curse and a cat named Kaspar?"

"I have no idea what you are talking about."

"Have you noticed that whenever you say 'I have no idea what you're talking about,' you are lying?"

"No," Priscilla said angrily, "I have not noticed that. When I tell you 'I have no idea what you're talking about,' it's because, in fact, I have no idea what you're talking about."

"My sources tell me that there was a dinner party in one of the private dining rooms. In order to avoid the curse that supposedly exists when there are thirteen guests, they brought out this sculpture of a black cat named Kaspar. So, then there were fourteen guests. That supposedly dispels the curse."

"That's the most ridiculous thing I've ever heard," Priscilla said shrilly.

"Further, I'm told that not long after James Harley's mother left that dinner party, she was found dead in her suite."

"I don't know who is telling you such nonsense," Priscilla said with all the authoritative vehemence she could muster. "None of it is true." Even though most of it was.

"I am pursuing that story," Percy stated formally, "the link between James Harley's murder, his mother's death and the so-called curse of the Savoy. I will be looking for a comment from the Savoy's press office."

"Don't you dare!" Priscilla spoke harshly into the phone.

"Incidentally, there's something else that always alerts me when you're not telling the truth."

"No, there isn't."

"Yes, there is. It's when you tell me you don't love me."

"I don't—"

"I will be in touch," Percy promised. Before she could fire off further protests, he hung up.

"Bastard," she said into the receiver.

Susie was back at the door. "Just as I thought," she said. "That *was* Mr. Banville's office."

"What does he want?"

"What else?" replied Susie glumly. "He wants to see you."

With El Sid unexpectedly absent from his usual guard post, Priscilla found Clive Banville in his office perusing copies of the day's papers laid out before him on his desk.

Uttering an unhappy *tsk, tsk, tsk*, Banville at last raised his fine head to acknowledge her presence—an acknowledgement, it was always Priscilla's impression, he would just as soon not have to make. "Miss Tempest…" he began.

"Good morning, sir," Priscilla said, hoping she brought the right cheery tone to her voice.

"I see you are all over the press this morning." For emphasis, as he spoke, his forefinger tapped the papers on his desk.

"Most unfortunate, sir. Many apologies."

Banville's frown evaporated. "No need for apologies, Miss Tempest. You were doing the task I asked of you, which was to find Lady Anne's son. Tragic the circumstances under which you found him."

"It was most unsettling, sir," Priscilla acknowledged. "Particularly so soon after the unexpected death of his mother."

"Most unfortunate," agreed Banville solemnly. Then he brightened. "However, that is not why I have called you here today." He had adopted what was as close to a pleasant expression as he could manage—highly unusual when Priscilla was in his presence. For some reason, Priscilla found that more worrisome than Banville with his customary frown.

"I understand congratulations are in order."

"I beg your pardon, sir?" Not quite understanding what Banville was getting at.

"On your new job."

"Excuse me? What new job?"

"I received a call from Jack Cogan earlier. He tells me that you will go to work for him shortly."

"He told you…*that?*"

"He seemed as pleased as punch." Given Priscilla's evident confusion, Banville began to look uncertain. "Is there something wrong, Miss Tempest?"

"I am not going to work for Mr. Cogan," Priscilla stated.

"You are not?" Banville appeared taken aback by Priscilla's denial. An edge of disappointment in his voice, if Priscilla was not mistaken.

"He offered a job, I suppose," Priscilla said, not adding that Cogan had done this after breaking into her flat and drinking too much Scotch. "But I certainly did not accept his offer."

"Jack seems determined to have you as part of his organization, Miss Tempest, so you can imagine my surprise upon hearing that you are reluctant to accept his generous offer."

Priscilla stared at him, speechless. "Are you suggesting I leave, sir?"

"I would not go so far as to say I am *suggesting* you do anything," Banville said, showing uncommon nervousness. "I thought the issue was settled. You are leaving us for a better position."

"Nothing has been settled. I told Mr. Cogan in no uncertain terms that I did not want to work for him. I am not sure that working for him would be a better job. Given Mr. Cogan's reputation, I would say it's to the contrary."

"Miss Tempest, I do not wish to upset one of the most powerful men in Britain, not to mention a highly valued occasional guest at this hotel." Banville had recovered his superior air of imperial authority. "If he says you have accepted a job with him, then I must take him at his word. You will reconsider joining him in the two-week period he has laid out for you."

Priscilla could not believe she was being summarily traded away to a job with someone she despised simply because Banville did not care to upset a powerful individual.

"If you'll forgive me, sir, there is ample reason at the moment why it is not a good idea to lose me."

"And what could that reason be?" Banville demanded archly.

"Reporters have called me inquiring about the Orson Welles dinner and the talk of a Savoy curse that has resulted from it. So far, I have been able to stop publication of such a story, but I fear what will happen if I am not here."

"I see," Banville said. His brow once again furrowed, a hint of doubt in his confident demeanour.

"There is also something else you should be aware of," Priscilla continued, deciding, in her desperation, to go for broke.

"And what would that be, Miss Tempest?" As though he could not imagine anything in the world that Priscilla could make him aware of that he didn't already know.

"On the morning following the Orson Welles dinner, I was called to Mr. Cogan's suite, where I found him bleeding from a knife wound."

"What?" Banville looked aghast.

"A letter opener, actually. Mr. Cogan wasn't badly injured, thank goodness. I managed to get him out of the hotel without a fuss. However, I believe the only reason he wants to hire me is to ensure my silence about the incident. I, of course, would say nothing."

"But you just did, didn't you, Miss Tempest?" Banville's voice was cold and accusatory.

"Only to you, sir, to explain why Mr. Cogan is anxious for me to work for him. But I would say that if the story does somehow leak, well, I would not want to leave with that possibility hanging over the hotel's impeccable name. I don't think we should take that chance. Do you?"

"No, no." For a moment, Banville allowed a despairing look, but then almost immediately he straightened and pulled himself together. "Above all, we must maintain calm."

"I couldn't agree more, sir."

"Continue to keep these matters out of the press," Banville ordered. "Do you think you can do that, Miss Tempest?"

"I will do my very best, sir."

"Do whatever it takes to accomplish this undertaking. Do you understand?"

"Yes, sir," asserted Priscilla, not at all certain about the limits of doing whatever it takes—if there were any limits. "And if I may ask, what about the position with Mr. Cogan?"

"You don't have to start with him for two weeks, is that correct?"

"Yes, but—"

"That should give you ample time to complete the tasks I have set out for you," Banville said.

"Yes, but sir, I—"

"That will be all, Miss Tempest," Banville declared peremptorily. "We can discuss anything else in due course."

CHAPTER SIXTEEN

Unforgiving!

Priscilla dearly would have loved to spend time luxuriating in feeling sorry for herself, considering all the calamities of her life, but regrettably Percy Hoskins was sprawled on her office sofa. He was dressed in a rumpled brown suit. Unless she missed her guess, he had slept in it.

"Whose bed did you land in last night?" she demanded.

Slightly taken aback, Percy said, "What makes you ask?"

"Wherever you ended up, she failed to supply you with a razor."

"I assume you keep one at your flat," Percy snarked.

"I do, but you will never get to use it."

Percy clutched a beer as he occupied himself warily eying Kaspar. Susie once again was nowhere to be seen. Priscilla really had to have a conversation with that woman, leaving the office unguarded and thus allowing unshaven louts like Percy to gain entrance—and a free beer to boot.

"This must be the notorious Kaspar."

"I don't want you in here," Priscilla said crossly.

"He does look as though he's more than capable of casting a curse or two." Percy showed no sign of moving.

"Percy, I'm serious. I want you out."

"Whatever do you mean?" He pulled his eyes away from Kaspar, doing a fine job of feigning offence. "Is this not the press office? Am I not the press?"

"I don't care what you are, get out."

Percy continued to huddle in place, angering her even more.

"I will call security," she announced heatedly, "if you do not leave immediately."

"The prospect of Major Jack O'Hara taking me by the scruff of the neck and tossing me out onto the street leaves me petrified with fear," Percy said, rising to his feet but hanging on to the beer. "However, you might be interested to know what brings me here."

"I am not at all," insisted Priscilla.

"I want you to know that I forgive you for not telling me about James Harley."

"Lucky me," snarled Priscilla.

"I have now acquired new information about the case. I thought I'd better drop around."

"I don't care about any information you may have," Priscilla lied.

"I didn't realize until I spoke to my contacts at Scotland Yard that the police have identified a person of interest in their investigation into Harley's murder," Percy went on, undeterred.

"And who would that be?" Priscilla asked nervously..

"I believe you know only too well who that person is." Percy's smile was indulgent. "Naturally, I don't believe you killed Harley."

"The police can't be serious," muttered Priscilla. "I keep telling them I never met the man."

"Until the day you arrived in his flat."

"Percy, what are you getting at?"

"Only that Harley had been accused of forcing himself on a number of women after first luring them to his flat. The police suspect that he may have assaulted you, and in the process of defending yourself, you might have accidentally cut his throat."

"What?" Priscilla's astonishment knew no bounds. "How precisely would I 'accidentally' cut his throat?"

"That's what I'm hoping you can tell me," replied Percy mildly.

"You absolute bastard," shouted Priscilla, restraining herself from finding something she could use to cut his throat.

"Now, I don't believe a word of it," he continued, sounding as though he might be all too willing to believe. "Even so, there are those suspicions out there. Tell me your side of the story. Given my status at the paper, I think I can guarantee you the front page."

"Are you out of your mind? I'm not about to give any credence to what the police are saying."

Percy either didn't hear what she said or pretended not to. "What's more, my paper is in a position to make it advantageous financially, and that would certainly help with any legal bills you might incur." Percy pointed a finger at Kaspar. "Of course, we would want Kaspar to be part of the story. The curse of the Savoy that haunts you, and all that."

"Listen, you bugger." Priscilla had lowered her voice to a seething boil. "I want you out of here—now!"

"You've got to at least consider what amounts to an extraordinarily generous offer." Percy appeared offended by the prospect that she wouldn't.

"Out!" shouted Priscilla. She found herself suddenly gulping back tears.

Percy stood there, the picture of confusion and uncertainty. "What's the matter with you?"

"The matter with me?" The tears were running down her cheeks. "The matter with you, you callous unthinking bastard. You think so little of me that it never crossed your mind that I might be innocent—damn you anyway!"

"I didn't say you were actually guilty," Percy protested. "I'm simply saying—"

In a fit of anger, she swept up Kaspar and heaved the sculpture at Percy. He ducked in time so it narrowly missed him and thumped against the wall before falling to the sofa.

"You're mad, you've gone completely mad," announced Percy angrily. "You might have killed me."

"Believe me, if I kill anyone, it'll be you!"

Percy departed, crouched as though expecting another missile aimed at him. "You'll want me back," he maintained. "It's a matter of time before I get a phone call from you."

"They will close the pubs on Fleet Street before that happens," avowed Priscilla.

As soon as Percy swept out the door, making sure as he departed to bristle in a state of high dudgeon, Priscilla sank to the sofa beside the fallen Kaspar. She refused to allow tears, even if they were of exasperation. Percy was a waste of any sort of tears. Kaspar lay on his side so that one black eye was trained on her, seemingly unconvinced. "Don't look at me like that," she admonished. "I'm finished with him. It's over."

Kaspar didn't respond.

CHAPTER SEVENTEEN

Johnny Get Angry

"Jazz at The Flamingo," announced the sign over the door at 33 Wardour Street, the address of the club said to be owned by Johnny Edgecombe. It was sandwiched between two Regents shoe shops.

The crowd that Priscilla made her way through on the street outside was mostly young, a mix of black and white faces. The men wore sports jackets and ties, looking like they'd just come from work at a bank. The women were dressed to kill: short skirts, puffed hair, lots of mascara and eyeshadow, little purses dangling from their arms.

Inside, the air was hot and choked with smoke. The night's featured band, Georgie Fame and the Blue Flames, was blasting out what Priscilla recognized as their hit, "Yeh, Yeh." The organ and sax were at such a decibel level that Priscilla had to shout to make herself heard by the bartender. "What's that, luv?" he asked, leaning into her.

"Is Johnny around?"

"Johnny? Johnny who? Lots of Johnnys in London."

"Johnny Edgecombe. The one and only Johnny Edgecombe," Priscilla purred into his ear.

"One Johnny, okay. I know *that* Johnny. You want something to drink?"

"Champagne—please," Priscilla shouted. "And Johnny—"

"Champagne coming up. Johnny? We'll see." The bartender nodded and went away.

Priscilla took in the heaving, sweating bodies around her. The bartender was back with a flute of champagne. "On the house," he called. At her questioning look: "Courtesy of Johnny."

"That's very kind of him."

"Johnny wants to make sure pretty birds are treated right."

"Where *is* Johnny?" Priscilla called back.

"All the ladies want Johnny."

"Yes, but you see, I'm a special lady."

"All Johnny's ladies are special."

"I'm the most special of them all," Priscilla fired back.

"I'll let him know," the bartender grinned.

Priscilla leaned against the bar, sipping the champagne. It gave her false confidence, but tonight she would take confidence any way she could get it.

She was beginning to think that whatever her charms, they weren't enough to lure Johnny, when a tall, slim black man slipped in next to her. "Hey there, my girl. You got your drink okay?" he asked in a sweet lilt. His torso-fitting white shirt was tucked into black trousers. His hair was cut close to his scalp. A Zapata-style moustache curled around the edges of his mouth. Heavily lidded eyes inspected her languidly.

"I'm not your girl, Johnny," Priscilla said leaning into him.

"Not my girl *yet*," he emphasized with a crooked smile. "But, hey, you want to see me, yeah?"

"A friend of mine suggested I look you up."

"Yeah? What kind of friend would that be?"

"Kirk? Kirk Strong?"

That got a frown out of Johnny. "You know Kirk?"

"He said that you know your way around the jazz scene in London."

"Yeah, well, he's right about that. Didn't think Kirk was much of a jazz guy. I know all the players. You take Georgie and his boys." He waved a slim hand in the direction of the bandstand. "I found him, yeah? Brought him to the Flamingo. Great, yeah? No one like Georgie." The frown had faded into a speculative look. "What's your name, baby?"

"It's Priscilla, but I'm not your baby, either."

"I hear you, baby. Champagne lady, yeah."

Johnny motioned for the bartender who arrived immediately with an open bottle of Dom Perignon to refill her glass.

"How do you know Kirk, yeah?"

"His girlfriend introduced us," Priscilla ventured, having no idea if Strong had a girlfriend.

Johnny seemed to buy the explanation. "Mariella. Yeah, Mariella she's something else. Don't know what she's doing with that dude."

"Business?" Priscilla was grabbing at more straws.

"Nah. Kirk and me, we do the business. Mariella, she's, yeah, Mariella."

"What kind of business do you do with Kirk?"

The frown was back. "You ask a lot of questions, baby."

"Just trying to make conversation, Johnny." She moved closer, feeling the warmth of his body. That seemed to settle him.

"Let's say it's the kind of business makes me real careful dealing with him," Johnny offered. "Making sure my wallet's still in my pocket when I leave, yeah?"

"Sounds like a dangerous kind of business," Priscilla observed.

"Business you do with a bloke like Kirk. American. Keep your eyes wide open with Americans, yeah?"

The bartender reappeared, apprehensive, motioning to Johnny. He leaned in to whisper in his ear just as Georgie Fame's band finished a song. Priscilla heard the bartender say, "He's here, man."

Johnny tensed. He nodded at the bartender and then without a word whipped around and disappeared into the mass of dancers. Somewhat stunned by his abrupt departure, Priscilla turned to the bartender. "Everything all right?"

"Fun time with Johnny is over," he mumbled, keeping his eyes firmly on the drink he had begun to pour.

Georgie Fame started up again. Dancers crowded the front of the bandstand. Priscilla left the bar and started across the dance floor.

A pair of scuffed metal doors opened into a hallway reeking of urine and stale tobacco. Priscilla reached a fire door. Behind her, she could hear a wailing Blue Flames saxophone. She pushed open the fire door and was immediately hit by a wave of cool night air. Johnny Edgecombe was down on his knees in the garbage-strewn alley. Two black men wearing dark glasses, neat in jackets and ties, leaned over him. One of the men, all muscles, kicked Johnny hard in the ribs. "I told you, didn't I? Didn't I warn you to stay away from her, you bastard."

The second man held the fedora he had been wearing so he could take his turn kicking Johnny. Johnny yelped in pain.

"Hey there," Priscilla demanded shrilly. "What's going on?"

Johnny's two attackers traded quick glances. The muscles man said, "Just having a friendly chat with Johnny."

"Doesn't look so friendly to me," Priscilla said, coming forward.

"Sometimes Johnny don't listen so good. This way he listens real good."

The man with the fedora delivered a final kick. "Come near her again and next time, I kill you. I swear I kill you." He then carefully arranged the fedora atop his head.

"Goddamn dead man," echoed the muscles man before they straightened around to cast fierce glances at Priscilla and then sauntered away along the alley.

Johnny whimpered and rolled onto his back. He was bleeding from his nose and mouth, his face already beginning to swell. Priscilla bent to him, resisted asking him if he was all right when he obviously wasn't. Johnny's hooded eyes blinked in recognition.

"My angel." He tried a smile that didn't work. "Get me out of here, yeah?"

"I'll help you back into the club."

"No, God no!" he said sharply. "Car down the alley…" He rolled onto his side and started to lift himself off the ground. "Gotta get…" He couldn't finish the sentence.

Priscilla helped him to his feet. The percussive sounds of Georgie Fame and the Blue Flames echoed and bounced along the alley as Johnny leaned against the wall, breathing hard, blood dripping down his torn white shirt. "Not far, darlin'…"

Johnny pushed himself away from the wall. She had to grab him to keep him upright. Half dragging, half walking him, she got Johnny to the Renault sedan at the end of the alley. Priscilla leaned him against the hood. "You drive," Johnny said curtly.

"What?" exclaimed Priscilla. "No, I can't drive you."

"Can't drive myself," Johnny slurred as he fished car keys from his pocket. "Can't stay here. Gotta disappear." He pushed the keys into her hands. "Please…" There was desperation in his voice.

Priscilla used the key to unlock the passenger door. She eased Johnny into the car, accomplished amid constant groans. Once he was inside, she went around and got behind the wheel. Johnny's head rolled back against the seat. He did not look good. "We should go to a hospital," Priscilla said.

Johnny shook his head violently. "No! No hospital. I'll be okay...just get me home..."

Priscilla said, "Where would you like to go, Johnny?"

"Swain's Lane," muttered Johnny. "Number eleven."

Swain's Lane? Priscilla groaned inwardly. Johnny's house in North London.

CHAPTER EIGHTEEN

Bad Lover

She must be out of her mind, she thought, not for the first time, as she drove north through Regent's Park. Entirely mad. Next to her, Johnny dispensed a loud grunt. She was driving through Camden Town when it occurred to her that she had no way of getting back. What was she thinking? But then that was her problem, wasn't it? The lack of thinking. That's what got her into messes like this.

A half-hour later, she turned onto Swain's Lane. No. 11 was lit on the ground floor but otherwise stood in darkness. As soon as she parked, Priscilla turned to Johnny and shook him. "Johnny," she said. "Johnny, wake up. We're here."

He jerked upright, his eyes full of confusion. "Where?"

"Your house," Priscilla said.

Johnny gave her a skeptical look. "You drove?"

"I did," Priscilla acknowledged. "Listen, I need to get you out of the car and inside."

"Sure," Johnny said distractedly. He fell back against the seat.

"Johnny, do you hear me?"

He didn't answer. Damn, she thought. Supposing he was about to expire next to her? What was she going to do then?

A sudden rap on the passenger window made Priscilla jump. A woman stared in and then yanked open the door. "What's going on?" she demanded.

"Who are you?" Priscilla asked.

"Who the devil are *you*?" She was in her twenties, Priscilla estimated, inches over five feet. Her lips were pouty and red, her eyes large and dark, her white-blond hair framed the heart-shaped face of an angel. Well, perhaps a decadent angel would be more accurate, Priscilla thought.

"Johnny was hurt at the club," Priscilla explained. "I drove him here."

"Good God, Johnny, you fool. What have you gotten yourself into now?"

Johnny responded with a moan.

"He wasn't hurt, as you put it," the woman corrected. "Someone's beat the shit out of him."

"There were two of them actually," Priscilla said.

"Silly bugger," the blond woman said with a contemptuous shake of her head. She glanced at Priscilla. "We're going to have to get him into the house. What is your name?"

"Priscilla."

"Very well, Priscilla, I'm Mariella. I have no idea how you are so crazy to be with Johnny, but now you must help me. Okay?"

So this was Mariella, supposed girlfriend of Kirk Strong. Out of the car, Priscilla got a better look at her and immediately decided that, with that face, Mariella could only be up to no good.

She was busily pulling at Johnny, who now began to howl in pain. "God, Johnny, shut up," she ordered impatiently. "You'll wake the neighbours." She frowned at Priscilla. "Don't just stand there," she ordered. "Help me."

Working together, the two women managed to extract Johnny from the car. He let out a sharp groan when Mariella wrapped her arm around his torso. "They were kicking him in the ribs," Priscilla advised.

"They should have kicked his skinny ass," Mariella said angrily.

Together they managed to move the semi-conscious Johnny into the house and onto a beaten-up sofa in a sitting room decorated with flowered wallpaper. Priscilla remembered the pattern, not fondly, from her grandmother's house.

"I don't want him getting blood on the sofa," Mariella said.

"It's too late to save this sofa," Priscilla countered.

They plopped him down, Johnny wheezing with pain.

Mariella disappeared from the room. Johnny's eyes fluttered open. He smiled bleakly, trying to sit up. Mariella was back with a wet cloth. She proceeded to wipe at the dried blood on his face.

"Any idea who might have done this to him?" Priscilla asked as Mariella worked on him.

"Who knows with Johnny. Somebody he screwed. Owes money to. Messed with their wife. Lots of possibilities." She finished with the facecloth and straightened to survey her hand-iwork. "I think he will live."

"I wanted to take him to a hospital, but he insisted on being driven here."

Mariella threw Priscilla a mystified look. "You really are the good Samaritan. What are you? His new bird?"

"I just met him tonight," Priscilla explained. "He's not your boyfriend?"

Mariella made a face. "You must be joking. Johnny does some jobs for *my* boyfriend, although I sometimes wonder why Kirk bothers with him."

"Isn't this his house?"

That inspired an annoyed laugh. "Johnny likes to say it is, but really he's just fronting for Kirk."

"Your boyfriend?"

"My *American* boyfriend," Mariella amended proudly.

"Is Kirk here?" Priscilla asked.

"He had to fly back to New York," Mariella reported sadly. "Some sort of emergency." She eyed Priscilla speculatively. "I probably shouldn't be telling you this, but he's *very* important in the American corporate world, my Kirk."

"That's impressive," Priscilla said.

"I just wish he hadn't left me behind in this dump."

"I love the wallpaper," Priscilla said deadpan.

Mariella chuckled resignedly. "See what I have to deal with? Fools like Johnny and terrible wallpaper." She paused to give Priscilla another look. "I guess I haven't properly introduced myself, have I?" She held out her hand. "I am Mariella Novotny. Welcome to my crazy life."

"Novotny? Is that Russian?" Priscilla asked, taking her hand.

"That's what everyone thinks. I was actually born in Essex. My parents are Czech, not Russian."

"Is it truly a crazy life?"

Mariella indicated Johnny passed out on the sofa. "What do you think?" She smiled. "I suppose you also know something about crazy living."

"I'm afraid I do," Priscilla conceded.

"Well, if you don't mind a piece of advice, as crazy as your life may be, you don't want to add Johnny to it. He is attractive when he hasn't been beaten to a pulp, but he is a very bad boy. And besides…" she leaned closer to Priscilla and whispered, "he is not a good lover."

"And you know this?"

Mariella smiled meaningfully. "I will tell you, when I was twenty, John Kennedy and his brother Bobby, they were both my lovers. I swear this is true. I have experience with good sex because of them. Only once with Johnny, but that was enough. He was not good. Not as bad as my husband, but bad enough."

"Your husband? You're married?" Why am I sounding so naive? Priscilla asked herself. This is London after all.

Mariella shrugged noncommittally. "William is not much of a husband."

"Not to worry," Priscilla said. "One night with Johnny is quite enough for me, no sex needed. Right now, I'm concerned about how I get out of here."

"Take the car—it's not his, incidentally—and leave it at the club."

"You trust me?"

"Why shouldn't I?" Mariella shrugged again. "It's a car. No big deal."

On the sofa, Johnny stirred to life. He sat up, bleary eyed as he took in Priscilla with Mariella. "Hey, baby."

Mariella regarded Johnny with rueful disappointment before turning to Priscilla. "Don't worry. He calls everyone 'baby.' But the thing to remember about Johnny…"

"What's that?" Priscilla asked.

"Nobody is ever his baby."

Ethel Cambridge, in her housecoat, a glass of brandy at hand, peered cautiously through the curtains of the parlour window that afforded a view of Johnny Edgecombe's house.

Tonight, as she sipped brandy, Ethel focused her interest on the young woman she remembered was called Priscilla, now getting into Johnny's car and driving off. Quite strange, she reckoned. Priscilla supposedly had come around looking for a rental. Why was she back at this time of night? And what was she doing with Johnny's car?

Should she make the phone call? That required another contemplative sip of brandy. A little more than a sip this time. A good-sized gulp. She hated to bother them if it was nothing.

But if it was something…

She trundled into the hallway to the side table where she had her phone.

She picked up the receiver and dialled the number she kept on a notepad beside it. While she waited for someone to answer, she finished what was left of the brandy.

CHAPTER NINETEEN

The Admiral

"Yes, Ethel, what is it?" Colonel Geoffrey Wolfe was just closing down his office when Ethel's call came in. He didn't bother to keep the impatience out of his voice. What was this damned woman doing phoning at this time of night?

"A suspicious bird, my luv," stated Ethel.

"What do you mean?"

"Named Priscilla—that's what she told me, Priscilla. She showed up yesterday saying she was looking for a place to rent in the area. Now she's been here again tonight, this time with Johnny Edgecombe."

"The same woman?" Wolfe stifled a yawn.

"Yes, yes, the very same woman. Priscilla. She said her name was Priscilla Tempest."

Wolfe recognized the name. He stopped yawning. "Priscilla Tempest? Are you sure that was the name she gave you?"

"Sure as rain. I don't know if it means anything, but I thought I'd better get in touch."

Wolfe closed his eyes. How could this be? *Priscilla Tempest?* Wasn't she the young woman in charge of the Savoy Press Office? What the devil would she be doing at Swain's Lane?

Ethel interrupted his reverie. "There's something else that I must talk to you about, my luv."

"What's that, Ethel?"

"It's about my recompense," Ethel said.

"Your recompense? What about it?"

"It's not enough, my luv. I've been doing this for you for some time now, keeping an eye on those mysterious buggers next door. Putting my life on the line, you might say. I do believe it's time for an increase."

"We are paying you quite enough, Ethel. Those people you're watching, they're thugs but they're not murderers." Wolfe was doing his best to keep the irritation out of his voice. Who did this woman think she was?

"That's easy for you to say, my luv." Ethel dropped her voice to indicate that she was now speaking confidentially: "I'm told that there might be some interest from the press in my story."

"You don't want to do that, Ethel," Wolfe responded carefully.

"Don't I? Then please, my luv, reconsider the amount you're paying me."

"You say you are 'told.' Have you been talking to others?"

"Not specifically, no, but that doesn't mean I wouldn't."

It was too late at night to be arguing with this infuriating old woman, Wolfe decided. "Let me get back to you," he said cautiously.

"Don't wait too long, my luv. I'm not getting any younger, I'm afraid, and I do get impatient."

Wolfe put down the receiver. God, he thought, was everybody blackmailing everybody?

He would have to do something about Ethel Cambridge.

Wolfe always referred to his boss, Lord Louis Mountbatten, as "the Admiral," the rank Mountbatten had held when Wolfe was a Royal Marine and served under him at the South East Asia Command.

In the campaign to retake Burma from the Japanese, Wolfe had lost a leg. He'd also suffered a nasty face wound administered by a *kyū-guntō* war sword before he managed to kill its owner, a first lieutenant. He had kept the sword as a reminder of the encounter. Another reminder greeted him in the mirror each morning—the ugly white scar that ran down the right side of his face, disfiguring what previously had been delicately handsome features.

Mountbatten, impressed with Wolfe's war record, his toughness in the face of adversity, his ability to keep his wits about him in a tight situation and do what was necessary when orders required it, had taken him on as his adjutant after the war. By now Wolfe was accustomed to the Admiral's many eccentricities, including obsessions with the genealogical charts he liked to study for evidence of his family's links to European royal houses and with the military uniforms and insignias he loved to design.

The admiral had other, darker obsessions too, obsessions that had to be kept hidden. Recently this part of Wolfe's job, what the colonel silently referred to as the Admiral's Secret Life, had produced a new problem—criminals out to ruin Mountbatten. Buggers who had to be stopped.

Wolfe found his boss in the library. The former viceroy of India, former admiral of the fleet, current member of the House of Lords, a man a bit lost in a world he no longer understood—at least in Wolfe's estimation—did not hesitate to show his annoyance at being interrupted in the midst of his nightly study of genealogical charts.

"What is it, Geoffrey?" demanded Mountbatten irascibly. The red-velvet smoking jacket he wore was the evidence that he had been about to turn in for the night.

"You wished to be kept apprised of any developments concerning the house at Swain's Lane."

"Damned blighters," Mountbatten grumbled, setting aside his charts.

"It may be nothing, but our informant has alerted me to a young woman who has visited the house on two occasions under suspicious circumstances."

"What sort of suspicious circumstances?"

As quickly as he could, Wolfe outlined what he had been told during the phone call from Ethel Cambridge. Wolfe made it clear he was uncertain of what to make of these visits Ethel reported, except the woman's name was familiar.

"And what name is that?" Mountbatten asked.

"I believe you have encountered Miss Priscilla Tempest of the Savoy Hotel."

Mountbatten scowled. "At the Orson Welles dinner. Didn't like her. Bit of a tart, I understand."

"Whatever she is, Miss Tempest would seem to have no business on Swain's Lane, and yet has been seen there twice, including earlier this evening."

Mountbatten's distress was all too evident on his ravaged patrician face. "Could be she is part of this extortion plot against me," he railed. "Blackmailing bastards! You know I cannot afford a scandal, Geoffrey."

"You've made that quite clear, sir," Geoffrey said in a conciliatory voice.

"I am known as the royal family's elder statesman, for God's sake. I'm Uncle Dickie."

"Beloved by everyone at Buckingham Palace," Wolfe said supportively.

"I'm about to be honoured by the Queen. Exposure would mean my absolute ruin. We must stop these people—stop them at all costs. Whatever it takes. Your man is on it, is he?"

"He is on it, sir. He will get the job done."

Mountbatten visibly relaxed. "You know," he said dreamily, "there was a time not so long ago when no one would have dared move against me. Yet here we are, my life, my career under threat. The end of everything I've worked a lifetime to achieve."

He looked to Wolfe for confirmation. Wolfe knew better than to offer it. Instead, he said comfortingly, "We are working to make sure that doesn't happen, Admiral. I've—"

"Dammit, work harder!" Mountbatten interrupted, angry again. "I am at my wit's end, I tell you! Take care of this woman. Do it quickly!"

"If I may, sir, I believe your friend, Noël Coward, knows this woman. Perhaps it might help to have a word with him."

Mountbatten considered this. "Yes," he said finally, "that's quite a good idea."

CHAPTER TWENTY

The Press Conference

The turnout for Orson Welles's afternoon press conference in the River Room surprised Priscilla. She would not have thought that at this stage of his career Orson could attract so much attention. But reporters from all the major London newspapers were arriving, as well as the hosts of shows on the BBC and ITV. The press filled the rows of chairs the hotel staff had positioned in front of a long table set with two microphones.

Priscilla stood beside Susie, surveying the room with satisfaction. "You've done a good job," Priscilla said.

Susie looked pleased with herself. "I wouldn't have guessed Mr. Welles was so famous," she said out of the corner of her mouth. "I guess it's because of that *Citizen* what's-his-name movie."

Priscilla showed her annoyance. "Kane, Susie. *Kane.*"

Susie was saying something in reply that Priscilla missed, distracted by the sudden arrival of Percy Hoskins.

"Is that Percy?" asked Susie in surprise.

"Don't tell me you invited him." Priscilla was equally taken aback.

"No, I didn't. Why would he be interested in Mr. Welles?"

"He wouldn't be," Priscilla said.

She crossed to Percy, who was leaning against the wall, his damnably insouciant grin firmly in place.

"What are you doing here?"

"What kind of question is that?" asked Percy, the picture of innocence. "This is a press conference, is it not? And I am press, am I not?"

"After what you did to me—"

"I didn't do anything," Percy interrupted. "Except try to help you."

"You're not welcome here," Priscilla declared.

"But here I am, and I suspect you don't want to make a scene," Percy said equably.

"What are you up to, Percy?"

"It could be that I'm a fan of *Citizen Kane*."

"Have you even seen *Citizen Kane*?"

"Not yet," Percy conceded. "But I've heard great things about it."

As more members of the press brushed past into the room, she eyed him with a mixture of anger and suspicion. "You're up to something," she hissed. "What is it?"

Percy ignored the question, glancing over her shoulder. "Aha, here is the great man now."

Priscilla turned as Welles sailed through the entrance doors, a great lumbering vessel swathed in cigar smoke, beaming at the multitude gathered to hear his words of wisdom. Providing, Priscilla thought ruefully as she watched him steam to the front of the room, there were words of wisdom to be heard.

"This should be interesting," Percy murmured as Priscilla started away.

That stopped her, radar on full alert, warning of trouble ahead. She went back and hissed in his ear. "Whatever you think you're going to do—*don't!*"

"Not to worry." Another of Percy's insouciant grins made Priscilla worry more than ever and fight an overwhelming desire to murder him on the spot.

A nervous-looking Harry Alan Towers trailed behind Welles, head down, shoulders hunched as though expecting a blow. He and Welles took their seats. Priscilla nodded to Welles as she sat down and then leaned into one of the microphones.

"Good afternoon, ladies and gentlemen. My name is Priscilla Tempest, and I am in charge of the press office here at the Savoy Hotel. Judging by the turnout this afternoon, our guest needs no introduction. I believe it is safe to say that Mr. Orson Welles is one of the great filmmakers of our time." She glanced over at the beaming Welles. "Mr. Welles, it is such a pleasure to have you with us today, and also your producer, Mr. Harry Alan Towers."

Towers barely raised his head, while Welles immediately grabbed for the microphone, at the same time deftly extracting the cigar from his mouth. "Thank you, Miss Tempest," he boomed amid a scattering of applause. "I cannot think of a better place to tell the world about my latest film than here at the Savoy." He gave Towers a quick glance. "Am I right about that, Harry?"

"Absolutely right, Orson," Towers agreed with a smile that, to Priscilla, looked more like a grimace.

"Mr. Welles," Priscilla piped up, "perhaps you can tell us about your new movie."

Welles smiled slyly and said, "It *is* a movie. There will be a beginning, a middle and an end." Again, he glanced at Towers. "What do you say to that, Harry?"

"A beginning, a middle and an end, Orson," Towers acknowledged.

An impatient stir rippled through the audience. Priscilla could see Percy, on his feet, moving from the back of the room.

"Provide us with the title of your film, Orson," someone called from the audience.

"A name?" Welles smiled playfully. "How about this? Pulled out of thin air—*The Other Side of the Wind*. There. That's a movie for you."

"Can you expand on the title, Mr. Welles?" asked Priscilla into the microphone, wondering what had happened to *The Deep* with Jeanne Moreau, the film he had mentioned earlier.

Welles waved his cigar around. "It will be a movie about movies," he divulged.

"Will you finish this one, Orson?" someone called from the audience.

"With Mr. Towers here providing financing, my film will most certainly be completed." He pointed his cigar at Towers. "Right, Harry?"

"That's right, Orson." Towers looked pained making the assertion, Priscilla thought.

"Orson." A female journalist was on her feet. "Ever since *Citizen Kane*, you have had trouble getting pictures made in Hollywood. Why do you suppose you continue to have these problems?"

"You're assuming that your statement is correct. I would argue that it isn't," Orson said mildly. "However, it's no secret that Hollywood doesn't like mavericks, and I, for good or ill, am a maverick."

"I have a question," Percy called out, raising his hand.

"Does anyone else have a question?" Priscilla leaned into her microphone, praying that someone did so she could ignore Percy.

"Excuse me." Percy raised his voice. "My question is for Mr. Towers. I'm Percy Hoskins from the *Evening Standard*."

The mischievousness on Orson's flushed face was quickly disappearing. Towers looked very uncomfortable, apparently disliking being caught in the spotlight as much as Welles hated losing it. "I'm not here to answer questions," he mumbled nervously. "I am here to support Orson."

"Nonetheless, Mr. Towers, I wonder if you might comment on reports that you were arrested in New York City and accused of involvement in a call-girl ring there."

"That's outrageous!" cried Towers.

"But is it true?" countered Percy.

"I have nothing to say about that." Towers's voice was back to a mumble.

"Mr. Towers, according to American news reports, there have been accusations that you are in fact a Soviet agent. Is that true?"

What had been a rustling of questioning voices became an explosion. Towers gaped at Percy, wide-eyed. Welles reacted by throwing his head back to let loose a burst of raucous laughter. "Harry," he called out, "I knew it! You're a spy!"

"Mr. Towers, could you please answer the question: Are you, as has been reported in the American press, a Soviet agent?" persisted Percy.

"Good God, no!" shouted Towers.

"Further, Mr. Towers, how will these accusations impact your ability to finance Mr. Welles's movie? And are you in fact receiving funds from certain international criminal elements, as has also been reported?"

"That's enough!" Towers was on his feet, eyes bulging, searching around, anxious for escape.

"Stop it, Mr. Hoskins!" Priscilla had also jumped to her feet. "This is unacceptable behaviour!"

Percy ignored her. "Mr. Towers! Are these allegations true? Why won't you answer?"

"He doesn't have to answer," shouted Priscilla. "Leave him alone!"

Towers bolted out of his chair, careening away, stumbling across the room and out the door. A dozen reporters were immediately on their feet, hotfooting it after him.

Percy caught Priscilla's eye with an expression of helplessness, as though he had nothing to do with the unfolding chaos. Orson, meanwhile, puffed serenely on his cigar. Priscilla noticed that his roguish smile was back, as though to acknowledge the impossible madness of life—and of making movies.

CHAPTER TWENTY-ONE

The Spirit Medium

Harry Alan Towers escaped through the Front Hall, chased by a swarm of reporters and photographers. Susie followed, waving her arms frantically, shouting that no photographs were allowed in the Front Hall. She was ignored.

With Susie preoccupied herding unruly reporters and photographers, Priscilla searched around for the reprehensible Percy. He was nowhere to be seen. Finally, she retreated to the comparative calm of 205 in hopes that Percy might have been foolish enough to go there, so that she could make good on her determination to kill him.

But Percy wasn't in her office. Rather, an old woman, leaning on a cane, stood glaring over the sculpture of Kaspar. "There is an aura of evil surrounding this cat," she announced, straightening slightly as Priscilla approached.

The woman wore a shapeless ankle-length purple dress. Her narrow face was a dry riverbed of intricate lines and creases. Bright blue eyes blazed, eyes that now focused on Priscilla with a fierce intensity. "You should not have this cat here," she said in a croak of a voice. "This cat is cursed."

"Who are you?" Priscilla demanded.

"I am Mrs. Whitedove. I have been *called*."

"Called? Called by whom?"

"I'm afraid it was me," said a frazzled Susie, hurrying into the office. "I called Mrs. Whitedove. I thought perhaps you should meet her."

"And why should I meet Mrs. Whitedove?" Considering that, right now, in the wake of the disastrous press conference, she didn't want to meet anyone.

"Mrs. Whitedove is a spirit medium," Susie went on. "She is well known for her ability to deal with curses."

Priscilla gave Susie an impatient look. "Susie, really?"

"Make no mistake," Mrs. Whitedove interrupted, her tone dire. "Based on what I am sensing in this room from this evil cat, you need me."

"I would like you to at least listen to her," Susie chimed in anxiously. "I mean, we keep thinking that Kaspar is the antidote to a curse. But maybe he isn't. Maybe Kaspar *is* the curse."

"There are evil spirits haunting this place," professed Mrs. Whitedove darkly. "They are everywhere."

"You mean to tell me there is more of a problem here than thirteen guests at dinner?"

"That is the least of your problems," said Mrs. Whitedove.

"Believe me, a silly curse that doesn't exist *is* the least of my problems," Priscilla maintained.

"You are a person who believes in nothing!" Mrs. Whitedove virtually spat out the words, eyes blazing anew. "You are oblivious to the spirits. They are unsettled and angry. Something terrible has happened here! There has been death! This cat is cursed!" She threw out a thin arm melodramatically, pointing a bony finger at Kaspar.

"You have it all wrong, Mrs. Whitedove," Priscilla responded impatiently. "As I understand this nonsense, the long-standing belief is that Kaspar *stops* the curse."

"Kaspar *is* cursed!" Mrs. Whitedove said with renewed passion. "No matter what you have been told, none of it is true. The curse surrounding this cat cannot be lifted until the spirits in this place are appeased."

"And how will we accomplish that?" Priscilla asked dryly.

"We must make contact, to discover what it is that makes them so unhappy."

"And you can do that, I suppose."

"I am able to communicate with the spirit world, yes. Whether I can contact the spirits here, I don't know. But I am willing to try." She paused and the intensity seemed to go out of her eyes. "You don't have a cigarette, do you?"

"I'm afraid not, Mrs. Whitedove," Priscilla said. "Tell me," she added sardonically. "Do the spirits like you smoking?"

"They understand me," Mrs. Whitedove answered shortly. "They indulge me and forgive my weaknesses."

"Well, thank you for coming," Priscilla said rising to her feet.

"I repeat, Miss Tempest." Mrs. Whitedove's tone had become sinister. "You *need* me." She aimed her cane at Kaspar. "The spirits must be appeased!"

Priscilla fought off the impulse to laugh derisively. "Let me speak to my associate, Miss Gore-Langton, and we will get back to you."

"Do not delay," Mrs. Whitedove warned. "Time is of the essence. More people will die unless you act."

"Don't you think that's a bit of an overreaction?" Priscilla was quickly becoming fed up with these threats.

"Is it?" Mrs. Whitedove threw back her skeletal head. "We will see!" She turned to Susie, notably quieter but no less demanding. "You promised me taxi fare."

"You're paying for her cab?" Priscilla gave Susie a reproachful look. Could this woman not have flown out on her broomstick? she thought.

"I *always* get cab fare," Mrs. Whitedove contended. "No one has *ever* refused me cab fare."

"Let me escort you out," Susie said to the medium. "I'll make sure we get you a cab."

Mrs. Whitedove raised her cane at Priscilla as though preparing to part the waters of the Red Sea—or crack her over the head. "For those who want the truth revealed," she chanted, her grating voice rising, "opened hearts and secrets unsealed, for now until it's time again, after which the memory ends."

"Please don't shake your cane at me, Mrs. Whitedove," ordered Priscilla, thoroughly fed up.

"Those who now are in this house will hear the truth of the curse from the spirit's mouth!"

With that, Mrs. Whitedove slapped down her cane and swirled out of the office. Susie cast a helpless glance at Priscilla before hurrying after her.

Susie was back a few minutes later, leaning into Priscilla's office.

"Tell me I'm crazy," she said meekly.

"You're crazy," Priscilla replied.

"I'm only trying to help," Susie said petulantly.

"I don't think a spirit medium is the answer to what is going on around here."

"It isn't the answer if you don't believe there's a curse," Susie replied. "But if you have any suspicion at all that it's real...well, maybe you should think about Mrs. Whitedove."

With that, Susie stormed away, bristling indignantly. But really, thought Priscilla, how could Susie possibly believe Mrs.

Whitedove's nonsense? No sane person would ever embrace such hocus-pocus.

Noël Coward appeared in the doorway. "Was that Mrs. Whitedove who just left?" he asked.

CHAPTER TWENTY-TWO

Dickie Is Worried

"You *know* Mrs. Whitedove?" asked Priscilla incredulously.

"I do, indeed," Noël said stepping into her office. "One of London's finest mediums. I met her many years ago. She was an inspiration for *Blithe Spirit*." He caught sight of Kaspar—apprehensively, Priscilla thought. "Whatever is *he* doing here?"

"No one knew what to do with him following Mr. Welles's dinner and so, me being the most expendable member of the staff when it comes to being cursed, I have inherited him. Mrs. Whitedove thought he was surrounded by an aura of evil."

"Yes, I suppose she would," Noël observed.

"I believe any aura of evil has more to do with the disreputable members of the press who have passed through here."

"Let us not forget the playwrights who have seen better days seeking a free glass of champagne," added Noël.

"Do you really believe she can summon spirits?"

"As I have stated previously, it is an idea worthy of consideration," Noël said.

"I'm not convinced but, based on your advice, I will give it some thought," Priscilla said.

"Very good," Noël replied. "Now if you have a moment, do you mind if I sit down?"

"Certainly. Please, have a seat."

Perched in front of Priscilla's desk, Noël was the picture of an elegant London flâneur, the Windsor knot of his tie done to perfection, a fresh carnation in his lapel. Only his brown suede shoes were at odds with his overall splendour.

"Why do I have a sneaking suspicion the subject of Mrs. Whitedove and spiritualism is not what brings you around."

"No, I'm afraid it isn't," Noël said.

"Afraid?" Priscilla didn't like the sound of that.

"I received a call this morning from Dickie Mountbatten. We have been friends for many years, although not good friends, and, if the truth be known, not a friend I particularly admire."

"A friend you don't admire," offered Priscilla. "Interesting. I must say I didn't exactly cotton to Lord Mountbatten when I met him at the Orson Welles dinner."

"Some of us are a bit more honest about who and what we are than others," Noël observed. "Dickie is not one of those people. I understand his reluctance, but it forces him into a secret life."

"I'm not certain what you're getting at Noël," Priscilla said.

"Dickie has confided in me that unnamed forces are threatening to expose certain things he is desperate not to have exposed."

"I'm sorry to hear that" was all a mystified Priscilla could think of to say.

"Dickie has reported to me about so-called intelligence that he has received about you, Priscilla."

"Me? I have nothing to do with Lord Mountbatten." Not quite true, thinking of the photos in her possession. But there was no way Mountbatten could know she had them—unless, somehow, he did.

"That's what I thought," Noël was saying. "Don't laugh when I say this, but from what I can gather, he suspects that you might be in league with an internationally based criminal group."

Priscilla first thought Noël was making some sort of joke. His grave demeanour told her he wasn't. "Are there such things as international criminal groups?"

"There are, yes," Noël said. "People organized to prey upon the rich and famous, digging up dirt on them and then threatening exposure unless they pay up."

"Is that what has happened to Lord Mountbatten?" Which would explain those compromising photos, she thought, angry with herself all over again for even thinking of taking them.

"I told Dickie I couldn't imagine that you were involved in anything like that. But then, given your tendency for getting yourself into what I might describe as unusual situations, I thought I might drop around and find out from you personally."

"What?" questioned Priscilla. "Do I belong to some sort of crime gang? Is that what you're asking?"

"Do you?" Noël asked in all seriousness.

"No!" Priscilla replied vehemently. But she could not help but think of the house on Swain's Lane. Had she stumbled into some sort of nest of crooks headed by the mysterious Kirk Strong? Were Mariella Novotny and Johnny Edgecombe part of it? They seemed unlikely master criminals. Could someone then get the idea that she was associated with these people? She thought again of the photos. Should she say something about them to Noël? A little voice deep inside her whispered no.

The playwright broke out a smile. "There we go, then. I imagined that Dickie was being paranoid, but he seemed quite adamant. He asked me to have a word with you."

"Nothing more?"

"A word," Noël said. "That's it."

Nothing about photographs then, Priscilla thought, feeling more uneasy than ever.

"If I could, Priscilla," Noël went on, "I would leave you with a tiny piece of advice."

"Don't join international crime groups?"

Noël allowed a faint smile. "I understand that it is 1968, and this is Swinging London, and everyone is taking off their knickers and all that, but Dickie Mountbatten represents an establishment in this country that exists in a bubble and thus largely remains—or tries to remain—oblivious to the changes roiling British society. Dickie and his ilk will fight any threat to their way of life. Dickie in particular, because he has a good deal to hide."

"What about you, Noël?" Priscilla asked coldly. "What would you do to protect someone like Mountbatten? How far would you go to cover up for him?"

"I fear you misunderstand the reason for my visit," Noël replied in a hurt voice.

"Do I?" Priscilla held on to her icy tone.

"You are inside the bubble, Priscilla. I know you think you aren't, but you work at the Savoy, thus you are deep inside. I merely want to make sure you are safe among the people it is your job to serve."

"Then I had best do my job and keep quiet, hadn't I, a Canadian kid from a middle-class family fortunate to serve the likes of Lord Mountbatten?"

"Now you're angry."

"I am trying not to be, Noël, but you're not making it easy."

"I have said my piece," he stated quietly. "Now I must be off, dear Priscilla."

As Noël stood so did Priscilla, enabling him to buss both her cheeks. His gaze was intense as it met hers. "If you need help, if there's anything I can do…"

"I'm fine Noël, really," she said with an assurance she wasn't feeling. "Tell Lord Mountbatten that he has nothing to fear from me."

Noël presented her with a soulful look and another kiss before exiting. Priscilla was left to contemplate why she was feeling somewhat let down by Noël.

When she got to London, fresh from Toronto the Good, Noël had become her safe father confessor, her gentle guide through the shadowy labyrinth of the London society that frequented the Savoy. He was part of that society, he told her, but not *one* of them. Therefore, he could remain at a safe distance, where he could keep his eye on the herd while not actually running with it. He said he knew these people for what they really were—venal, nasty, highly manipulative and determined to hang on to their secrets no matter what.

What Noël had failed to mention was that when it came right down to it, in order to protect his place at the edge of the herd, he would make the necessary compromises. But then Christine Keeler had warned her about just this sort of thing, had she not? Her words echoed back hauntingly: "*All I know is if there are people out there blackmailing establishment blokes like Lord Mountbatten, there are other people bound to stop them by any means necessary.*"

Arriving back at her flat later that evening, Priscilla switched on the lights and ignored the all-too-familiar mess of the place. One of these days she would clean up. But not tonight. Tonight, she would bathe—and forget. She stripped off her clothes—she would retrieve them from the floor later—and then ran hot water into her small bathtub, adding bath oil.

She sank with relief into the warm water, inhaling the soothing lavender scent and wishing she had thought to pour herself a glass of wine. Ah well, she thought, dropping her head back against the tub's porcelain surface, this would do for now.

This would do just fine.

Eventually, her mind wandered back to Noël's visit and his warning about Lord Mountbatten. International criminals blackmailing Lord Mountbatten? Was that possible? Apparently it was. Now, not only was she a person of interest, as the police described her, for the murder of James Harley, she was also suspected, possibly as a result of investigating Harley's murder, of being in cahoots with extortionists. And she wasn't even taking into consideration the dreaded Jack Cogan and his determination to put her to work for him.

Maybe she should simply remain in this tub for as long as it took for all the madness to pass.

But then the madness never actually passed, did it?

Thus, she had no choice but to rise like a soapy Venus from her bath. Dripping wet, she was reaching for a towel when the phone in the other room began to ring. No, she thought, she would not answer it. This was her night alone. She would clean up the flat, wash the dishes; there would be no intrusions.

The phone kept ringing.

She issued a frustrated expletive and then, dropping the towel, dashed into the living room.

The tall man in the dark coat seated in the easy chair adjusted his glasses and pointed his gun at her as he said, "Don't bother to answer it."

CHAPTER TWENTY-THREE

Priscilla Unclothed

The telephone finally stopped ringing. The tall man in the easy chair readjusted his glasses and kept his gun where Priscilla could see it. How should she react? she thought vaguely. Cover her breasts? What good would that do?

"Who are you?"

"I'm your friend Kirk Strong," he said. "I understand that's how you have described me."

He was tall, if not taller than previously advertised. Jet-black hair fell in an unruly swatch across his forehead. Even seated, he possessed a certain coiled power that overcame the professorial look the glasses might otherwise have provided him.

Watching Strong, Priscilla had no trouble believing him as the mastermind of a gang dedicated to blackmail and extortion. In his black coat and matching black turtleneck, holding a gun on her, he was perfectly cast.

"What are you doing here?" she managed in a strained voice.

"Advising you to get a better lock on your door," said Strong.

"I wasn't expecting company this late," Priscilla said, maintaining a level of cool that, under these circumstances, she wouldn't have thought possible. "Usually, the people with guns show up a little earlier."

"I was delayed by traffic," Strong said. "It's getting worse all the time."

"I don't suppose I could cover myself."

"I don't know." Strong allowed the hint of a smile. "I kind of like you as you are."

"Still…"

"Don't do anything silly."

"Like standing naked in front of a man with a gun?"

"It looks as though there is a trench coat on the rack by the door," Strong said. "Why don't you go over there and put it on?"

He again pushed at his glasses, watching her walk to the coat and lift it off its hook. As gracefully as she could manage, she shrugged into it, wrapping it around her so that she could cinch the belt. She turned back to Strong. "Now what?"

"Now I must ask you how it is you got mixed up with Johnny Edgecombe. And what makes you think I'm your friend?"

"You're not?"

"I'd never laid eyes on you until a few moments ago, with or without clothes," Strong said.

"Most of my friends have never seen me without clothes," Priscilla said.

"You were less than honest in your encounters with Johnny and then Mariella."

"I'm not sure I was dishonest with either of those people," Priscilla countered. "I tried to help Johnny, that's all. As for Mariella, I understand she's your girlfriend."

"I don't have girlfriends." Strong said. "What I do have is headaches, and right now, Priscilla Tempest, you are my biggest one."

"You break into my apartment and threaten me with a gun because I give you a headache?"

"You're a headache because, for the life of me, I can't figure out what you're up to. And I didn't break in. The door was open."

"Fine, you didn't break in and that isn't a gun in your hand and you're not part of an international crime group—"

"But I do want to know what you think you're doing."

"So, you *are*."

"I didn't say that."

"Maybe I'm trying to figure out what *you're* up to."

"Then that's the problem. You shouldn't be trying to figure that out. You should be staying far away and getting on with whatever it is you do at the Savoy. But you're not and that, as I mentioned, is giving me a big headache."

"I'm sorry to hear that."

"What are you doing, Priscilla? Why are you inserting yourself into a place that is only going to get you hurt?"

"Someone murdered James Harley. I happened to discover his body. The police think I might be implicated. Let's say that in trying to clear my name with the police, I ended up on Swain's Lane."

"I didn't have anything to do with Harley's murder," Strong said quietly.

"What about the photographs? Do you have anything to do with those?"

Strong's eyes narrowed behind his glasses. "What photographs are you talking about?"

"Photos I found in Harley's flat. Christine Keeler and Lord Mountbatten. Both compromised in ways they wouldn't want the public to know about."

"Where are those photos now?" Strong asked carefully.

"I destroyed them," she lied.

"Why would you do that?"

"I didn't want the possible scandal to reflect back on the Savoy. After all, both Lord Mountbatten and Miss Keeler were at the Orson Welles dinner that you financed."

"Lord Mountbatten and my group are involved in a business venture," Strong said evenly. "Nothing more complicated than that."

"Business venture. Is that what you call extortion these days?"

"Like I told you before, Priscilla, I want you to stay out of this. Lord Mountbatten's friends are even more dangerous than I am." Strong lowered the gun as he got to his feet, towering over her. The light glinted off his glasses. She noted that the professorial quality they lent him was obscured by his size. Dressed head to foot in black, Strong appeared more sinister than ever.

"Every time you open your mouth, you make me think you're a whole lot more trouble than I could have imagined."

"Tell me why you paid for that dinner," Priscilla stated flatly.

"Let's say Mr. Towers operates as a consultant to our business," Strong acknowledged. "It was good for us to support him on that occasion."

"But then—" Priscilla started to say.

"Damn you," blustered Strong. "Quit asking me questions or I *will* shoot you."

"I will add that to the list of threats I've been receiving lately," Priscilla said dryly.

"Make sure you put me at the top," Strong said. "Not to worry. I'll see myself out."

Relief flooded through her—until he reached the door and came to stop. What now? she groaned inwardly. He turned to her. "Incidentally..."

"Yes?"

"I thought you looked pretty good without your clothes on."

Priscilla frowned. "Only pretty good?"

He smiled and went out the door.

That's when the phone started to ring again. And ring—and ring.

Priscilla closed her eyes briefly, took a deep breath and picked up the receiver.

"Is this Miss Priscilla Tempest?"

"Yes," replied Priscilla. "Who is this?"

"Miss Tempest, this is Ethel Cambridge. I have been trying to get hold of you."

"Yes, Ethel, what is it?"

"You left me your number in case I heard of rental properties that might become available."

Priscilla relaxed. At least Ethel wasn't threatening to kill her—not yet. "Is that why you're calling me?"

"No, Miss Tempest, that is not the reason. I know you're not actually looking for a flat. I know what you're up to and so it is imperative that we meet. I have been betrayed by certain people, and I believe you can provide me with the advice I need."

"Can't this wait, Ethel? It's very late."

"Now—tonight!" The anguish in Ethel's voice was palpable. "I am in fear of my life, lovey. You must come around—now!"

Ethel rang off.

I can't do this, Priscilla thought as she hung up. It's too much, she told herself as she entered her bedroom, shedding the trench coat. She eyed her unmade bed longingly. She should simply turn out the lights and crawl into it and get a good night's sleep, and then in the morning concentrate on the business of the Savoy. Until it was time to go to work for the dreaded Jack Cogan, of course. She struggled into olive-coloured cords, pulled on a University of Toronto sweatshirt and laced up a pair of saddle shoes.

She grabbed her shoulder bag and keys to the Morris Minor as she left the flat.

CHAPTER TWENTY-FOUR

Dying Among the Dead

Priscilla guided her car along Swain's Lane, past No. 11. Further up the street she pulled over to the kerb beside a cemetery. The headstones and looming crypts stood out starkly in the moonlight. She shuddered involuntarily. If this life was at an end, she thought morosely, at least she was close to where they could ditch her body.

She passed the wrought-iron fence that separated the cemetery from the street, and then, keeping to the shadows, reached Ethel Cambridge's house. No lights were visible. Next door, No. 11 was also dark.

She went up the walkway to Ethel's house and rang the bell. No lights came on. She rang again. Still nothing. She tried the latch, praying that the door was locked, that it would not open, that no one would answer, that she could turn around and go back to her car and drive away.

The door swung open.

Priscilla swallowed hard, pushed the door open further and stepped into a darkened vestibule. She closed the door behind her and then called out, "Ethel? Are you here?"

No one answered.

"Ethel, where are you?" Priscilla called again as she ventured along the hall.

Suddenly Ethel Cambridge lurched out of the dimness, her face twisted in terror. "Get out!" she cried. "Get out!" A loud pop resounded and Ethel was flung forward.

Priscilla caught a glimpse of a dark figure. She turned and bolted, crashing out the door and jumping down the steps onto the street, the gunman behind her.

Priscilla charged full bore along the street, which was lined with high brick walls on either side. There was an opening in the wall. She turned into it, convinced that at any moment she would be shot.

On either side of the footpath where she found herself, grey and weathered headstones tipped at odd angles. Statues honouring the dead were concealed among towering trees bathed in moonlight. Veering from the path, she shot past gothic tombs and beds of wildflowers, then broke onto a cobblestoned expanse surrounded by curving archways sheltering neoclassical vaults. She plunged down a series of steps, tripped and went flying, landing hard at the bottom.

The breath knocked out of her, vision blurred, down on all fours, she heard a voice say, "What's this about, then?"

A London bobby, moustache bristling, iconic custodian helmet catching the gleam of the moon.

Following the frantic run for her life through what was, according to attending officers, historic Highgate Cemetery—Karl Marx was buried there, advised one copper chattily—Priscilla wasn't sure of anything except an intense desire to be finished with the police and go home to bed.

An hour or so later Detective Constable Oliver Brock showed up. The detective sat beside her on a bench beneath an archway in front of the vaults in the part of the cemetery known as the Circle of Lebanon. He was young, with a round clean-shaven face, short-cropped brown hair and the kind of inquisitive blue eyes that, Priscilla decided, a good detective should always possess. Kind of cute, although this was not the time or the place to be appraising the cuteness of police officers. She couldn't help wonder, after he'd been with her for a time, if his interest in her extended beyond the professional. Or was her imagination running wild? Given the evening's events, it very possibly was.

"We have attended at the house on Swain's Lane that you described to us, and I'm afraid we found it deserted," DC Brock reported.

"It belongs to a woman named Ethel Cambridge," Priscilla replied in a tired voice. "As I told the other officers, I saw her being shot. The man who shot her then chased me to this cemetery."

DC Brock had his notebook out and was scribbling away as she spoke. He raised his head. Such nice blue eyes, she thought. "Well, I'm afraid we found the place deserted. As we did the other house you mentioned, next door—No. 11, I believe?"

"It's a house occupied by a criminal group," Priscilla proclaimed, sounding rather more melodramatic than she intended.

"A what?" Confusion clouded the DC's round face.

"That's what I understand. An American named Kirk Strong is in charge." Priscilla spoke slowly, trying to make what she was telling the detective sound reasonable, as though murderous criminal groups could often be found dwelling next door. She added for good measure, "I believe his people may have shot Ethel to keep her quiet."

DC Brock gave her a look that was partly sympathetic and, she thought, a bit patronizing. "But she wasn't able to tell you anything, is that correct?"

"Yes," Priscilla said with a nod. "She was shot as soon as I got there. That's when I ran for my life."

"I'm afraid the attending officer who found you said there was no sign of anyone who might have been chasing you."

"That's because whoever it was ran off when the officer appeared. Thankfully. The officer probably saved my life."

DC Brock finished scribbling into his notebook and once again raised his eyes. "Miss Tempest, I'm aware you took a pretty hard tumble this evening. I wonder if we shouldn't take you to hospital just to make sure everything is all right."

"I'm fine, Detective. I want to go home." She eyed him uncertainly. "Why do I suspect you do not believe a word out of my mouth?"

"It's not that I don't believe you. It is just that, thus far, we have not been able to find any evidence to back up your claims."

"So you think I am mad?"

"Not at all. We will follow up on what you have told us but, for now, if you feel you don't need medical attention, we should allow you to go home."

And stop hallucinating about things that aren't true, Priscilla added to herself.

"My car is on Swain's Lane," she said.

"I think it's best if I drive you," the detective said. "That way we can make sure you're safe. I'll arrange to have your car picked up in the morning."

"That's very kind," Priscilla said. A wave of exhaustion swept over her, washing away any inclination she might have had to drive.

"My car is close by." He put away his notebook and started to rise. "Are you okay to walk a bit?"

"Yes, certainly." But when she stood, Priscilla immediately felt dizzy. DC Brock reached out to steady her. "Are you sure you're all right?"

"Just really, really tired," Priscilla said.

"Then let's get you home," he said in a voice unexpectedly filled with warm assurance.

She gave him an appreciative smile. It couldn't possibly be, of course, but for a moment there she could have sworn her clean-cut young detective wore armour that shone.

"I'm told you work at the Savoy Hotel," DC Brock ventured. He kept his eyes straight ahead, both hands on the wheel, as they sped south through mostly deserted streets occasionally illumin-ated by pools of amber light and occasionally by the flicker of a neon sign.

Priscilla, beside him, fighting to stay awake, was on her guard immediately. "Who told you that?"

"My boss, Detective Chief Inspector Robert Lightfoot. I understand he's had several previous encounters with you."

"Oh dear," Priscilla groaned. "Charger Lightfoot."

"No one would dare call him that to his face," Brock said gently.

"I can't imagine what he's told you about me," she said, thinking that she could well imagine—and that none of it was good.

"He suggests you have problems when it comes to telling the truth."

"I see." Which would make her account of the evening's events even more suspect.

When DC Brock drew up to her flat, he said, "I very much respect my chief and the wisdom he brings with his many years of experience at Special Branch. However, I do insist on making up my own mind about whatever case I'm working on."

He stole a quick glance at Priscilla, which she blessed with a smile.

"Are you sure you're going to be all right?"

"Yes, but I am very tired."

"Hopefully you can get some sleep, Miss Tempest. I will be in touch."

"Thank you for the ride." She opened the passenger door.

"Glad to do it," said DC Brock.

"You know, Inspector Lightfoot regards me as what he calls a person of interest in the murder of James Harley."

"Yes, I'm aware of that."

"I didn't kill him, and I *am* telling you the truth about what happened tonight."

"Like I said, I make up my own mind about things."

Priscilla nodded. "If you need me, I can be reached at the Savoy."

"That will be a first for me," he said with a grin.

"How's that?"

"I've never phoned anyone at the Savoy Hotel before. A bit above my pay grade, I must say."

"It's very easy to reach the hotel," said Priscilla. "All you have to do is pick up the phone."

"Ah, but there is an ocean between those who can easily phone the Savoy and those who would never ever have any reason to do it."

"Well, it looks like I've given you a reason, Detective," Priscilla said. "In fact, if you come around, I can give you a tour."

"I'll keep that in mind," he said noncommittally.

Was she flirting with the detective? she wondered as she got out of the car. Or simply trying her best to make him believe her?

Maybe a bit of both, she thought.

CHAPTER TWENTY-FIVE

A Dinner Invitation

"Goodness gracious, what happened?" Susie demanded when Priscilla entered 205 late the next morning.

"What are you talking about?" Priscilla retorted, thinking that it was one thing to feel like a wreck, quite another to look like one.

"Did you not get any sleep last night?" Susie settled a bit, realizing she might have overreacted.

Hardly a wink, Priscilla thought, but just as well Susie didn't know. "I'm fine," she said aloud. "Let's get on with it. What have I missed?"

"Not much. A Mr. Leach has called a couple of times. He wishes to meet you in the American Bar for a drink at five o'clock."

"He does?" Should she finally have that drink with him? In the name of keeping an important guest at the Savoy happy, how could she say no?

"Don't play coy," Susie said smugly. "Was it Mr. Leach who kept you awake all night?" she asked naughtily. "Or was it that Cary Grant?"

"Susie, enough." Trust Susie not to know that Mr. Leach was in fact Cary Grant. "What else?"

"Percy Hoskins's piece about Harry Alan Towers has appeared," Susie answered promptly. "According to Percy's story, his sources at MI6 tell him that Mr. Towers was an informant for them—but hasn't been for some time."

She thought of what Kirk Strong had told her about Towers. Maybe he was still an informant for MI6—not a revelation Kirk Strong would appreciate.

She entered her office certain that Kaspar was giving her a malicious eye as she took her seat behind the desk and pressed the waiter button. Something had to be done about that damned cat, she thought, resisting the urge yet again to consider, based on recent events, that there might be something to Kaspar's curse.

Susie stuck her head in the door. "I almost forgot. Mrs. Whitedove called. She's wondering if you might be having second thoughts."

In a moment of weakness, Priscilla almost said yes. Maybe the medium could provide the answers she hadn't been able to get elsewhere. She resisted—for now at least. "No, it's all right, Susie."

Susie looked chastened. "Well, if you change your mind…"

Karl appeared with morning coffee mounted on a silver tray. He made a face when he saw Priscilla. "Late night?" he inquired.

"God, do I look *that* terrible?"

"You look wonderful, as always, but perhaps a trifle tired this morning," Karl revised diplomatically, placing the coffee on her desk.

"She won't tell me who kept her up all night," Susie reported. "But I do believe it was a Mr. Leach."

"Mr. Leach?" Karl allowed himself to look uncustomarily taken aback. "Don't you mean Mr. Cary Grant?"

Susie appeared perplexed. "How—"

"That's enough, Susie," insisted Priscilla. "Thank you for the coffee, Karl. Let us all get back to work."

"I really am confused," Susie said as she followed Karl out the door.

"I'll explain it to you, Susie," Karl said, closing the door behind him.

Left alone, finally, Priscilla took gulps of coffee, thinking about, well, she was thinking about that copper, wasn't she? DC Oliver Brock. Not that she should. She shouldn't be thinking about any man right now. She should be thinking about the people who were trying to either put her in prison or, even worse, put an end to her life. Her gaze fell on Kaspar, perched malevolently across the room. "Well, you're certainly no friend," she said aloud. "All this started because of you."

Kaspar had no response. Bugger of a cat, she thought, sipping her coffee.

Still, in a world of enemies there was perhaps one ally she could count on.

Cary Grant never let down Grace Kelly or Audrey Hepburn. He wouldn't let her down either.

Would he? Well, she would soon see.

Among the pasty London faces captured in the late afternoon light of the American Bar, Cary Grant's stood out, the ageless ideal of glowing, sun-kissed good health.

If there was a single crease in his dark blue suit, it was not visible as Cary stood to greet her. His smile was, well, what could she say? That Cary Grant smile bursting with good cheer but at the same time somewhat quizzical, as though he went through life uncertain about what would happen next but eternally optimistic that it would all work out.

She was already feeling better.

"There you are, dear Priscilla," he said, taking her hand and kissing her cheek. "Right on time."

As Cary held a chair for her, those pasty London faces did their best not to stare at the movie star among them. But a film legend had descended, and so they failed badly at pretending not to notice. Priscilla suspected that no one in the American Bar would mistake Cary Grant for Archie Leach. Or Stewart Granger for that matter.

"You're certainly attracting attention," Priscilla said when she was seated.

"No, no, my dear, it's you. An elderly fellow with a beautiful young woman. Everyone suspects the worst, I'm sure."

"Of you? Or me?"

"Oh me, definitely," Cary said. He motioned for a waiter, who immediately hastened to their table, his face flushed with excitement. "Yes sir, Mr. Grant. What may I get for you?"

"What will you have, Priscilla?"

Priscilla ordered a Buck's Fizz while Cary satisfied himself with soda water. "I'm far too old for booze, I'm afraid."

"It's why you look so healthy," Priscilla said.

"Why I'm such a bore," Cary countered. "That is why I must live vicariously through you, Priscilla. Tell me what adventures you've been up to without me."

If only you knew, Priscilla thought. Aloud, she said vaguely, "Not much to report, I'm afraid."

"I keep running into Orson's producer, Harry Alan Towers. He glares every time he sees me. As if I should be in Orson's movie, and I'm not. I understand he and Orson had a disastrous press conference the other day."

"I'm afraid so," Priscilla said as the waiter returned with their drinks.

"Chin-chin!" Cary said, raising his glass. Priscilla clinked his glass with hers and then sipped the Buck's Fizz.

"Poor Orson," Cary said as he set his drink aside. "In order to finance his films, he gets mixed up with all sorts of scoundrels and frauds. I'm afraid our Mr. Towers is one of them."

"Do you mind if I ask how you came to be invited to that dinner?" Priscilla asked.

"Hitch received the invitation. I came along as his date. That way he could pepper me with pleas to do his next film."

"Which you have resisted?"

"I think I finally convinced him," Cary said. "He's off to France to start filming without me. Unlike Orson, Hitch has no trouble getting financing."

"What are your plans, Mr. Grant?"

"Soon I must return to Los Angeles, but for now I've been invited to dinner next week at Buckingham Palace. Black tie required. Are you impressed?"

"How could I not be," said Priscilla. "Very impressive indeed."

"I'm so glad you feel that way," Cary said. "You see, I'd like to bring you along."

"Me?" Priscilla nearly choked on her drink.

"Yes, you," Cary said. "I can't imagine you haven't been to the palace before."

"As a matter of fact, I haven't."

"Then it's high time you met Her Majesty the Queen."

"Will she be there?"

"Unless she's moved, she lives there."

"This is very kind of you, Mr. Grant." Priscilla coughed a couple of times to clear her throat. "But as I've mentioned before, Savoy employees aren't allowed to date the hotel's guests."

"But you see, I have checked out of the hotel. I am no longer a guest here. Nothing to do with you, I hasten to add. A friend of mine has lent me his flat until I go back to Los Angeles. I am bunking in there. Free accommodation. I couldn't resist."

"I see," said Priscilla, at a loss as to what else to say. "I wasn't aware you had left us."

"Therefore, you have no excuse," continued Cary. "Will you be so kind as to accompany me to Buckingham Palace to dine with the Queen?"

"Can I ask what the occasion is?"

"As it happens, Her Majesty is hosting a dinner to honour an old friend of mine."

"Lord Mountbatten?"

"I've known him forever," Cary replied.

Of course he had.

"Well, what do you say, Priscilla?"

She should say no. Sight unseen she was already in trouble with Mountbatten. She couldn't imagine what would happen should she waltz into a celebratory dinner hosted by the Queen. Priscilla would say no. She had to say no.

"Yes," someone said out loud. It was a moment before she realized the voice was hers.

Returning to 205 in a bit of a daze—an invitation from Cary Grant and a second Buck's Fizz could do that to a young woman— Priscilla saw that Susie had left for the day. Mrs. Whitedove was headed out the door, lugging Kaspar.

Priscilla blocked her exit. "Mrs. Whitedove," she said crossly, "what do you think you are doing?"

"A great favour," proclaimed Mrs. Whitedove, drawing Kaspar to her chest protectively. "This cat must be destroyed!"

"Whatever else said cat is, it is hotel property and you are not allowed to remove it," insisted Priscilla irately. "Please put it back."

"No!" shouted Mrs. Whitedove, holding on to Kaspar more tightly than ever.

"Mrs. Whitedove, either put that cat down or I am calling security."

"You are a *fool*, Miss Tempest. You have no idea what you're dealing with."

"Put the cat down."

Mrs. Whitedove gave a great, heaving sob of defeat and then thumped Kaspar down on Susie's desk. "I have tried to help, and I have failed. *Evil wins!*"

"There are much better ways to deal with evil than stealing hotel property."

"Then you must agree to a seance, Miss Tempest. That is the only way. We summon the spirits who can rid you of this terrible curse."

"Really, Mrs. Whitedove, I think you are being far too melodramatic."

"Am I?" Mrs. Whitedove flared back, eyes wide with alarm, an impressive demonstration of the melodrama Priscilla had just accused her of. "I feel the evil vibrations from this cat. This cat has caused death! There have been murders! I know this is true!"

Priscilla had to concede that the old woman was right— more or less. That is, if one allowed oneself to believe in Mrs. Whitedove's histrionic assertions. Priscilla wasn't about to do that—not in front of the woman at any rate.

Still...

"All right, Mrs. Whitedove. I will consider the possibility of a seance. But no more sneaking in here and trying to make off with hotel property. Agreed?"

"Let me know a day and time, and I will make the necessary arrangements."

"I'm not promising anything, mind you. But I will give it some serious thought."

The phone started to ring in Priscilla's office. "I had better get that."

"Please do not wait," Mrs. Whitedove warned. "The longer you delay, the stronger evil grows. More people will lose their lives."

With that, Mrs. Whitedove swept away. Priscilla lifted Kaspar gently and transported him back to his station on the side table in her office. He gazed at her impassively, neither admitting to evil nor denying it, open to any interpretation one might care to apply to him.

The phone continued to ring. Priscilla forced her eyes away from the cat and picked up the receiver.

"I didn't know if I would get you at this hour or not," said the voice on the other end of the phone.

"Who is this?"

"Sorry. It's DC Oliver Brock."

"Detective, hello." She had to stop herself from adding, "I was just thinking about you." Instead she forced out, "Good of you to call." That wasn't her heart beating faster, was it? No, it couldn't be.

"Listen, we need to talk, but I don't think it's a good idea to do it over the phone. Are you available to meet?"

"Why don't you come to the hotel?" Priscilla said. "I will give you that tour we discussed and then we can talk in my office."

"I'm about ten minutes away, if you're free," said the detective.

That was quick, Priscilla thought to herself. "I'll meet you in the Front Hall."

"Front Hall?"

"It's what we call the lobby."

"Ah yes, the Front Hall it is," said the detective. "I'll see you in a few minutes."

Well, well, she thought, isn't this interesting? Then her stomach sank. Perhaps this wasn't a personal visit. Perhaps Oliver Brock was now DC Brock and this was official business that might include—what? Arrest, given her circumstances, was not out of the question.

Her gaze once again fell on Kaspar, certain that damned cat had taken on a gleefully malevolent air.

The Detective's Tale

Priscilla barely got to the Front Hall before Oliver Brock appeared. He wore a tweed jacket and a dull brown tie. His round face appeared freshly shaved and his brown hair was neatly combed—he was the picture of the young, organized copper, Priscilla decided as she watched him take in his surroundings. With a bit of a frown, she thought as she crossed to him.

"What do you think?"

"Smaller than I might have imagined," he said. "But lovely flower arrangements."

"Our staff puts out fresh flowers each day," Priscilla said. "It's one of the hotel's traditions."

"A privileged world full of fresh flowers," he said vaguely.

Priscilla ignored the gibe. "If you will follow me, Detective, I'll provide you with a bit of history along the way."

"That's very kind of you," Oliver said.

"The hotel was the creation in 1889 of Richard D'Oyly Carte, who was best known as the producer of Gilbert and Sullivan's operas," Priscilla explained. "As you can see, the Front Hall, or lobby, retains vestiges of its original Edward VII elegance—out of another time, but timeless."

"A very rich time, I imagine," put in Oliver.

"D'Oyly Carte's ambition was to create a place of elegance and comfort much like the hotels he had visited in New York and

San Francisco. In London, it was thought the rich were inclined, when they travelled, to stay with friends on their estates. The hotels of the time weren't very good, and so the rich never went near them."

"But this chap proved them wrong, I suppose."

"Very much so. My favourite piece of trivia about this hotel is that before Mr. D'Oyly Carte arrived on the scene, the Victoria Hotel, at the time the height of luxury, provided four bathrooms for five hundred guests. At Mr. D'Oyly Carte's insistence, every suite at the Savoy had its own bathroom. That was, believe it or not, revolutionary."

"Anything to make the lives of the rich more comfortable, I suppose," Oliver said coolly.

"In any event," she continued, "the same high standards that D'Oyly Carte originated in 1889 continue to be carefully maintained at the Savoy today."

"And you help to maintain those standards, do you, Miss Tempest?" Oliver was following her along the corridor to her office.

"I do my best," Priscilla said over her shoulder. "Everyone here at the Savoy does."

"Good to hear."

Priscilla led him into her office. "And this is where I work."

Oliver's gaze landed on Kaspar. "That's a frightening-looking cat," he observed.

"That's Kaspar," Priscilla offered, deciding not to explain anything more about him than she had to.

"I don't like cats," Oliver said. He looked at Priscilla. Slightly accusatory? "But I suppose you do."

"I'm not a cat person," Priscilla said, perhaps too quickly.

"Yet you have a cat sculpture in your office," Oliver countered.

"Yes, I do." Leaving further explanations about Kaspar at that. No matter, as Oliver was already moving on to the celebrity photographs above the sofa.

"Have all these people stayed at the Savoy?" Oliver kept his eyes on the wall.

"They have," Priscilla said tightly, increasingly concerned about the direction this conversation was taking.

"I actually recognize some of them," Oliver said.

"I get the impression you don't think much of the rich or the hotels that house them."

Oliver turned to face her. "I don't mean to offend you."

"I'm not offended at all," said Priscilla. "I understand the Savoy is not everyone's, shall we say, cup of tea."

"Yes, I don't suppose it is," Oliver said. "Money might have something to do with those who can stay here and those who can't."

"Then why don't you have a seat and tell me why you're here," said Priscilla formally.

Oliver sank onto the sofa, noticeably relaxing. "That's better," he said.

"Is something wrong?" Priscilla took her place behind her desk. "You seem in pain."

"A bit of trouble with my knee, that's all."

"From chasing bad guys?"

"Something like that." Oliver massaged his right knee as he spoke. "Anyway, what I wanted to tell you—between the two of us for now, if you don't mind—"

"We pride ourselves on our discretion at the Savoy," Priscilla said emphatically.

"Naturally, the private lives of the rich and privileged must be carefully guarded."

"Get to the point, Detective," Priscilla said, weary of Oliver's jabs.

"The body of Jack Cogan has been found." Oliver, as she feared he might, had left the room, replaced in authoritative tone by DC Brock.

In the silence that followed, Priscilla grappled with what she had just heard. "I—I'm not sure what to say," she managed.

"Then you know Mr. Cogan?"

"Yes, I've had dealings with him here at the hotel, where he's been an occasional guest. Why is that important?" Priscilla asked, beginning to sense that her knowledge of Cogan might be working against her.

"Mr. Cogan was discovered by passersby in a secluded part of Highgate Cemetery."

"You can't be serious," Priscilla said, still trying to come to terms with Oliver's news.

"I thought I had better talk to you," Oliver said. "Nothing has been announced yet, and the investigation is ongoing, but the preliminary conclusion is that he died by a self-inflicted gunshot wound."

"Given what I know of Mr. Cogan, that hardly seems possible," Priscilla said, thinking of the pompous, self-important—drunk!—individual who had pushed his way into her life.

"You knew Mr. Cogan well enough to come to that conclusion?"

"Enough to be highly skeptical that he would have any reason to take his own life."

"Well enough to have some idea as to who might want to murder him?" Oliver asked.

Priscilla flashed on Christine Keeler plunging a letter opener into Cogan's shoulder. Christine Keeler blackmailed by the now-murdered James Harley. "I don't know anyone *that* well,"

Priscilla said. "But I do have to say that Mr. Cogan was not a particularly nice man. I can only imagine there is no shortage of people who might wish him harm." At least she was dealing with Oliver and not Inspector Lightfoot and the inspector's insinuations that she was somehow responsible for Cogan's death. Still, she had to dare to ask the question: "Do you have *any* evidence that Mr. Cogan was murdered?"

"There is no evidence of foul play at the moment," Oliver said, "but given what you have just told me, I thought I would ask."

"I see."

"There is a second reason why I came here," Oliver offered hesitantly.

"And what is that reason, DC Brock?"

"I've been told by my superiors that you are considered unreliable, and accordingly I must tell you that I've been ordered to drop any further investigation into events on Swain's Lane."

Another shock to the system, thought Priscilla. Was there no end to them? "You mean to tell me that you have found Ethel Cambridge alive and well?"

"I'm not saying that," Oliver said. "But at the moment, there is no evidence that she has been shot."

"What do you think, DC Brock?" she asked in a strangled voice. "Do you think I'm unreliable?"

"I would be inclined to believe you," Oliver answered. "But it seems the sort of people who stay at the Savoy and wield the power in this country do not."

"What about the house next door to Ethel, the people at No. 11?"

"That idea was dismissed as soon as I brought it up," Oliver said. "The house is owned by a rather notorious chap known to police, Johnny Edgecombe. I interviewed him this afternoon.

He said the house hasn't been occupied for some time, and he was thinking of selling it. He was rather convincing."

"Johnny is a convincing liar," Priscilla said. "Look into an American named Kirk Strong. He was staying there. I believe he could be involved in blackmailing prominent individuals, Lord Mountbatten among them."

Oliver, Priscilla noticed, was trying his best not to look skeptical. He wasn't very successful. "Those are pretty wild accusations," he said.

"Kirk Strong might well be a suspect if your superiors ever decide Cogan's death wasn't a suicide."

"I don't imagine my superiors will agree," Oliver said.

"The *Evening Standard* will be looking into the manner of Mr. Cogan's death, as well as the death of Ethel Cambridge," Priscilla stated boldly, certain that the horrible Percy Hoskins would be interested in such a story.

Oliver did not appear particularly concerned. "Should I assume that you would be the source?"

"This is the press office," she answered, lifting her hand into the air to indicate their surroundings. "I know lots of reporters."

"You are something, Miss Tempest, I must say. A gadfly at the Savoy, I can't help thinking."

"It has been said," Priscilla acknowledged.

"As a matter of fact, I know Special Branch has been investigating Mr. Strong on other matters, so his name isn't unfamiliar to me. Will you give me a few days to look into your allegations before you go to the press?"

"Kirk Strong all but admitted to me that his group is blackmailing Lord Mountbatten. You might start there if you're looking into his activities."

"I will do that," Oliver said, rising to his feet. "Can I count on your discretion for the time being?"

"For the time being, yes," she said, thinking that finally someone was taking her a little more seriously.

"I'd better be going," Oliver said.

"I will walk you out."

"That's not necessary."

"I want to make sure no rich people try to corrupt you on the way."

Oliver laughed. "Didn't I mention it? I'm incorruptible."

"And here I thought all policemen were corruptible."

"Not this one," Oliver said.

Their footsteps echoed against the black-and-white tiles of the mostly deserted Front Hall. "The rich are quiet at this time of night," he observed as they reached the entrance.

"They're up in their suites counting their money."

"That's what I thought," Oliver said. He stepped closer to her and dropped his voice. "If I hear anything, can I call you?"

"You can call me anytime," Priscilla said, immediately worrying the declaration might give him the wrong idea. Or perhaps hoping that it would.

"Take care, Miss Tempest." He reached out and took her hand.

A handshake, Priscilla thought—not very romantic. But his handshake did succeed in producing a tingling sensation up and down her body.

CHAPTER TWENTY-SEVEN

Johnny Talks

Priscilla should have gone home. That might well be the inscription on her headstone: *She should have gone home.* Yet there she was, nowhere near home, back in the noise and the smoke of the Flamingo Club looking for Johnny Edgecombe. Johnny had lied to the police about a lot of things, including Kirk Strong. It was her job, she had decided, to convince him not to lie. She did not hold out a lot of hope, but she had to give it a shot.

Recognizing Priscilla, the bartender gave her a you've-got-to-be-kidding look. "Don't tell me you're looking for Johnny," he said with a weary shake of his head.

"And a glass of champagne," Priscilla added.

"Champagne, no problem. Johnny, I'm not so sure about."

"Tell him his girlfriend is here."

"Which one?"

"The one who saved his bony derrière."

"The only one who would use the word *derrière*," he said with a grin.

Johnny slid in beside her a few minutes later. His bruised and battered face registered the effects of the beating Priscilla had interrupted. "My angel," he said into her ear so that he could be heard over the din.

"What do you say, Johnny?"

"I've been behaving," Johnny asserted with a smile.

"I wonder about that."

"I've been thinking about you."

The bartender put a flute of champagne down beside her. Priscilla said, "We need to talk."

"About our future?"

"Let's get out of here to where it's less noisy."

Johnny's eyes sparkled. "Where would you like to go?"

"How about No. 11 Swain's Lane? I hear you're telling the police it's unoccupied."

Johnny's eyes lost some of their sparkle. "I got an office right upstairs. Let's go there. Nice and private. No one will bother us, yeah?"

"Why don't we do that?" said Priscilla, pasting on an artificial smile.

"Bring your drink," Johnny ordered.

Johnny led the way as they waded through the crowd to a set of stairs roped off by a chain barrier. Johnny unhooked the chain and then ushered her up a narrow staircase. The air filled with the smell of marijuana as she came onto a landing. Johnny opened a door and then went through. "Step into my office." The sparkle was back in his eyes.

A banged-up metal desk and a couple of straight-backed chairs stood near a big daybed. Priscilla didn't like the look of that bed. She took a fortifying gulp of champagne as Johnny closed the door behind her.

"What do you think?" Johnny asked as he moved in on her.

"It's a bedroom," Priscilla said.

"A workspace," Johnny said with a smirk. "Plenty of work gets done up here, yeah." His grin disappeared as he asked, "What were you doing talking to the police?"

"Ethel Cambridge, your next-door neighbour, called me last night. When I went around to her house, someone shot her and then chased me through Highgate Cemetery."

"That's what you told them?"

"You know anything about that?"

Johnny's expression slipped into neutral. "First I've heard about it."

"Now the police tell me no one got shot, no one chased me and no one lives next door at No. 11."

"Okay, the last part is true. Like I told the coppers, yeah. No one at my house."

"Kirk Strong and Mariella have moved out?"

"Never heard of them." Johnny's voice was reduced to a mumble.

"Mariella. Novotny, I believe is her last name. She was nursing you the other night when I got you home. Do you remember? She told me she's Kirk's girlfriend."

"No idea." Johnny's face had turned sullen.

"What's going on, Johnny? What are you involved in?"

"Right now, I'm at my club with a bird who asks too many bloody questions for her own good." His bruised face had become flushed with anger.

"The police are coming back for you, and they are going to ask a lot more questions than I will," Priscilla said. "You are in a load of trouble."

"How could I be in trouble? I haven't done anything." Johnny was back to looking sullen.

"I might be able to help you, but I need you to talk to me— honestly."

"I don't know shit, okay?" Johnny said.

"Tell me what you do know."

The loud percussive beat of the music coming from below filled the room.

"All right," Johnny said, exhaling a long breath. "You can keep me out of trouble with the coppers, yeah?"

"I will do my best," said Priscilla, without having a clue as to how she would keep a character like Johnny out of police hands.

"Look, Mariella got me into this, yeah? She knew a guy, she said, an American looking for someone who could front the sale of a house, some good money in it for me, okay?"

"This was Kirk Strong?"

"Yeah. Turns out Mariella had met him in New York and she was shagging him now that he was in London. I didn't want to get involved at first but there was nothing much to it and it looked like I owned a place, not a bad thing. I went along. The next thing I know, Mariella moves in with this Kirk Strong bloke and I'm pretty much out in the cold. Then this joker Harry Alan Towers starts to show up, and it seems like he and Strong are hatching some sort of deal together. All sorts of mysterious comings and goings. People becoming real quiet every time I show up."

"Any idea what kind of deal?"

"Sounded like they were after someone big, blackmail thing. That's what Kirk does. He goes after big shots, gets dirt on them in exchange for money. Other than the house, and putting up with Mariella, I stayed away from the whole deal. Never should have gotten mixed up in it. Blame Mariella, yeah."

"What about Kirk Strong? Any idea where I can find him?"

"Your guess is as good as mine, baby."

"I'm not your baby, Johnny."

"You might be right about that," Johnny said regretfully. "You're like all the other birds in my life—not to be trusted."

"What about Mariella? Where is she?"

"Talk about birds you can't trust. As far as I know, Mariella's with Kirk."

"Okay, Johnny, I'm leaving," Priscilla said. She moved to the door. "There's not going to be a problem, is there?"

"No problem with me, baby. With some of these other people you're dealing with, hey, you got big problems, yeah."

Out on Wardour Street, Colonel Geoffrey Wolfe could not take his eyes off the couples embracing in the shadows. What was wrong with these young people? Had they no sense of morality? Apparently not, he huffed to himself, keeping an eye on the entrance to the Flamingo. Swinging London and all that claptrap. The country was going to the dogs, what with the state of the culture—music, movies, fashion. Far too permissive, the lot of it. And now emerging from the club was Miss Priscilla Tempest, the tart giving his boss a headache, although for the life of him, he couldn't understand why.

Was she part of the effort to extort money from His Lordship? That particular problem had been dealt with, perhaps more harshly than he might have liked, but the extortionists now were either dead or gone to ground. It was hard to imagine this Tempest was part of it, or what harm she might present. The police were suspicious of her for a number of reasons and therefore discounted anything she told them. A very unreliable person, barely clinging to her job at a hotel that should never have employed her in the first place.

Wolfe followed her to Shaftesbury Avenue, which was still busy at this time of night. Hailing a cab, Priscilla was caught in the glow of the traffic along the avenue—her short skirt and those long legs on full display. Sure enough, a black cab stopped for her almost immediately. As she slipped into it, Wolfe felt angry. She was another problem that had to be dealt with.

CHAPTER TWENTY-EIGHT

The Jackal Is Dead

If there was any doubt that Jack Cogan had committed suicide, it was not reflected in the headlines of the next morning's papers: PRESS BARON FOUND DEAD. G'NIGHT FOR THE JACKAL. DEAD DAY OF THE JACKAL.

"Mr. Banville has called," Susie gulped as soon as Priscilla came into 205.

"What did he want?" As though she didn't know.

"You!" Susie announced it like a death sentence.

By now Banville would have read of Cogan's death. He would know that his strategy for ridding himself of the bothersome Priscilla Tempest had died with Cogan. What was Banville cooking up now? Nothing good, she suspected as she made her way to his office.

To her relief, the terrible Sidney Stopford was nowhere to be seen when she arrived at Banville's outer office. One less obstacle to overcome this morning. The door to Banville's inner sanctum was slightly ajar. Taking her usual deep bracing breath, she pushed the door open further. Banville looked up from his copy of *The Times.* The frown already on his face only deepened. "There you are, Miss Tempest. Come in. Sidney has the day off."

Banville put his paper aside as she took up her position in front of his desk. "I presume you have seen the news today."

"I did, sir, the death of Mr. Cogan. Most unfortunate."

"The police seem to believe he committed suicide."

"That's what I understand," Priscilla agreed.

"I must say he didn't seem like the suicidal type."

"No, he didn't," Priscilla said.

"A generous supporter of this hotel," Banville added vaguely, as though hard-pressed to find something more positive to say.

Occupying suites so he could entertain his mistresses, Priscilla mused.

"What are your thoughts, Miss Tempest?"

"About Mr. Cogan? Naturally, I am saddened at the news of his death." Not exactly, if she was being honest, but presumably that's what Banville wanted to hear.

"No, no," Banville said impatiently. "Your thoughts about your situation here at the Savoy."

"My situation, sir?"

"You were to leave to work for Cogan. What are your plans now?"

"As you may recall, sir," Priscilla said, speaking quickly, "I informed you of certain incidents involving Mr. Cogan that I have been working to keep out of the press."

"What are you telling me, Miss Tempest? Jack Cogan did not commit suicide? You murdered him in order to protect the reputation of this hotel?"

"Hardly, sir," Priscilla quickly assured him. "But that's not to say someone else wouldn't have."

Banville, as he often did when dealing with Priscilla, looked perplexed. "What are you suggesting?"

"I have it on good authority that the death of Mr. Cogan might not be a simple case of a man taking his own life."

"Murder?"

"I believe the police are investigating that possibility."

"Someone killed Jack Cogan?" Banville stated this in such a way that it sounded unimaginable.

"Murder is a possibility."

Banville closed his eyes momentarily. "God in Heaven."

"My point being, sir," Priscilla continued, "a murder investigation would bring renewed scrutiny from both the police and the press. Almost certainly that scrutiny would unearth affairs Mr. Cogan conducted at the Savoy. I believe it imperative that I continue to do everything in my power to safeguard the good name of this institution."

Banville was rubbing his temples as Priscilla finished. "Very well," he said with a resigned exhalation of breath. "Do your best to keep the press away."

"Exactly what I intend to do," Priscilla said.

"And make sure you keep me informed as to developments. Is that understood?"

"Understood completely, sir." Priscilla began to make the pivot that would take her out of his office to relative safety. "I will get on this immediately—and thank you, sir."

She nearly made it to the door before Banville said, "And while I think of it…"

She turned to him. "Sir?"

"I received a phone call from a chap named Geoffrey Wolfe. Is that name familiar to you?"

"It's not," Priscilla said tightly.

"He works for Lord Louis Mountbatten. He wished to confirm that you are employed here."

"Why would this person be interested in me?"

"You never know," Banville said. "Lord Mountbatten might want to offer you a position of some sort."

"Why would he want to do that, I wonder."

"I have no idea," Banville said. "But you never know…"

He sounded far too hopeful.

CHAPTER TWENTY-NINE

Under Suspicion

"Is everything all right?" Susie asked as soon as Priscilla returned to 205.

Priscilla pasted on a smile. "Everything is fine, Susie. We are back to business as usual."

"What is business as usual around here?" asked Susie, mystified.

"We have a hotel to promote!" Priscilla announced with forced enthusiasm.

"Before we do that, I should tell you I just got off the phone with Mrs. Whitedove. According to her, you agreed to consider a seance."

"With the stress on 'consider,'" Priscilla added.

"She wanted to remind us that as long as Kaspar remains here, this hotel is very much a place of evil," Susie went on anxiously, as though a place of evil was a given, not to be disputed. "I think she's right, if you want my opinion. I must say I find the atmosphere in this office creepy and scary ever since that cat arrived. I am all for a seance that would rid us of any curses lingering about."

"I am still considering her proposal," Priscilla said.

"But Priscilla, there *is* an aura of evil in this office. I can *feel* it. Honestly. It frightens me."

"I will inform the management that you cannot work here any longer because the entire hotel is cursed by a cat sculpture."

"Oh Lord," exclaimed Susie in horror. "Don't tell them that!"

"Then quit going on about curses," Priscilla admonished.

Susie made a nasty face but said nothing.

Priscilla escaped into her office and closed the door. She made it a point not to look at Kaspar as she went to her desk. The Savoy was a place of evil? *Ha!* she thought to herself. If Susie was looking for true evil, let her try No. 11 Swain's Lane. Mrs. Whitedove should hold a seance there!

Throughout the afternoon, Priscilla occupied herself with the parts of her job that did not involve getting killed. She prepared the weekly newsletter that went out to the press alerting them to all the wonderful things that were happening at the Savoy.

The American jazz legend Louis Armstrong, always a welcome guest, was due to arrive in a couple of weeks and would host reporters in his suite. A newspaper in Canada, the *Toronto Star*, asked to send its food writer to report on how, in the spirit of the legendary chef Georges Auguste Escoffier, the Savoy had continued to maintain its reputation as a celebrated food mecca; supper at the Savoy a tradition still of London nightlife.

This, Priscilla reminded herself, *was* what the Savoy was about; this was the business of the hotel with its great history and traditions that she had come to love. Yes, it was possible someone like DC Oliver Brock had a point in that the hotel catered mainly to the wealthy, royal and famous but, after all, everyone was welcome at the Savoy. Even DC Brock. He was particularly welcome, she thought, as she finished with the newsletter. She would not at all mind making him welcome.

Stop it, she told herself. She must keep her mind on her job. Doing her job would save her job.

The calm, disciplined routine of a well-run press office...

"Do you have a moment for us, Miss Tempest?" Inspector Lightfoot stood on the threshold. His tone did not suggest Priscilla had an option.

"Yes, of course, Inspector," Priscilla said, working to hold herself together.

"You already know DC Brock," the inspector said as Oliver appeared behind him, the expression on his face steadfastly neutral.

"Yes," Priscilla nodded at Oliver.

"Good day, Miss Tempest." His voice was as neutral as his expression.

"Do you mind if I sit down?" Inspector Lightfoot was the soul of courtesy—entirely feigned, Priscilla was certain.

"Please, Inspector, make yourself at home. You, too, DC Brock. Can I get you gentlemen anything?"

"No, I think we're fine, thank you," Lightfoot said, seating himself in the chair facing Priscilla while Oliver settled on the sofa behind him. As he crossed his legs, Lightfoot strained around to gaze at Kaspar. "I see you have a new addition to the office since last I visited."

"His name is Kaspar," Priscilla said. "Something of a fixture here at the Savoy."

"A forbidding creature, I must say." Lightfoot straightened around to face Priscilla, his cop's countenance hardening. "I'm afraid what brings us here today, Miss Tempest, is official police business."

"How can I help you, Inspector?" Priscilla felt a cold shudder run down her spine.

"The body of a woman named Ethel Cambridge has been discovered in a remote section of Highgate Cemetery. She was shot to death."

"This is what I reported to DC Brock," Priscilla said. "I was soon told that no such incident had taken place."

"Yes, well, all that has now changed," Lightfoot said mildly. "Perhaps you might go over with me what you previously told DC Brock about the incident you say involved the shooting of Mrs. Cambridge."

"As I told your officer, Mrs. Cambridge telephoned and said she wanted to see me. That it was most important. She said she feared for her life."

"Did she say why?" interjected Lightfoot.

"Ethel said she would explain when I got there."

"Go on."

"I went around to her house and found the door unlocked. Concerned about her safety, I entered and called out to her. At first, she didn't respond. Then she suddenly appeared. There was a gunshot and she fell. I immediately turned and ran from the house. As I further related to DC Brock, Mrs. Cambridge's assailant chased me through the cemetery. Thankfully, a uniformed police officer happened on the scene, and my would-be killer ran off."

"And why would Mrs. Cambridge have called you? Why did she think you might be able to save her life?"

"I don't know," Priscilla answered. "I didn't have a chance to talk to her before she was shot."

"I'm a bit confused," Lightfoot stated, arranging at the same time to appear suitably confused. "How was it you even knew this woman?"

"I had met her when I helped her with her groceries."

"You happened to be driving by and you saw this elderly woman struggling with groceries and you stopped to help her?"

"I would say that is accurate," Priscilla said brightly, as though helping elderly ladies was something she did all the time.

Lightfoot shifted slightly so that he could look in the direction of a stone-faced Oliver. "You said something to DC Brock about Americans next door—criminals?"

"I had reason to believe that, yes," Priscilla said uncomfortably, for now not wanting to get into why she believed this.

"DC Brock has thoroughly investigated your claim and hasn't been able to find evidence of criminal activity." He turned to Oliver. "Is that not so, DC Brock."

"It is, sir," Oliver confirmed.

Lightfoot gave a satisfied nod. "Nor have we been able to find any substantiation for a gunman chasing you through the cemetery." Lightfoot's voice had become harsh. "The officer who found you in the cemetery says he saw no sign of your so-called assailant. He says you were alone and seemed to be running away."

"I was running away from the man who shot Mrs. Cambridge." Priscilla practically shouted the words.

"Or, conversely, you were making your escape after shooting Mrs. Cambridge." Lightfoot spoke so conversationally that it took Priscilla a moment to register what he appeared to be accusing her of.

"You are not suggesting that I murdered Mrs. Cambridge?" .

"What do you say to that, Miss Tempest?"

"I would say that you are completely out of your mind." Priscilla's eyes darted to Oliver. He remained damnably impassive. What was wrong with him anyway? Why didn't he come to her defence? "Why in the world would I want to shoot Mrs. Cambridge?"

"Perhaps to keep her quiet. She called you because she was about to expose some of the ridiculous allegations you have been making about the house next door. In a fit of rage, you shot her and then ran from the house."

Dumbfounded, Priscilla could only stare for a time into the inspector's placidly accusatory face. He gave off the distinct impression he was waiting patiently for her to confess to murder so that he could get on with his day.

As calmly as she could, Priscilla said, "That is ridiculous. This is not the first time, Inspector, that you have made wild accusations against me. You also have me, I believe, murdering James Harley. Up to my elbows in blood. It's amazing I have time to come to work."

Inspector Lightfoot appeared unmoved. "Miss Tempest, it is my duty to inform you that you remain very much a person of interest in this investigation and also the one that involves the Harley murder."

"What about Jack Cogan? I suppose I murdered him, too."

"I am not in charge of that inquiry, but my understanding is that Mr. Cogan took his own life."

"Don't you see, Inspector? Something is happening. If I am not killing these people, and I'm not, then who is? And if the criminals at the Swain's Lane house are not figments of my imagination, as you seem to think, then what is going on?"

"You tell us, Miss Tempest. What is going on?"

"I would suggest that an American named Kirk Strong is part of a criminal enterprise that is or was working out of No. 11 Swain's Lane. Their aim is to extort money from well-known individuals. Their most recent mark, I suspect, is Lord Louis Mountbatten."

Inspector Lightfoot's response was a slight but noticeable tightening of the muscles around his mouth. He cast a quick glance at Oliver, who showed all the emotion of the side of a cliff. "Even if what you're telling us were true—and we at Scotland Yard have no evidence of such a plot against Lord

179

Mountbatten—then why do you suppose people are getting killed?"

"I'm not sure," Priscilla had to admit. "But I believe they are somehow all connected."

"Or maybe it is this curse I keep hearing about," Inspector Lightfoot said, barely restraining a smirk. "I understand curses at the Savoy are something of a tradition."

Not choosing to wait for Priscilla's response, Lightfoot turned to Oliver. "What do you say, DC Brock, do you have anything to add?"

"Only that Miss Tempest did appear terribly upset when I arrived at Highgate Cemetery. I had no reason to disbelieve her story."

Finally, a defence—of sorts—Priscilla thought.

"Yes, well, thank you, DC." The inspector showed his dislike of Oliver's reply with a frown as he stood. "And thank you for your time today, Miss Tempest. May I make a suggestion as we take our leave of you?"

"What kind of suggestion, Inspector?"

"Get some legal representation—as soon as possible."

Priscilla was having trouble breathing as Inspector Lightfoot went out the door. She held a faint hope that Oliver would cast a sympathetic glance back at her. He didn't.

As soon as they were gone, Susie appeared, the bewilderment plain on her face. "What was that all about?"

"Apparently, I am out there murdering half of London," Priscilla said.

"And here I thought you were seducing half of London," said Susie.

CHAPTER THIRTY

Fish and Chips

An hour later, Oliver phoned. "Priscilla, I am so sorry." He really did sound remorseful, Priscilla had to concede.

"For some reason, I thought you were on my side," Priscilla said in a disappointed voice.

"I *am* on your side," Oliver protested. "Inspector Lightfoot doesn't really believe you're a murderer."

"He's doing a very good job of pretending he does," Priscilla said.

"The inspector is under a great deal of pressure to somehow make all this go away. Powerful people are closing ranks to protect themselves."

"From whom?"

"Perhaps from you."

"Yes, I am a danger to the upper classes, no question," Priscilla said sardonically.

"I don't think anyone is suggesting that," Oliver said.

"Incidentally…"

"Yes?"

"That was the first time you've called me Priscilla."

"This is totally inappropriate," Oliver said.

"That I am a murder suspect?"

"That I'd like to see you."

"Yes," she said.

"Yes, what?"

"Yes, I'd like to see you, too," Priscilla blurted, saying exactly what she shouldn't say—exactly the sort of thing that got her into trouble. With men. With everything. The next words out of her mouth only got her in deeper: "Why don't you come to my place tonight?"

"Are you sure?"

"I can cook dinner."

"Do you cook?" Oliver sounded doubtful.

For good reason. "No."

"Then why don't I bring some takeaway?"

"I'll see you at eight," Priscilla said.

She hung up and aimed a helpless glance at Kaspar. "Don't look at me like that," she admonished. "And don't you dare suggest I don't know what I'm doing, because I truly don't, and don't need to hear it."

Priscilla had enough time after she got to her flat to do what she often said she would but seldom ever did: clean up. Clothes were hung in closets or stuffed into drawers. The cosmetics that had littered the bathroom forever were stowed away in the cupboard under the sink (pray he wouldn't open it!). Since there was nothing particularly incriminating in the medicine chest beyond Aspirin and a bottle of English Ivy Cough and Cold syrup, she left well enough alone.

There was time left to make herself presentable, reapply makeup and add lipstick while imagining how the evening might end—appropriately, she decided, with perhaps a chaste kiss on the cheek. No dragging her victim into the bedroom on a designated first date. Oliver didn't seem like a first-date kind of guy when it came to sex.

He showed up at promptly at eight, as she imagined he would. The Oliver Brocks of the world were never late. The

Oliver Brocks were dependable. Why were the Oliver Brocks so foreign to her experience? she wondered as she opened the door to him.

"Good evening," he said formally.

"There you are," she replied, moving back so that he could enter carrying takeaway wrapped in newspapers and smelling to high heaven. "Fish and chips?" she inquired, closing the door.

"Said to be the best in London," he offered.

Every fish and chip shop in London was the best in London, she thought.

"I hope you like fish and chips," he said, uncertain suddenly about London's best fish and chips.

"Doesn't everyone?" Priscilla answered cheerfully, exercising first-date diplomacy.

He held up a paper bag. "I wasn't sure if you'd like red or white wine."

"White is fine."

He made a face. "I brought red."

She smiled and said, "Wonderful, Oliver."

She took the wrapped fish and chips from him.

"I can open the wine," he offered. "That is, if you have a corkscrew hanging about."

"I think I can find one." She deposited the fish and chips on the trestle table dividing the sitting room from her open kitchen. Meanwhile, Oliver took in his surroundings. Priscilla gave a silent prayer of thanks that she had made herself tidy up.

"This is a nice flat," he said admiringly while she rummaged around in a kitchen drawer and found the needed corkscrew.

"It's not mine, I'm afraid. It's owned by the Savoy. I'm just a tenant."

"One of many perks, I'm sure," he said.

"Why don't you open the wine?" Priscilla suggested by way of deflecting the prospect of more sarcastic remarks about privilege. She handed him the corkscrew.

Oliver set about struggling with the cork. Fumbling with the cork was a better description. Perhaps not a wine connoisseur, Priscilla thought. He looked positively relieved when the cork finally burst free.

"Bravo," she said.

"Yes, bravo, indeed."

He set the wine on the table. Priscilla laid out a couple of plates and then opened up the fish and chips. As usual, a mountain of chips dwarfed what she supposed was the halibut. Priscilla wondered why they didn't call it chips with fish bits added.

"Wine glasses?" Oliver stood with the wine bottle in one hand, the corkscrew in the other. He looked quite out of place but kind of cute, thought Priscilla. Boyishly cute. Not at all like a copper.

"In the cupboard above the stove."

He brought down two wine glasses and set them on the table—clean, thank goodness—and then filled them with the red wine. Too full, she thought. Definitely not a wine connoisseur.

She lifted her glass. "Cheers."

He raised his. They clinked glasses awkwardly. He took a sip and then said, "You should know I'm pretty damned nervous."

"You?" Priscilla grinned at him and resisted saying, "Yeah, that's quite evident." She chose instead the more diplomatic first-date retort, "A hard-nosed Scotland Yard detective like yourself? Hard to believe."

"Who's never had, well, a date with someone like…you," he said somewhat abashedly.

"Me? What's so special about me?" As though she didn't know.

"Well, you know…" Oliver actually looked a bit sheepish.

"No, Oliver, I'm afraid I'm completely in the dark." Priscilla was not about to make this any easier for him.

"The Savoy...the life I'm certain you lead...celebrities... royalty..." He stopped, at a loss for words. Then: "You're...*you*..."

"That's very kind. At least, I believe it's very kind..."

"It is, it is..." The Scotland Yard detective had become quite flustered. "And also, well, you are quite attractive..."

"Quite attractive?" Hardly a ringing endorsement. She couldn't help thinking how much better Cary Grant was in the compliment department. Of course, merely *being* with Cary Grant was a compliment. Cary would never show up with fish and chips. But she mustn't think about Cary Grant. Focus on DC Oliver Brock, she told herself.

"No, no," Oliver said insistently. "Quite lovely, actually."

"Yes, but please keep in mind that your boss thinks I kill people," Priscilla counselled. "Or is that what makes me...*me*?"

"He's wrong about that," Oliver stated categorically. "About killing anyone, I mean."

"How can you be so sure?" Priscilla asked, warmed by the wine, feeling quite flirtatious, enjoying being in control with this boy detective.

"I know a killer when I see one," Oliver said with authority.

"You've had experience in identifying killers?"

"Enough to know you don't fit the profile."

"I must say, Oliver, you don't quite fit my idea of a detective either."

"I don't know if that's a compliment or an insult," Oliver said, smiling.

"I mean it as a compliment," Priscilla said. She touched his arm. "Very much a compliment."

"It's all right, my father says the same thing." He lowered his voice a bit. "'Ya don't look like one of us, lad. Works to your advantage.'"

"Your father is a police officer too?"

"Retired. Inspector Tommy Brock. Thirty years on the force. Quite a name in his day."

"And you're following in his footsteps?"

"Let's say I'm creeping along," Oliver said with a wry smile. "There was no one like my father. I'm the weak imitation—as he likes to remind me from time to time."

"Oh dear," said Priscilla.

"It's all right, really," Oliver hastened to add. "After all, he's Tommy Brock and, well, I'm not…"

"You are Oliver Brock, and you don't think I'm a killer. That makes you a very good detective as far as I'm concerned."

"I would say you're definitely not a killer."

"Now if you can only convince Charger Lightfoot," Priscilla said.

"I am doing my best."

It then seemed the most natural thing in the world to kiss this boyish fellow, this son of Inspector Tommy Brock, so fumbling and unsure but somehow so endearing.

And she did.

"Do you mind if I ask what you are doing?" he said. His face was flushed.

"Doing my best to convince you that I am not a killer," she said.

"Very convincing." This time he kissed her.

"You don't seem so nervous now," Priscilla noted.

"My training as an officer of the law," Oliver said. "I have learned how to respond to unexpected situations."

"Is this unexpected?"

"Totally," he said.

In the blur of everything that ensued, Priscilla wasn't sure how they ended up in the bedroom undressing one another, but it was shortly after that she decided that Oliver wasn't so awkward or boyish after all. He knew what he was doing.

So much for a chaste first-date kiss. And the fish and chips.

What You Must Never Do at the Savoy

"He's left the hotel!" Susie exclaimed as soon as Priscilla was in the office the next morning.

"Who has left the hotel?"

"Mr. Harry Alan Towers!"

"For heaven's sake, Susie. As impossible as it seems, and although I'm sure they hate to do it, our guests do eventually leave."

"But Mr. Towers has left without *paying!*"

One could be forgiven almost any indiscretion at the Savoy. What could not be overlooked was the failure to settle one's account. The Savoy, after all, trusted its guests and would never ever consider being so impolite as to ask about payment until one checked out. Then and only then was the account discreetly presented.

"Are you sure he's left?"

"One of the housekeepers went into his suite this morning and discovered all his luggage was gone. Since she had no record of him checking out today, she phoned the front desk. Mr. Tomberry said he was not due to depart until next week. Can you imagine? Leaving the Savoy without paying!"

He was stealing away with more than the unpaid bill in his luggage, Priscilla mused. A few inconvenient secrets had left with him—secrets he would not have to divulge if he simply disappeared.

"Do me a favour, will you, Susie? Make sure Mr. Welles hasn't checked out, as well."

"You think he has?" Susie was more wide-eyed than ever.

"God, Susie, just check on him, please."

Priscilla escaped into her office, closed the door and tried not to look at Kaspar, who would not be happy if he knew what she had been up to the night before. The boyish cop who turned out to be, well, so much more.

Oliver left around one, thus avoiding the potentially messy business of deciding if he would—or should—stay the night. How did she feel about him, she asked herself, her finger on the waiter button. Was Oliver a one-night stand or was there more? Was she far too much of a snob to be dating a policeman—even a cute one? She told herself she hadn't expected to go to bed with him, but then quickly decided she wasn't exactly telling herself the truth.

Karl arrived with coffee. "You look very bright and rested this morning, Miss Tempest," he opined as he placed the cup and saucer on her desk so that it was within easy reach. "You must have had an early night of it."

Why did everyone always think she was out and about in London until all hours? Maybe because, all too often, she was. "I had a good night's sleep, thank you, Karl," she acknowledged.

Susie appeared in the doorway. "You will be glad to know Mr. Welles has not left us and is, in fact, currently occupying his suite."

"I understand we have a guest who neglected to pay his bill before slipping away in the dead of night," Karl said.

"Dead of night?" Priscilla raised her eyebrows.

"That is what I hear."

As Karl left, and before Priscilla could reach for her coffee, in barged Major Jack O'Hara, moustache twitching, a balding hound dog on the hunt for big game. "You haven't seen your Mr. Towers, have you?" he demanded accusatorially, as though the man might be hiding under her desk.

"He's hardly *my* Mr. Towers, Major," Priscilla objected.

"Damned blighter," said the Major. "I've argued for years that we should have security in the Front Hall at night. To stop buggers like your Mr. Towers slipping away with their luggage."

"Shall I call the police, Major O'Hara?" Susie was in the doorway.

Major O'Hara looked horrified "Police? Good Lord, no. This is the Savoy, Miss Gore-Langton. We do not air our dirty laundry in public. We take care of these situations ourselves!"

With that, Major O'Hara was gone. Susie and Priscilla traded looks. "Now you know," Priscilla said with a grin.

She allowed herself a couple of sips of her already lukewarm coffee, deciding what to do next. Rising from her desk, she told Susie that she would be back soon. She took the lift up to Welles's suite.

"Who's there?" Welles demanded in an apprehensive voice from behind the door. By the time he responded, she had knocked numerous times.

"It's Miss Tempest, Mr. Welles. I'd like to speak to you."

The door slowly opened. Welles peered out at her. "Are you alone?"

"Very much alone, Mr. Welles," Priscilla said.

Welles opened the door wider and then stepped back so that she could enter his darkened suite. It stank of cigar smoke. The brocaded silk robe he wore was like a tent over his immense girth. "And what can I do for you this fine morning, Miss Tempest?"

"I came to see if Mr. Towers is hiding in your closet."

Orson responded with a twinkling smile. "He's not under the bed either. Although it was all I could do to convince your security fellow that he wasn't."

"Major O'Hara has been here already?"

"He certainly has. I managed to convince him not to put me in handcuffs—just yet."

"Do you have any idea what happened to Mr. Towers?"

"I'm afraid not. But he is a producer and thus capable of just about anything. It is most inconvenient when the man you're counting on to finance your movie disappears without paying his hotel bill."

"I must say, Mr. Welles, you don't seem very upset," Priscilla said.

"When you travel the world in search of people with money, you do encounter the most curious characters, grifters and charlatans as well as the occasional moneyed angel—a rare and endangered species, I must say. Alas, it has become apparent that Harry is no angel."

"I'm afraid Mr. Towers was not at all what he seemed," Priscilla said.

"They never are," Welles said equably.

"I fear he took advantage of you."

"I know what the papers are saying. Harry the spy and all that. And there was that young reporter who threw the press conference into disarray. Harry was adamant that he is no such thing. But then Harry was also adamant that he could finance my movie and so anything he says must be taken with a large grain of salt."

"Do you have any idea where he might have gone?"

"That fellow, Major what's-his-name, asked me the same question. Harry left without a word to me. I'm afraid the answer is no. I haven't a clue."

"What will you do now?" Priscilla asked.

"As is usually the case with me, my future is somewhat up in the air." He paused before he went on. "I am, however, in something of a quandary myself."

"What sort of quandary?" Priscilla didn't like the sound of that.

"You see, one of the agreements I extracted from Harry was that he would pay for my stay at the Savoy. Now that he has skedaddled, I'm afraid I'm in somewhat of a bind."

"You can't pay your hotel bill?"

"I am somewhat tapped out at the moment." Welles reported this information without the slightest hint of embarrassment. He added: "I don't suppose you're in a position to help me, Miss Tempest?"

Priscilla wasn't sure how to respond. She was barely holding on to her job, let alone able to come to the aid of a penniless guest—even if he was a world-famous filmmaker. "How long do you plan to stay?" she asked.

"Indefinitely—until I can come to some accommodation with the hotel. Thankfully, the Savoy does not come looking for payment until one makes an exit. Very civilized. Any help you could provide, Miss Tempest, would be very much appreciated."

"Let me see what I can do," Priscilla said, without having the slightest idea of what she could do. "In the meantime, perhaps you will find other means to settle your bill."

"Yes, well, we all live in hope, do we not?"

Before Priscilla had a chance to reply, the bathroom door opened and a tiny blond woman draped in a towel appeared.

"I am tired of waiting in there," Mariella Novotny said petulantly.

"Ah, Mariella, there you are," Orson said, as though she was an unexpected arrival.

"This is the second time this morning I have been forced to hide in the bathroom," she snapped. "No more. Enough!"

"Mariella," Orson said with infinite calm, "I'd like you to meet Miss Priscilla Tempest. Miss Tempest is in charge of the press office here at the Savoy."

"We have met before," Priscilla said.

"You must be mistaken," Mariella replied aloofly. "We have never met."

"In that case, I must be mistaken," Priscilla said hastily.

"Yes, you are," Mariella said confidently.

"Miss Tempest has promised to help me out with a minor problem I've encountered."

"I'm just on my way out," Priscilla said.

"It is a pleasure to meet you," Mariella purred, taking Orson's arm possessively.

"You wouldn't by any chance know where I might locate Mr. Harry Alan Towers?" Priscilla addressed Mariella.

The question appeared to startle Mariella. "I do not know this person," she said haughtily, as though it was an imposition to even ask such a question.

"Sorry, I must be mistaken. I thought you did."

"No, I do not," Mariella stated.

"The two of you look lovely together," Priscilla said, lying through her teeth. Mariella was all but lost against the vast brocaded tent in which Welles was wrapped. "Do you mind if I ask how you met?"

"An American friend of Harry's," Welles said. Mariella looked uncomfortable.

"A friend of Mr. Towers, you say?" Priscilla pressed. "Even though Miss Novotny doesn't know Mr. Towers."

"Now that Orson mentions it, yes, I do remember that I have met this Towers—very briefly," Mariella, unabashed, countered with lightning speed.

"Perhaps this friend could be of some help in contacting Mr. Towers."

Mariella darted a nervous glance at Welles.

"Unfortunately, Harry's friend, Kirk Strong, has returned to America," he swiftly answered. His smile was frozen in place.

"Perhaps you can help me with an address for Mr. Strong."

"I had only a nodding acquaintance with the man," Welles said with feigned breeziness. "I would have no idea how to contact him."

"That's disappointing," Priscilla said.

"I hope to hear from you soon, Miss Tempest," Orson said, having quickly regained his equanimity. "Any help you can provide will be very much appreciated."

Orson's smile, as Mariella clung possessively to his arm, was much like that of the cat who had swallowed the canary.

Priscilla, as she left, pondered how long it would be before Mariella wiped the smile off his face.

Mariella's Advice

Everyone was lying, Priscilla mused as she entered the Front Hall. So many lies in the age of Kaspar. Harry Alan Towers lied about his ability to finance Orson Welles's movie. Orson was lying, mostly to himself, about getting his movies made with the likes of scoundrels such as Towers. And then there was Mariella. She had no idea who Harry Alan Towers was. Had never met Priscilla. The name Kirk Strong, a.k.a. her American boyfriend, meant nothing to her. Lies, lies and more lies.

With murder thrown in for good measure.

That was not to let herself off the hook. Priscilla, too, had become a pretty good liar. Or at least someone able to relocate the truth in order to—what?—survive? Yes, in the world in which she existed lately, one had to do what was necessary in order to survive.

Or so she told herself.

"That copper called for you," Susie reported as soon as Priscilla entered 205.

"Which copper would that be?" Dreading that it might well be Inspector Lightfoot calling to arrest her for murder.

"The young one, DC Brock," Susie said. "I left his number on your desk."

Pleased that he was taking the initiative, she rang the number he had left. Oliver came on the line directly. "I thought I should give you a call," he said. He was back to sounding a bit like the nervous suitor. Absent was last night's confident lover.

"*Should* call?" Priscilla said.

"That came out wrong," he sputtered. "I *wanted* to call you. I mean I didn't want you to think that it was, you know, a one-night—"

"Stand?"

"Yes—or…no, no. I didn't want you thinking that."

"I'm glad to hear from you," she said, not sure what she was thinking today. Perhaps it was, in fact, a single night with Oliver. In the harsh light of the day, her view of DC Oliver Brock was more complicated than it had been the night before, when there didn't seem to be any time for questioning. Now, unfortunately, there was too much time.

But then wasn't that usually the case?

"I really had a wonderful time," Oliver said.

"It was fun," Priscilla said, more guardedly than she might have intended. "But we never did get to the fish and chips."

"No, we didn't," Oliver said. "The next time, for sure—that is, if you're up for a next time."

"I don't see why not." True enough, she thought. Why not?

"That doesn't sound very enthusiastic," Oliver said unhappily.

"No, I must apologize, Oliver," she said, feeling a little guilty about her lack of response. "It's just that it's a busy day around here, many distractions."

"I'll let you go," Oliver said.

"Please call me later. We'll figure something out—promise."

"I'd like that," Oliver said, sounding much more cheerful. "Listen, before I go there's something—"

The office door burst open, Susie crying out an objection as Mariella pushed past her. "I must talk to you," she insisted loudly. "It is imperative!"

"Oliver, I have to go," Priscilla said. She hung up as Mariella flew in. The scowl did not fit well on the heart-shaped loveliness of her face. She plunked herself down in front of the desk. Susie looked beside herself, not sure what to do next.

"It's all right, Susie," Priscilla said. "I will handle this."

"I'm just outside if you need me."

"You will not be needing her," Mariella said with a sneer.

Mariella had discarded her towel in favour of the short black skirt she was probably wearing when Orson lured her to his suite. Or was it the other way around? Priscilla leaned toward the latter.

"You shouldn't barge in like this, Mariella," Priscilla scolded.

"Shouldn't?" Mariella's dark eyes blazed with indignation. "Perhaps I could say the same about you."

"I knocked," Priscilla reminded her. "Mr. Welles let me in. I had no idea you were hiding in the bathroom."

"I wasn't *hiding*, as you call it." She stopped and glanced around, as though aware suddenly of where she was. "There are too many ears here," she announced. "We must go somewhere private—then we can talk."

"Talk about what?"

"Talk of many things that will be of interest to you." She focused on Priscilla. "Where can we go?"

The Victoria Embankment Gardens, located behind the Savoy, was home to the Sir Arthur Sullivan Memorial. The bust of Sir Arthur, W.S. Gilbert's esteemed musical collaborator, was set imperiously above the bronze of a woman pressed against the pedestal, forever enraptured by the oblivious Sir Arthur, her nakedness covered only by a piece of cloth draped strategically across her buttocks.

"It's reputed to be the most erotic statue in London," Priscilla explained to Mariella as they settled on a bench. "I suppose I'm a bit envious. I do wonder if I present as remarkable a back to the men in my life."

Mothers pushing prams, a bowler-hatted fellow on a bicycle, a knot of noisy uniformed schoolchildren passed by while Mariella pursed full red lips, inspecting the memorial.

"I would not wonder at all," she responded confidently. "I know I have a beautiful back, the best. Very sensual. This is what Orson tells me—who, for your information, is in love with me."

"That was quick," said Priscilla dryly.

"That is why I do not want him receiving any wrong ideas about me."

"Like the idea that your boyfriend, Kirk Strong, is an American criminal who blackmails people for a living, with some help from Harry Alan Towers?"

Mariella looked miffed. "That Kirk is a son of a bitch. I don't know him because he is no longer my boyfriend. Does he do bad things? How should I know? He has left me and gone back to America."

"Are you sure about that?"

"He is not here. He has disappeared. Where else would he go?"

"What about Mr. Towers?"

"Harry, ah yes, Harry." Mariella sounded amused. "Harry was used by Kirk. Very simple. Kirk wanted entry into this hotel so he could find more prospects. Harry was associated with Orson Welles. Who could resist the Great Orson? He could attract important people, which is what Kirk wanted—and that was the real reason for the dinner."

"It's too bad Harry couldn't have made the movie he promised Mr. Welles—or paid his hotel bill."

"That's Harry for you," Mariella said with a shrug. "Unless he absolutely has to, he never pays for anything. He makes lots of promises to everyone. Sometimes he comes through on those promises. Most of the time he doesn't. Welcome to Harry's world."

"How much of this have you told Orson?"

Mariella looked horrified. "My God, I have told him nothing— and you must not say anything either."

"Did Kirk ever say anything to you about Lord Mountbatten?"

"You mean the cousin of the Queen?"

"You're aware of Lord Mountbatten?"

"Naturally, I am British after all."

"Did Kirk talk about him?"

"You should not be asking me these questions." Mariella abruptly seemed uncertain.

"Why not, Mariella?"

Priscilla was able to enjoy birds chirping away in the nearby mature trees while Mariella took her time deciding whether to answer. "If I help you, what do I get in return?" she asked finally. "I tell you. I get nothing but trouble, that's all I get. More trouble, I don't need."

"I can help you with Mr. Welles," Priscilla said. "That's what I can do for you."

"You will not tell him anything?"

"I can make sure he remains oblivious—at least when it comes to you."

"What difference does any of this make to you?" Mariella looked perplexed. "You have a good job at this grand hotel. Why do you want to jeopardize it?"

"Is that what I'm doing?"

"Yes, you are."

"Tell me what you know about Lord Mountbatten, Mariella."

"Kirk never told me anything. He denied everything. When I asked, he told me to mind my own business. But I have ears. I heard a few things that perhaps I shouldn't have. And then there was Johnny, who couldn't keep his mouth shut. He also heard things."

"I don't trust, Johnny. What did *you* hear, Mariella?"

"That is Kirk's business you understand. He finds rich people who have secrets they don't wish to have revealed. Then he puts them in vulnerable positions and makes them pay for, let us say, their vulnerability."

"Is that what he's done with Lord Mountbatten?"

"There was a young man. Kirk arranged for him to meet Lord Mountbatten. I am not sure, but I think photographs were taken. It was suggested Kirk would be happy to give Lord Mountbatten those photos in return for a substantial financial consideration."

"Blackmail, in other words."

"A business arrangement. That is how I heard Kirk describe it. Like I say, he never told me much, but—" She finished her sentence with a knowing look.

"What else did you hear?"

"In the situation with Lord Mountbatten, there were unexpected problems that began to concern Kirk."

"What sort of problems?"

"You keep asking me things I am not so certain about, but when this man, an associate of Kirk's, James Harley, was murdered—"

"What was someone like Harley doing with the likes of Kirk Strong?" Priscilla interjected.

"Harley needed money. I understand there were gambling debts. Kirk could provide it and he could use Harley. It was

Harley, I believe, who introduced the boy in question to Lord Mountbatten."

"And so Harley is dead, then what?"

"That seemed to frighten Kirk. He was on edge. Harry was also scared, convinced that he could be next. I imagine that's why he has left."

"What about Kirk Strong?"

"I keep telling you. Back to America. I have no idea where."

"Leaving you hanging," Priscilla put in.

"He is like all men; he is a bastard."

"What about Orson?"

"He will turn out to be a bastard, too. But for now…" Mariella gave are resigned shrug. "That is why you must be very quiet and not say anything to Orson. Also, it is just as well he doesn't know that I have slept with the Kennedys."

"My lips are sealed as long as…"

"As long as what?" Mariella asked with a frown.

"If you hear from Kirk, I want you to let me know. All right?"

"I will not hear from him," Mariella said adamantly.

"But if you do."

She shrugged. "I will let you know, believe me. But Kirk is in the past. Now I am with Orson. They say he is a genius and rich! Before he turns out to be a bastard just like all the other bastards, he will take me to America, where I will be safe from all this."

Priscilla didn't have the heart to tell her that, as things stood, Orson couldn't even pay his hotel bill.

Mariella jumped to her feet, startling a young couple as they passed hand in hand. "Now I must leave you. I have told what I know, which is nothing really, and I shouldn't have said anything. But there you go." She pointed a warning finger at Priscilla. "You are very nosy, Priscilla. You must be more careful. Whoever has been killing these people, whoever has scared off my Kirk and Harry Towers, this person is out there somewhere. You are asking too many questions of too many people. What you are doing is very dangerous. It could get you killed—and for what?"

"I'm not sure," Priscilla conceded.

"All the more reason to stay away. Orson tells me something about a cat that was brought to his dinner. A curse. The curse of the Savoy! You should leave the place, Priscilla," she warned. "Nothing but bad can come if you stay." Mariella started down the pathway that cut through the park. It had begun to rain.

CHAPTER THIRTY-THREE

Let's Not Tell the Queen

Having arisen as usual at 8 a.m. and breakfasted, as always, in the Green Tea Room—Special K cereal, toast with marmalade, fresh-squeezed orange juice and the Darjeeling tea she loved—Elizabeth, again as customary, arrived in her office at 10 a.m. Routine and tradition, those are what she liked. She crossed the plush carpet to the large desk where, seated on a green-baize chair rimmed in gold beside a curtained window overlooking the gardens, she daily wrote letters and read correspondence. Calls were received on a white desk telephone adorned with eighteen buttons connecting her to various sections of the palace. A clutter of family photographs filled a nearby table.

Her equerry, Wing Commander John "Johnny" Slater, formerly of the Royal Air Force's 33 Squadron, stepped in carrying the red leather-bound Menu Royal that had been prepared by the chef. The Menu Royal contained the week's meal suggestions pending Elizabeth's approval. Objections and changes were noted with a pencil in the margins.

"The chef has prepared the menu for the Lord Mountbatten dinner you are to host," Slater advised.

Elizabeth opened the Menu Royal and immediately raised her eyebrows. "*Hanche de venaison?*"

"At His Lordship's request," offered Slater. "His Lordship loves venison, I am told."

"Yes, that." Elizabeth made a slight face. "Remind me why I have agreed to do this."

"I believe the rationale for the dinner is to put to rest the rumours surrounding your recent conversations with His Lordship," Slater said.

"You mean the tongue-lashing I gave him for his unacceptable behaviour?"

Slater nodded. "I would think of it more as a reassurance that His Lordship is your cousin, beloved by your son and Prince Philip and still very much a member of the family in good standing."

"Yes, I suppose that is the idea," Elizabeth said without enthusiasm.

"I have the tentative guest list with me," Slater said, approaching her desk.

"Let me have it." Elizabeth pushed aside the papers she had been about to read.

He placed the list in front of her.

"Twenty for dinner?"

"So it seems," agreed Slater.

Elizabeth tapped her pencil against the list as she moved down the names. "The usual unusuals. Although I see Cary Grant is to be with us."

"He is in town. A longtime friend of Lord Mountbatten's, I am told."

"I like Cary Grant," Elizabeth stated. Then she frowned. "But why is the name below his struck out?"

"That is the young woman who was to accompany Mr. Grant."

"And why was her name taken off the list?"

"I believe that was Commander Trueblood's doing."

"Our all-too-often-annoying head of the Walsinghams," Elizabeth said with an impatient sigh.

"Commander Trueblood and his group are tasked with protecting the family, ma'am," said Slater, feeling it his duty to defend Trueblood even though, personally, he disliked the commander. He added delicately, "Let us say, he is dedicated to his job."

"You call him dedicated. I choose annoying." Elizabeth adjusted her glasses to peer more closely at the list. "Priscilla Tempest. Is that the young woman's name?"

"It is ma'am," stated Slater. "I understand Miss Tempest works at the Savoy Hotel."

Elizabeth's frown deepened. "Why would Commander Trueblood remove her name?"

"I have no idea," said Slater. "The list came back from his office with the name struck off."

"This is quite ridiculous," Elizabeth said, pushing the guest list away and sitting back. "I do find our Commander Trueblood quite tedious at times."

"Indeed," agreed Slater.

"He is supposed to be protecting us, not censoring guest lists."

"Perhaps he sees this young woman as some sort of threat."

"A threat presented by someone who works at the Savoy?"

"Apparently."

"Do we know what this Miss Tempest does there?"

"From what I understand, she heads the hotel press office. This is how Mr. Grant met her."

"What then? Fears that Miss Tempest will go running to the newspapers to report on dinner at Buckingham Palace?"

"I suppose that might be the case," said Slater noncommittally.

Elizabeth sat up, adjusting her glasses once again as she brought the list closer, tapping her pencil against it. "We are intrigued."

"Are we?" Slater would never have allowed her to know it, but Elizabeth's unexpected interest puzzled him.

"Let us find out more about the young woman who has succeeded in raising the alarm in Commander Trueblood's office."

"And how do you propose to do that?"

"We invite her to tea."

"We do?" replied Slater, not so much puzzled now as taken aback.

"Invite Miss Tempest. It will annoy the annoying Commander Trueblood. And remind him that he cannot go about arbitrarily adjusting our guest lists."

"Can we do this?" inquired Slater in a concerned voice.

"Yes, we can," Elizabeth said. "After all, I *am* the Queen of England."

Susie called from the other room. "There's someone on the phone for you. Says he's from Buckingham Palace."

Priscilla didn't quite catch what she said. "From where?"

"Buckingham Palace."

"You're kidding." Who would be calling her from Buckingham Palace? Priscilla picked up the phone. "This is Priscilla Tempest. How may I help you?"

"Miss Tempest, my name is Wing Commander John Slater." The voice on the other end certainly contained the beautifully modulated tone of someone who might call from Buckingham Palace. "If you are available tomorrow afternoon at four, Her Majesty would like to invite you to tea."

"Who are you?" asked a bewildered Priscilla.

"John Slater, ma'am, although everyone calls me Johnny. I am equerry to Her Majesty. I am calling on her behalf."

"On behalf of the Queen—of England?"

"That's the one," Slater replied. "Are you available tomorrow afternoon?"

"Forgive me for asking if this is some sort of joke. Did you say Wing Commander?"

"That is correct?"

"You command wings, do you?"

Slater chuckled. "I assure you, Miss Tempest, Her Majesty does not joke when it comes to her afternoon tea. She is quite serious about it. Moreover, although she understands it is short notice, she would most appreciate it if you could join her."

Priscilla was speechless.

"Miss Tempest? Are you still there?"

"Yes, sorry," said Priscilla quickly.

"May I tell Her Majesty you will join her?"

"Yes, that would be—well, it's very kind of Her Majesty."

"If you could come to the palace at 3:30 p.m. They will have your name at the gate and will direct you to the Green Tea Room. I will meet you outside and escort you in."

"Is—is there anything I should know?"

"It's very informal," reassured Slater. "You might give a bit of a curtsy when the two of you meet."

"A curtsy, yes."

"If there is nothing else, we will see you tomorrow afternoon."

"Yes," she said.

She hung up as Susie appeared in the doorway.

"What was that all about?"

"I'm not sure," Priscilla replied. "But unless this is an elaborate hoax, I have been invited to Buckingham Palace for tea with the Queen."

"But you dislike tea."

"Yes, but let's not tell Her Majesty."

CHAPTER THIRTY-FOUR

Tempest in a Teapot

Nervous as all get out, Priscilla arrived at Buckingham Palace's central gate at 3:30 p.m. Security guards checked her identification and, although she worried that they wouldn't, they quickly found her name on a list and, with warm, welcoming smiles, admitted her into the palace grounds.

She thought someone might accompany her across the grand inner court but, no, she was on her own. Once inside the palace, a liveried footman directed her along vaulted halls to a foyer outside what she imagined was the Green Tea Room. She stood, heart beating fast, catching her reflection in a nearby mirror, praying that the knee-length Jaeger skirt, the Liberty print blouse, the kitten-heel Clarks shoes—and didn't she have a time digging that combination out of her wardrobe—would pass muster with Her Majesty. That is, if Her Majesty actually showed up.

At the other end of the hall, she spotted movement and thought it must be Wing Commander Slater, the Queen's equerry, come to fetch her. But then she saw that it couldn't be Slater because, unless her eyes were totally deceiving her, she had just caught a glimpse of DC Oliver Brock of Scotland Yard.

By the time she realized who he was, Oliver had passed out of view. What was he doing at Buckingham Palace?

She quickly glanced around—still no one in sight. She then hurried along to the end of the hall, turned a corner just as Oliver got on a lift. The floor indicator showed that the lift had gone down. She paused a moment or two, still expecting someone to come along inquiring—politely, naturally—what she thought she was doing wandering about the palace unescorted. But no one appeared. She pressed the call button. A couple of moments later, there was a rattle of machinery and the lift doors opened. Priscilla stepped into the tiny enclosure. The doors closed and the lift slowly, noisily descended. As had happened far too often lately, she was struck by the thought that she was out of her mind. The lift settled with a thump that shook the cage. The doors opened and she stepped out into an unlit hallway. She moved past two kitchens, deserted, their shadowy interiors aglow with light reflecting off dozens of hanging copper pots.

She paused, hearing voices in the distance. Voices coming toward her. Frantically looking around for cover, she ducked into one of the kitchens. The voices drew closer. She could hear Oliver saying, "She's here now?"

"With the Queen in the Green Tea Room is what I understand."

"Are you sure about this?"

"I'm as surprised as you," said the other voice. "But there you have it."

"Then what would you like me to do?"

Peering through the confusion of hanging pots, she caught a glimpse of Oliver with another man. The man limped. A long white scar slashed down the side of his face.

An instant later they were gone. Their voices drifted away, Oliver's question unanswered.

"Excuse me. May I ask what you're doing here?"

She swung around to find a man wearing a chef's cap and a challenging expression.

"I'm afraid I'm lost," she said quickly.

"Where are you supposed to be?"

"The Green Tea Room," Priscilla said.

"My goodness, you *are* lost," said the man in the chef's cap. "Come along with me. I'll get you straightened around."

Wing Commander Slater, looking deeply perturbed, was pacing in front of the Green Tea Room when Priscilla returned. He looked relieved when he saw her.

"Wherever have you been, Miss Tempest? I was quite concerned."

She was tempted to say something like, "I've been in the basement overhearing my lover talking about me with a strange man." But she resisted the urge and instead said, "Sorry. Nobody was here when I arrived. I was afraid I might be in the wrong place."

"My apologies," Slater said. "I'm running a bit late this afternoon. So is Her Majesty. But she's all set now—and here you are. Shall we go in?"

As its name suggested, the Green Tea Room was done in pale green. There was a lovely view of the flowers, trees and shrubs in the palace gardens. The Queen wore a green dress that matched the room. A tiny woman with flawless white skin framed by a helmet of brown hair, a half-smile carefully in place and—to Priscilla's way of thinking—curiously hollow eyes that were like shields preventing onlookers seeing into her inner self.

"Your Majesty," intoned Slater, "I would like to present Miss Priscilla Tempest of the Savoy."

Priscilla's attempt at a curtsy actually drew a full-on smile from Her Majesty. "Rise, Priscilla of the Savoy."

"I'm afraid that wasn't much of a curtsy," Priscilla said, straightening. "Shall I try it again?"

"No, no," admonished the Queen. A gleam had lit those hollow eyes. "That's fine, Miss Tempest." She glanced at Slater. "Thank you, Wing Commander."

Slater gave a quick bow and then left the room. "I was about to have a cup of tea. Won't you join me?" The Queen indicated a Chippendale table covered with a blazing white damask cloth embroidered with the royal coat of arms. The table was set with silver dishes containing sandwiches, biscuits and tiny cakes. "The teapot is part of a silver service favoured by Queen Victoria, who always believed, as do my husband and I, that tea tastes best in silver," offered the Queen as she seated herself at the table. "Please, sit down. May I call you Priscilla?"

"Yes, please do," Priscilla said seating herself across the table and wondering how she should address the Queen. If she was Priscilla, was her host Elizabeth? She thought not.

"I do hope you like tea," the Queen said.

"Yes, indeed," said Priscilla, doing her best to sound enthusiastic, drowning out her inner voice.

"The cups and saucers are from Queen Mary's collection," the Queen went on. She had Victoria's teapot in her hands and was pouring into Priscilla's cup. "Queen Mary, like me, was an avid tea drinker, very particular about her tea. We have Earl Grey today, one of my favourites." She finished pouring and said, "Would you care for a sandwich? A cake?"

"Thank you, I'm fine for the moment," replied Priscilla, balancing the cup daintily on its saucer, nervous about breaking a cup that had been around since Queen Mary, yet thankful to have something to do with hands that she feared would otherwise be fluttering about everywhere.

"Tell me about yourself, Priscilla. You are Canadian, I understand." The Queen took her time setting her tea cup on the table. "My husband and I love Canada."

"That's right, ma'am. I'm from Toronto." Good God, she thought. Was the Queen really interested in her boring life? There was no choice but to plunge on. "My parents are still there. Mom thought I should become a secretary and then find a good man to marry. I didn't want to be a secretary and I couldn't find any good men, at least none I wished to marry. I suppose I was looking for adventure and I certainly wasn't finding it in Toronto. And so I came to London."

"Swinging London," the Queen put in unexpectedly. "Although I'm afraid I haven't been able to do much swinging."

Priscilla flashed on an image of the Queen in a Mary Quant minidress—swinging. Her mind immediately readjusted that image. "Yes, well, I didn't have much time either." A little fib, Priscilla thought. "I had no money and was in desperate need of a job. I found something at a small public relations firm, little more than the secretary my parents thought I should be. About a year later, I landed at the Savoy."

"And how was it you came to be at one of the finest and most historic hotels in London?"

"There are those at the Savoy who believe I got my position under suspicious circumstances," Priscilla explained. "But in fact there wasn't much to it. I was dating one of the vice-presidents at our advertising firm. He introduced me to the hotel's chairman of the board of directors. The next thing I knew, I was being interviewed, not thinking much of it. As much to my surprise, as I'm sure it was to Mr. Banville, the general manager, I was hired."

"Are you good at your job?" the Queen asked bluntly.

Priscilla paused to consider the question. It was unexpected. "Yes," she stated confidently. "I believe I am. The circumstances can be quite difficult, as you might imagine. I am a woman in a man's world, with all the attendant prejudices and complications."

The Queen fixed Priscilla with a knowing smile. "I'm afraid I am all too familiar with your situation. The male of the species. The men tend to think they know it all and therefore regard us as inferiors they don't have to listen to."

"Yes, I certainly am familiar with that kind of condescension," agreed Priscilla, marveling that even the Queen felt the pressure of trying to navigate through a world of powerful men.

"And what about adventure?" the Queen asked. "Have you found the adventure that brought you to London?"

"You might say that, yes," Priscilla said, vastly understating the truth of that statement. "Sometimes, much more than I bargained for." A trifle less understated.

"That's interesting," said the Queen attentively. "And what about a good man, if I may ask?"

A question she would never have anticipated from the Queen of England. "No good men yet," Priscilla answered and then thought she had better add, "not good enough, at any rate. It may have something to do with me not being very interested in marriage." Priscilla had to remind herself that the voice blurting out these things was hers. She was baring her soul to the Queen of England, for heaven's sake.

"You're still young," the Queen volunteered. "Plenty of time for settling down, marriage, family, that sort of thing. Getting married was part of the job I inherited when I was your age. It's not part of yours, I imagine."

"There are many, many rules one must follow at the Savoy, but so far, thankfully, none of them requires employees to be married."

"Tell me something—and please, do be honest with me." The Queen was leaning forward earnestly.

"I will certainly try," Priscilla said, and immediately experienced pangs of regret. Was it a good idea, given her circumstances, to be too honest with the Queen of England? Had she already been far too honest?

"I am curious as to why someone here at the palace would wish your name to be taken off the guest list for Lord Mountbatten's dinner."

"I can only assume that Lord Mountbatten does not want me there," Priscilla answered, all too aware of the possibilities behind why her name might be removed.

"And why would he not want you to attend?"

"I will tell you, if you wish," Priscilla said hesitantly, more concerned than ever about crossing the line to a place the Queen did not want to hear about.

"I am told things all the time that I don't necessarily wish to hear," the Queen said. "It comes with the job. Please, continue."

"Lord Mountbatten could believe that I suspect he is the victim of an attempted extortion plot orchestrated by an American-led group that specializes in blackmailing prominent individuals."

If the Queen was at all disturbed by what she was hearing, she gave no indication of it. "You are an employee of a London hotel," she said matter-of-factly. "How could you know about plots to extort Lord Mountbatten?"

"Believe me, I wish I didn't. But for now, I probably should not say anything more."

"I would ask you about what these people know that enables them to blackmail Lord Mountbatten, but I'm afraid I am all too aware of what they should not know but seemingly do."

"For what it's worth, Lord Mountbatten may have been set up by these people."

"Exploiting Louis's many weaknesses, I'm sure." The Queen pointed to Priscilla's cup. "Your tea has grown cold. Can I refresh it for you?"

"Thank you, no," said Priscilla.

"You don't like tea, it seems."

"You could tell?" Priscilla asked with a sheepish smile.

"I have had to develop a sense of when I am being told the truth and when I am not. You were not telling me the truth about the tea."

"And the rest?"

"Put it this way, Priscilla. You strike me as a very honest young woman. If anything, you are being too careful and holding back. That's fine. Discretion is as admirable as honesty." The Queen fell silent, touching an index finger to her lips, as if in contemplation. Then she smiled at Priscilla, the sign that she had reached a decision. "You should attend my dinner for Lord Mountbatten. I am ordering your name returned to the guest list."

"I'm not sure that's necessary," Priscilla said. "But I do appreciate it."

"I must be honest with you and say that I'm also taking into consideration that if you are excluded, your date, Mr. Cary Grant, might take umbrage and decide not to attend. Being an admirer of Mr. Grant's movies, we don't want to do anything to upset him, do we?"

"No, definitely not," said Priscilla. "He is a very charming man, I must say."

"A little old for you, though."

"A delightful friend," Priscilla gently amended. "No more than that."

"Cary Grant aside," the Queen went on, "we must say we are impressed with you, Priscilla. What is the phrase? A breath of fresh air? Yes, that's it."

"I'm—I don't know what to say, Your Majesty."

"You don't have to say anything. Unlike, I'm sure, the males with whom you work, I have no doubt that there is something quite extraordinary about you. I could be wrong, but I don't think I am. Although there is one thing you haven't told me."

"What's that, ma'am?" asked Priscilla, her mind turning over frantically as she tried to think of what Her Majesty could be referring to.

"The curse at the Savoy."

Priscilla blanched. "You're aware of the curse?"

"We've had to deal with several curses at the palace over the years," the Queen said. "Balmoral Castle, too."

"You believe in curses?"

"Let us say I don't discount them. Have you been in touch with the estimable Mrs. Whitedove?"

"You know Mrs. Whitedove?"

"She's been a great help to us over the years. If you haven't already, you might consider contacting her."

"I will take it under advisement, ma'am."

"And one more thing, if I may."

"Of course," said Priscilla.

"I would like to take advantage of you, if I can."

"Ma'am?" Priscilla wasn't sure she liked the sound of that.

"I want you to act as my eyes and ears in connection with the Lord Mountbatten affair. The fact that my cousin has made himself susceptible to extortionists disturbs me immensely. I don't think I can always trust those around me, but my intuition tells me that I can trust you, Priscilla. I want you to report back to me—and *only* me—anything you discover. Will you do that for me?"

"I—I suppose I can," Priscilla said uncertainly.

"I'm going to give you a number." She withdrew a pen and a small white card from her purse, jotted a number and then handed the card to Priscilla. "My direct line. It may be that Wing Commander Slater will answer. In which case, tell him that you wish to speak to me and he will know to transfer you."

"I hope I won't disappoint you, ma'am," Priscilla said.

"I hope so, too," the Queen said soberly. "I am not used to being disappointed." Her Majesty rose from her chair. "It has been a pleasure, Priscilla."

"For me as well, ma'am," said Priscilla, struggling to her feet.

"Wing Commander Slater will see you out."

The Queen made her way to the door and then stopped. She turned back to Priscilla. "Don't forget to call Mrs. Whitedove. You will find her most helpful."

CHAPTER THIRTY-FIVE

A Detective Calls

"Then what would you like me to do?"

Oliver's question echoed in Priscilla's head all the way back to the Savoy. What was it they wanted Oliver to *do* with her? Nothing good, she could only imagine. For now, he was added to the growing list of people she couldn't trust.

She knew she could trust the Queen, though. After all, Her Majesty had found her "quite extraordinary." Not that Priscilla had been feeling particularly extraordinary lately. Quite the opposite in fact.

"How did it go?" Susie asked excitedly as soon as Priscilla was back in 205. "What was Her Majesty like? What did she say?"

"She was exactly what you would expect the Queen of England to be," Priscilla replied, not wanting to give too much away. After all, she was now a confidante of Her Majesty, was she not? "She was…queenly."

"What did she say?"

"She said she liked tea."

"That's it?" Susie looked disappointed. "Did she say why she invited you?"

"I think it's because of Cary Grant," Priscilla said. "She likes Cary Grant."

Susie was unconvinced. "If you don't mind my saying, that doesn't seem like much of a reason to invite you to tea at Buckingham Palace."

"She's a queen," Priscilla said. "Who knows what queens are thinking."

Susie gave her a look with narrowed eyes. "I don't believe you. You're not telling me everything."

"I am," Priscilla protested. And she was—more or less. "No one ever said royalty was particularly interesting." Priscilla's phone started ringing. "I'd better take that."

"The only time you want to answer the phone is when you don't want to talk to me," grumbled Susie.

"Here's something that should please you," Priscilla said as she walked to her office. "I've decided to take you up on your suggestion and hold a seance. Will you please arrange it with Mrs. Whitedove as soon as possible?"

As Priscilla picked up the receiver, Susie called: "It's about time!"

"Hello, Priscilla?" Oliver Brock's voice startled her. Not the caller she was expecting. She almost hung up on him and then thought better of it.

"Priscilla, are you there?"

"Yes, I'm here, Oliver," she said coldly. "What can I do for you?"

Priscilla's tone appeared to unsettle the detective. "Uh, well, I called to see how you're getting on."

Getting on? "Getting on very well, thank you."

"What have you been up to?" *Discovering you are not at all what you seem,* Priscilla thought.

Out loud, she said, "It's been very busy here. How about you, Oliver, any news?"

219

"No, not at the moment," he answered vaguely. "However, our investigation is ongoing."

"Well, it's always ongoing, isn't it?"

"Actually, I was calling to ask if I might see you again." He sounded quite formal. The next thing, she thought, he'd be down on his knee proposing marriage.

"I don't know," Priscilla said, debating silently whether she should see him or stay as far away as possible. "As I said, it's very busy around here."

"I understand," Oliver said, doing his best not to sound disappointed. "I was thinking perhaps we might have dinner at some point."

"Why don't I check my schedule and get back to you?" Priscilla said. Even to her that sounded awful. "I'll get back to you" being the kiss of death for any relationship.

"Uh, I really enjoyed our time together the other night." Oliver was flopping around—back to being the boy out of his depth, Priscilla noted with satisfaction. "I hope," he continued, "I, uh, I hope I haven't done anything to upset you."

"Why would you think that?" Priscilla asked. Would the fact that Oliver was an untrustworthy liar have anything to do with her attitude? It certainly might, she thought.

"I'm sure it's nothing," Oliver stumbled on. "It's just that..."

"What?"

"You seem different, that's all."

"No difference, Oliver. But like I said, it's a bit mad around here. Why don't I call you once things calm down?"

"I would like that," Oliver said, adopting an impersonal tone.

"Thank you for calling," Priscilla said with a brightness that was as artificial as it was forced.

As soon as Oliver rang off, Susie reappeared in the doorway, looking pleased with herself. "It's all arranged," she announced.

"What's all arranged?" Priscilla was fighting to refocus.

"The seance," Susie said in exasperation. "I spoke to Mrs. Whitedove. She has agreed to do it tomorrow night. In the Pinafore Room. I've already reserved it."

Priscilla nodded agreement. "Let's go ahead."

"Mrs. Whitedove requires the presence of as many as possible who attended the original dinner. I've already been in touch with Mr. Grant. He will be glad to attend. I've also left a message with Mr. Welles and with Miss Keeler. What about Mr. Coward?"

"I will speak to him."

Her phone began to ring again. "I'd better take that."

Susie frowned in annoyance at the interruption.

"Priscilla, it's Larry...Larry Olivier," the voice on the other end of the line said.

"Larry, a pleasure to hear from you," Priscilla said. "Is everything all right?"

"Emergency Gossip's Bridle meeting within the hour, dear girl." Olivier's tone would have been right for calling a meeting of the United Nations Security Council. "We need you there. Noël's in a bit of a dither."

"Don't tell me he's had a bad review," Priscilla said, intending a bit of levity.

"Worse than that, I'm afraid." Olivier might have been announcing the start of a war. "American Bar. One hour."

He rang off.

Priscilla hung up, mystified. What now? she thought. Not more trouble, surely.

Priscilla's fellow Gossip's Bridle Club members looked surprisingly miserable when she arrived in the American Bar. Perhaps their sullen moods had something to do with the fact that the

221

bar was nearly deserted at this time of the afternoon, thus there were none of the usual admiring glances of recognition cast their way from nearby tables. Momentarily, anyway, they were nothing more than three aging anonymous men. That couldn't possibly make them happy, Priscilla speculated. Gielgud and Olivier did manage weak smiles as she sat down. Noël, however, declined to meet her gaze, concentrating instead on the intricate business of fiddling with his cigarette holder.

"How is everyone?" Priscilla asked the gloomy group.

"As I told you on the phone, we have our Noël in an unexpected funk," Olivier explained. "Even a Buck's Fizz has failed to rally his spirits."

"I'm absolutely fine," stated Noël desolately. "Never better."

"We've been here for a full half-hour and he hasn't once insulted me," Olivier said miserably.

"I've had to fill in for him," added Gielgud.

Priscilla placed a comforting hand on Noël's arm. "What's bothering you?"

"He is despondent over actions that may have resulted in an end to his friendship with you," Olivier explained, choosing his words with unusual care. "It's put him into a terrible state. Thus, the reason for our meeting."

Priscilla tightened her grip on Noël's arm. "Is that true?"

Noël finally regarded her sorrowfully. "I fear I have betrayed you, dear Priscilla. I will never forgive myself, and I suspect you will never forgive me."

"He's been listening to that awful Mountbatten." Gielgud's mouth twisted into a scowl as he spoke His Lordship's name. "Despite everything we tell him, he insists on believing the man is his path to a knighthood."

"If that were ever true, it isn't now," protested Noël.

"I would point out, most humbly, that I received my knighthood before anyone else at this table," Olivier interjected.

"You must be referring to me, Larry," Gielgud said irascibly. You beat me to a knighthood. You beat me to everything."

"I don't know that I've mentioned it before, that's all."

"Only about two hundred thousand times."

"Not to worry, that will end soon," Larry said with a prideful smile. "I am, as you may know, soon to become a lord."

"Whatever you are, you will remain always a pain in the ass," Gielgud retorted wearily.

"I must concede that Louis is not the friend I thought he was," Noël said sadly. "He is in thrall, I believe, to that scar-faced devil who does his dirty work."

"Excuse me," Priscilla interrupted, "but what scar-faced devil?"

"Colonel Geoffrey Wolfe," Noël explained. "He acquired the scar fighting for king and country in Burma. Mountbatten fell in love with him during that campaign. Wolfe has been his lapdog ever since."

Colonel Wolfe must have been the scar-faced man with Oliver at Buckingham Palace, Priscilla thought. But what was Oliver doing taking direction from him?

"Are you all right, Priscilla?" Olivier asked, expressing concern in the wake of Priscilla's distracted silence.

"Dear Priscilla, I do owe you an apology." Noel's eyes were filled with remorse. Priscilla had never seen him like this. "I have been feeling wretchedly guilty ever since our last conversation."

"I've felt terrible, too," admitted Priscilla.

"I get far too carried away defending so-called friends who should not be defended and institutions that should be rocked, not protected. I allow myself every so often to forget that these people are not really friends. They bribe us with knighthoods and lordships, when we in fact are outsiders, mere actors.

It wasn't so long ago they were running us out of town, not handing out knighthoods."

"All very well for you to say, considering you have neither a knighthood nor a lordship," said a miffed Olivier.

"Nonetheless, he is right," said Gielgud.

"Well, that is your opinion, certainly it is not mine," mumbled Olivier.

"You are the nonconformist, Priscilla," Noël said admiringly. "A glorious gadfly who I should have been celebrating, not stifling."

"I'm not any of that, Noël, not intentionally," Priscilla protested. "I'm simply fighting to keep my head above water at this hotel, trying to extricate myself from the trouble I somehow find myself stumbling into."

"I'm just not sure how far we should go with this anti-establishment business," said Olivier apprehensively. "At least until I have received my lordship."

"Oh God, Larry," moaned Gielgud. "They have swallowed you up hook, line and sinker."

"They have swallowed us all," replied Olivier. "And frankly, I don't see a problem with becoming a lord."

"Well, have at it, dear boy," Gielgud said, barely containing his anger.

"Let's not fight over this," interjected Priscilla. She turned to Noël. "I hope we are still friends."

"I pray you can forgive me my many trespasses."

"They are forgiven and forgotten, if only because I need a favour from the three of you."

"Anything, dear girl."

"Perhaps not *anything*," cautioned Olivier.

"Don't worry, Larry, I'm sure Priscilla would never interfere with the attainment of your lordship," said Gielgud sardonically.

"I need the three of you to attend a seance," Priscilla said.

"A seance?" said Noël enthusiastically. "Bloody good!"

"Utter nonsense," declared Gielgud. "But for you, Priscilla, I will gladly go along."

"Whatever is this seance for?" asked Olivier doubtfully.

"It is to rid the Savoy of its curse!" pronounced Noël.

"This is a completely ridiculous idea," sniffed Olivier.

"Is it? I don't think so." Noël's eyes had taken on a challenging gleam. "Then come along with us, Larry. Prove me wrong."

"Proving you wrong, dear boy," Olivier growled, "will be one of my greatest pleasures."

"I have been proven wrong before," said Noël, sitting back confidently, fishing for another cigarette. "I just can't remember when."

"You were a mere youth," put in Gielgud, deadpan. "You were convinced Britain would never give up the American colonies."

Susie was gone for the day. The phones in 205 were not ringing. For the time being anyway, all was pleasant silence. Priscilla sat at her desk looking at her phone, balancing the pros and cons of making the call. She picked up the receiver.

"Oliver, it's Priscilla Tempest calling," she said when he came on the line.

The detective actually hesitated before answering, as though not sure who it was or what he should say. "Priscilla, yes," finally came out of him. "I wasn't—wasn't expecting to hear from you."

"I realize it's short notice, but are you free this evening?"

"This evening? Yes, I can be."

"No cases you have to solve before morning?"

"I've solved all the crimes I can for one day," Oliver said with a hint of humour.

"How about my flat, say eight o'clock? We can have a drink—but promise not to bring any red wine."

"How about fish and chips?" Oliver said venturing further into humour.

"If you do, Inspector Lightfoot's suspicions about me may prove to be correct."

"No fish and chips then," Oliver said with a laugh.

"See you tonight," Priscilla replied. She hung up feeling satisfied with herself. What was Oliver Brock doing at Buckingham Palace with the man who did Lord Mountbatten's dirty work? Two people who would seem to have no reason to be together. Two people who would seem to have no reason to be talking about her.

CHAPTER THIRTY-SIX

The Spider in Her Web

A few clothes shoved away, a bed more or less made, a quick removal of dishes from the sink and Priscilla's flat was all set for what?

Seduction?

Since she had already seduced, or been seduced by, Oliver, was it correct to define anything that might occur this evening as a seduction? And should she go so far as shagging him in order to discover what he was doing with this Wolfe character at Buckingham Palace?

She might be further ahead to simply confront him with a blunt question rather than waste time on the rituals of seduction.

Except, she had to admit, the rituals of seduction could be more fun.

If she chose the femme fatale approach, the question then became what should Mata Hari wear? Whatever she decided on, she didn't want to be obvious.

Or did she?

Going through her closet, she opted for her recently acquired silk Pucci jumpsuit. She held the ensemble in front of her before a mirror. Yes, that could do the trick. Whatever the trick might turn out to be. Perfume? Part of any decent seduction. Arpège, subtly applied, would surely drive him mad with passion.

In the kitchen, she considered a glass of Chablis to calm her nerves. Except, she discovered, her nerves did not require calming. The evening involved a man, thus she was more or less on familiar ground. Anything else and a glass of wine was a necessity. Perhaps two.

As she knew he would, Oliver arrived promptly at eight o'clock. Once again he was the well-appointed picture of the presentable copper, out there protecting the upper classes he appeared to disdain. Ensuring that the lower orders did not get out of line—or provide a threat to the likes of Lord Mountbatten and his henchman, Colonel Wolfe. Something of a hypocrite, she told herself.

"You smell wonderful," Oliver said once she'd closed the door behind him. As promised, he had arrived empty-handed.

"That sounded more or less like a compliment," Priscilla said.

Oliver looked immediately chagrined. "That came out wrong, didn't it?" This was the boyish Oliver. Another, better Oliver had been introduced in the bedroom.

"Not at all," Priscilla said. "I accept all compliments, even the subtle ones."

"Is it safer to say that you look extraordinary?" The second attempt came out in a rush, slightly garbled. Not only was the boyish Oliver back, so was the nervous Oliver.

"You look like you could use a drink," Priscilla said. "I have Stoli in the fridge."

"I'm not really a hard liquor drinker—"

"Have a drink with me," she said insistently.

"Okay, that's fine," he said, accepting the glass and inspecting its contents with a distrustful frown, as though it might contain poison.

She sat beside him and raised her glass. "This is how we started to get into trouble the last time."

"I don't remember any trouble at all," Oliver said. He clinked her glass. "Cheers."

"Cheers it is." She took a deep gulp of the vodka then watched as he sipped his and coughed. He caught her gaze and looked uncomfortable. "Not much of a drinker, I'm afraid."

"How can you be a detective if you don't drink?"

"That's what my father tells me."

"Ah yes, the famous Tommy Brock. You talked about him the other night. In his shadow, right?"

"Somewhat, yes." Oliver stared at his glass.

"Honoured by the Queen, I would imagine. For his remarkable service."

"Not by the Queen, but by Princess Margaret near the end of his career."

"Well, that's close enough, isn't it?"

"He was a bit disappointed it wasn't the Queen. As we all were. But there you go."

"I should tell you I was at Buckingham Palace yesterday. Tea with the Queen." As though she regularly had tea with the Queen.

"You don't say." As though he knew she regularly had tea with the Queen.

"I saw you there," Priscilla said, deciding to slap her cards on the table and see how he reacted.

He reacted quite coolly, to her disappointment. "Why didn't you say hello?"

Priscilla played it just as cool—or tried to. "You seemed quite busy. I didn't want to bother you."

"It wouldn't have been any bother at all," Oliver said matter-of-factly.

"I was having tea with the Queen, of course," Priscilla, pushing a bit. "What were you doing there?"

"I wasn't having tea with the Queen," Oliver said, smiling. An evasive smile, she thought.

"You visit Buckingham Palace regularly, do you? You don't strike me as an ardent monarchist."

"Hardly," Oliver said. "I was meeting with a chap named Wolfe."

Priscilla studied him closely, somewhat thrown by what came across as Oliver's matter-of-fact honesty. "A chap named Wolfe? An important chap?"

"I assume Colonel Wolfe is important. He works for Lord Mountbatten. Apparently, they've been getting threats and are apprehensive about security for an upcoming dinner at the palace. Mountbatten is to be honoured and they want to make sure there are no problems. But I'm sure you know all about this dinner, since I understand you will be there."

Priscilla gaped at him. "How do you know?"

"Wolfe told me," Oliver said straightforwardly. "He said that the film star Cary Grant was attending and bringing along a young woman from the Savoy Hotel. I inquired as to whether it was you. Colonel Wolfe was quite surprised that I knew you."

"I can imagine," said Priscilla, feeling unexpectedly comforted by what appeared to be a logical explanation for Oliver's presence at the palace. "Why did this Wolfe meet you there?"

"I suppose because that's where the dinner is being held, and it might have been that he was trying to impress me."

"Were you? Impressed, I mean?" Priscilla asked pointedly. She wondered if the vodka was starting to get to her.

Oliver seemed to pull back a bit. "As you suggested before, I'm not exactly a rabid monarchist."

"Yes, I did say that, didn't I?" The vodka, as she finished her glass, sent a delicious warmth through her body.

"Can I ask you something?" His expression had become subdued.

"Certainly."

"This Cary Grant fellow."

"What about him?"

"He's quite a famous film star, is he not?"

"A legend," Priscilla corrected. Was that a teasing quality in her voice? Careful of the vodka, she reminded herself. Mustn't get too carried away.

"Do you mind if I ask if the two of you are..." Oliver seemed at a loss for words. Priscilla could see no reason to help him out. "I guess what I'm trying to ask is, Is this Grant chap your boyfriend?"

The rather forlorn expression on his face made Priscilla decide to let him off the hook. "Mr. Grant was a guest at the Savoy," she explained. "He needed a date for this dinner, and he asked me to come along with him."

"That's all?"

"Isn't that enough?"

"Colonel Wolfe thought there might be more," Oliver said. "He wondered what I thought about that."

Which could help to explain the snippet of conversation she overheard.

"How could he possibly know about the two of us?"

"I may have said more than I should have." The sombre expression was replaced by one of sheepishness.

"Did he happen to mention that Lord Mountbatten does not want me at that dinner?"

"He may have said something about your appropriateness?"

"Appropriateness?" Priscilla began to feel the heat rise.

"I should say I also spoke to my father about you."

"Your father?"

"Frankly, he doesn't think I should be dating someone...well, someone with your background. I'm afraid Colonel Wolfe feels the same way. Which is why your name has been taken off the guest list."

"Possibly," Priscilla said, measuring out her words, "you might inform me as to what is wrong with my background, as you call it?"

"Dating around. With film stars and such."

"And such?" Priscilla found herself not so much shocked as furious. "Is this how you feel?"

"I do have to take my father's views into consideration," he said. "He's been a great influence on my life. I do my best not to upset him."

"As long as you don't upset your father, never mind about me."

"I didn't mean it quite that way."

"Yes, you did." Priscilla sprang off the sofa. "I think you should take your father's views somewhere else."

Oliver looked nonplussed. "I'm sorry if you're angry."

"I'm not angry," Priscilla shot back. "You and your father and Colonel Wolfe have merely pissed me off."

Oliver jumped to his feet. "Clearly I've made a mistake coming here tonight."

"You have made a huge mistake."

By the time she got the sentence out, Oliver was already at the door. He opened it, looked back and seemed to come to a decision. "There was a reason why I wanted to see you tonight."

"Other than to insult me?" snapped Priscilla.

"That bloke you talked about. Kirk Strong?"

"What about him?"

"He's suddenly on our radar at the Yard. I was going to ask if you had any information that might help us find him."

"I'm told he's left for America," Priscilla said.

"No, he hasn't," Oliver said firmly.

"How do you know that?" asked Priscilla in surprise.

"Our information is that he is still in London. If you hear anything, perhaps you'd be so kind as to give me a call."

"I would be so kind," said Priscilla coldly.

"Good night, Priscilla." Out the door Oliver went, leaving her numb and breathing hard, not sure what had just happened. Somehow the tables got turned. The seductress rejected. Instead of holding him to account for his behaviour, her behaviour had been called into question. Boyish Oliver's lout of a father had deemed her, sight unseen, as unworthy of his attentions. Colonel Wolfe, too, someone else who had never met her.

And Kirk Strong was not in America after all. If Oliver was to be believed, Strong was right here in London.

The phone began to ring. It was too late for phone calls. She wouldn't answer it.

But the phone kept up its incessant noise.

"Priscilla?" asked a distressed voice as soon as she put the receiver to her ear.

"Who is this?" Priscilla asked.

"It's Christine—Christine Keeler." Breathless. "I'm in trouble. There's been an accident. I need help." Of course, thought Priscilla fleetingly, how could Christine be in anything else? How could anyone associated with that awful dinner? The curse of the Savoy...

Pigs Eat Angels

"I—I didn't know who else to call. There was no one else I could trust." Christine's voice had become more breathless in its desperation.

"Where are you?"

"A police station on Lavender Hill. Number 176. I'm so scared, Priscilla. I'm afraid they're after me. I didn't know who else to call."

"Who's after you?"

"They drove into my car on the Upper Richmond Road, tried to kill me. The police don't seem to give a damn. Please—this is awful—please, could you come and get me?"

"Stay where you are," Priscilla said. "I will be there as soon as I can."

It was drizzling rain as Priscilla stopped her Morris Minor in front of the Lavender Hill Police Station's bland facade. Christine was a forlorn figure in a trench coat, huddled in the lee of the entranceway. As soon as Priscilla sounded the horn, Christine hurried down to the car and got in the passenger side. Her hair was plastered against her head from the rain and she looked ashen. She reached out to take Priscilla's arm, saying, "I don't know how to thank you."

"Where would you like to go?" Priscilla asked, pulling away from the police station.

"I can't go home." Christine's hand tightened on Priscilla's arm. "They know where I live…there's no one else I feel safe with."

"You want to stay with me?" Priscilla asked in astonishment.

"Would you mind terribly? Just for tonight. Until I get things sorted out."

Priscilla's windscreen wipers weren't working very well and the rain was increasing as she drove along Lavender Hill. She chanced a quick glance at Christine whose eyes were wide with fear. Priscilla had sworn to herself on the drive over to the police station that she would not feel sorry for this woman. Now she was feeling sorry for her.

"Very well," Priscilla said, resigned. "My flat it is."

Christine's hand came away from Priscilla's arm. "You're an angel," she breathed.

No, I'm not, Priscilla thought. A pushover, maybe. But no angel.

"Oh good, someone who's not as messy as me," Christine said as soon as they were inside Priscilla's flat.

As long as she didn't get a peek at the chaos in the bedroom, thought Priscilla. "Can I get you something? I don't have tea, but there's coffee."

"Is there something stronger?" Christine was in the process of shedding her trench coat, revealing a navy-blue dress. Already, Priscilla noted, the colour was back in Christine's cheeks and she seemed calmer.

"I think there's some vodka left."

"Perfect." For the first time since Priscilla had picked her up, Christine was smiling. "I could also use a moment in the loo."

"Through there." Priscilla indicated the closed bedroom door. "Please forgive the mess."

"It can't possibly be as bad as my flat." Christine sailed away.

Priscilla retreated to the kitchen and the vodka stored in the icebox. The bottle was half full, perhaps enough to get them through the night.

Christine was back at few minutes later, her hair more or less dry, swathed in Priscilla's white terry cloth robe. "I hope you don't mind," she said brightly. "I just had to get out of that dress."

Actually Priscilla did mind, although she was trying not to. "Not at all," she managed and then indicated the vodka bottle mounted on the kitchen table.

"That will do the trick," Christine said eagerly.

"Neat?" Priscilla held the bottle aloft.

"Naturally," Christine said, smiling.

Priscilla poured vodka into each of the glasses and handed one to Christine. "God bless," Christine said before downing a big gulp. Her cheeks flushed. "I must say, whether it's looking at photos of oneself naked or dodging people trying to kill you, vodka always helps."

"How are they trying to kill you, Christine?" Priscilla asked.

Christine finished off her glass and then helped herself to more before she answered. "A green military-style truck," she said. "It drove straight into the back of my car, sent me flying out of control off the road. The truck didn't stop. Lucky I wasn't killed."

"You're sure it wasn't an accident? Hit-and-run?"

"They'd like me to think so, but it was deliberate, I'm certain." She was sipping at the vodka. She gave Priscilla a pensive look. "Although, you know what? The moment it happened, I thought of that bloody dinner and the silly curse. Only it crossed my mind that perhaps the curse wasn't so silly. After all, I was the second person to leave that night, wasn't I?"

"Presumably so that you could go up and wait for Jack Cogan in his suite," Priscilla said. "Hours before you stabbed him with a letter opener."

"The police actually questioned me about Jack's death," Christine reported glumly.

"I didn't know." Hardly a surprise, though, given their history.

Christine's inquiry was casual enough but her look was wary. "I wondered if you might have told them about Jack and me. You know, what with the photographs you found."

"Not a word," Priscilla stated vehemently. "Not about you and not about the photos. Since they seem to think I might have something to do with Cogan's death, I thought I'd better keep my mouth shut."

"You don't still have those other photos, do you?"

Priscilla hesitated before she said, "I'm not sure what to do with them."

"Keep quiet about them would be my advice." She issued a plaintive laugh. "Two suspected killers drinking vodka together on a rainy night in London—cheers!" She raised her glass.

"Cheers," Priscilla responded and took a sip.

"It's been very difficult for me these past few years," Christine continued quietly. The anxiety Priscilla had seen earlier in her eyes was back.

"I'm sure it hasn't been easy for you."

"I—I'm virtually penniless," Christine said sullenly. "I didn't even have enough money for cab fare so that I could leave the police station. The lawyers, the tax people, they've taken everything. They were out to ruin me and, bully for them, they pretty much did. But even so, that doesn't seem good enough. They either want me arrested for murder or—better yet—dead."

"You keep saying 'they.'"

"The pigs in clover, the people who run our world, who don't want people like myself—or perhaps like you, too, Priscilla—shaking things up." Christine waved her empty glass around. "I think that's why they tried to kill me tonight."

"Because you shake things up?"

Christine nodded sagely. "Because I know *far* too much." She paused. "But if I tell you, then you're in danger too, if you're not already—it's the curse!"

"Not a curse," Priscilla corrected, "but evil people, yes, who don't need a curse to do what they do."

"What I should like," said Christine sombrely, "is to get away from this city. Escape to where it's safe. I have a friend in the Douro Valley in Portugal. A farm. Groves of olive trees. Wandering cattle."

"I have difficulty seeing you with cattle, wandering or otherwise."

"Not to worry," said Christine with a frown. "Without a farthing to my name, as they say, I'm stranded. The pigs are coming for me."

"What do you think? Did the pigs come for Jack Cogan, too?"

Christine snorted derisively and waved her glass around some more. "Jack, well, if ever there was a male ripe for the murdering it was our Jack."

"He wanted to hire me." As soon as the words came out of her mouth, Priscilla regretted them. But they seemed to do no more than amuse Christine.

"Are you serious? He was going to hire you? Why?"

"To keep me quiet about the two of you."

Christine was shaking her head. "I don't believe it."

In response, Priscilla got up and went to the closet. The leather bag containing the five thousand pounds Cogan had given her was on the top shelf, where she had placed it the night he was in her flat.

She plopped the bag down on the coffee table in front of Christine and then unzipped it. Christine leaned over to get a better view of the wads of banknotes inside. "Well, well," she said. "How much to keep your mouth shut?"

"Five thousand."

"My goodness," exclaimed Christine.

"Money that I don't want," Priscilla said.

"Yet, here it is," said Christine with a catty smile.

"I've probably said too much."

"Or not enough," responded Christine. "The police don't know about the photos. Do they know about that money?"

Priscilla gave her a look. "It's late and I'm tired," she said with a yawn.

She grabbed the empty vodka bottle and deposited it in the kitchen. She went to the closet and retrieved the duvet she used for any guests who weren't sleeping in her bed.

"You have the sofa," Priscilla said, throwing down the duvet.

"You are most kind," Christine said with a grateful smile. "Really, Priscilla, you are an angel. But you must be careful."

"Must I?"

"No matter what you think, no matter what they may tell you—and believe me at one time I heard it all from them—you are not one of them. The five thousand pounds is meaningless to them. They will use you and then destroy you."

"Not tonight," Priscilla said. "We will see what happens tomorrow. Meanwhile, let's get some sleep."

Priscilla didn't want them to, but Christine's words persisted in her head as she crawled into bed and, aided by the vodka, fell into a deep sleep.

Dreaming of pigs in clover.

Priscilla awoke with a headache and no idea how long she had slept. She lay there for a few minutes, pondering what to do about Christine. Were wicked people really after her? It was certainly possible, particularly if Christine was right and she really did know too much. Priscilla got up and opened the bedroom door and padded barefoot into the living room. Her robe was draped across the folded duvet on the sofa.

There was no sign of Christine. Or the bag containing five thousand pounds. There was, however, a note.

Off to Portugal. Thank you. You truly are an angel. Be careful out there. The pigs eat angels. Cheers, Christine. P.S. This way you don't have to explain five thousand pounds to the police.

Maybe she was an angel after all, Priscilla thought, holding the note, beginning to laugh at the madness of it all.

CHAPTER THIRTY-EIGHT

Calling All Spirits

Susie refused to go near Kaspar, so it was left to Priscilla to transport the cat to the Pinafore Room. From outside, appropriately, given the evening's seance, came the loud roll of thunder as rain pounded down on London. The gods summoning the spirits of the dead? wondered Priscilla as she bore Kaspar into the room.

Susie, her face ablaze with excitement, directed Priscilla to put Kaspar down on the round table she had set up. Orson Welles, Cary Grant, Noël Coward, John Gielgud and Laurence Olivier looked on with varying levels of interest. The novelist Norman Mailer had returned to New York unscathed. Christine Keeler, as far as Priscilla knew, was safely on her way to Portugal. The banker Quinn declined to come anywhere near Orson Welles, not so much fearing spirits but a movie director desperate for money.

The only light this evening came from the candles placed around the table. A properly eerie atmosphere, Priscilla decided. Kaspar's sleek black-ink surfaces gleamed in the candlelight.

"My God, that cat looks to be evil incarnate," said Olivier nervously.

Gielgud regarded his friend with mischievous delight. "I haven't seen you look so frightened since the time you forgot your lines making your entrance in *Murder on the Second Floor*."

"I *never* forgot my lines," stammered Olivier angrily. "That's a blatant lie!"

"Old chap, I was in the audience," Gielgud said with equanimity.

"Bloody hell you were!" thundered Olivier.

"Larry, you forgot your entrance in the second act of *Private Lives*," said Noël, the provocative gleam having moved from Gielgud's eyes into Noël's.

"I was given the wrong bloody cue!"

Olivier was searching around for support in such desperation that Priscilla felt sorry for him. "Gentlemen, please," she said quietly, "we should get started."

"Actually, I'm enjoying these three old hens pecking away at each other," said an amused Welles.

"I'm afraid we are still awaiting the arrival of Mrs. Whitedove," said Susie.

"Possibly having trouble getting her broomstick started," offered Orson. "Tell me, Noël, are you responsible for this evening's rain-drenched little drama?"

"Guilty as charged," Noël said. He added, "Tonight, if all goes well, the hotel will be rid of the evil spirits Mrs. Whitedove believes are responsible for the curse that haunts the Pinafore Room."

"I still say it's all utter nonsense," said Welles scornfully.

"Do keep in mind, Orson, that the current incarnation of the curse originated with the dinner you organized. You carelessly ignored my advice and sent Kaspar away. Since then all sorts of nasty things have happened, including murder."

"My goodness, old chap, you are not blaming me because I sent away the sculpture of a cat."

"No blame, just a reminder of the facts, that's all," said Noël placidly.

The doors to the Pinafore Room swung open to admit Mrs. Whitedove. "I have arrived," she announced—in a voice loud enough to wake any lurking spirits, thought Priscilla.

The spirit medium was bedecked in flowing robes of ivory and purple, her ravaged face bright with mascara and highlighted by a crimson smear of lipstick Priscilla imagined could be seen for miles.

"Well, well," murmured Cary, "there's an entrance for you."

Susie bolted over to lead Mrs. Whitedove, who seemed uncertain on her feet, to the table.

Mrs. Whitedove stopped when she spotted Kaspar, her face exploding with horror. "Evil is in this room," she croaked loudly. "*Evil!*"

"Really, Mrs. Whitedove, please restrain yourself," admonished Noël calmly. "We have a long evening ahead of us and so the fewer melodramatics, the better. You are going to drive the non-believers away before we even get started."

Mrs. Whitedove set piercing eyes on the playwright. "There you are, Noël. I am still waiting for the royalties from *Blithe Spirit*, seeing as how I inspired it."

"I have no idea what you're talking about, dear lady," Noël replied.

"You should know years ago that I cast a spell on you and your awful play," Mrs. Whitedove announced.

"That may explain why I have yet to receive my knighthood," said Noël mildly.

"It certainly explains the second act," observed Gielgud.

Susie touched Mrs. Whitedove's arm, and the older woman jumped. "Don't *touch* me, girl! I am not to be touched!"

"Apologies, Mrs. Whitedove," said a contrite Susie. "I believe we are all set for you. Please tell me if you need anything."

"Let us get everyone seated," said Mrs. Whitedove, abruptly all business. "I can already feel the presence of the spirits. Unhappy spirits, I might add. We must act quickly."

She swept to the table, her fierce eyes riveted on Kaspar. "This cat must be removed immediately!"

"What's wrong?" demanded Priscilla, coming over to Mrs. Whitedove. "Isn't Kaspar what this is all about?"

"Ah, there you are, Miss Tempest," said Mrs. Whitedove, throwing back her head as if in triumph. "I see you have decided to partake in the spirit world after all."

"Let's say I am willing to let you do what you do," Priscilla replied. "Let us proceed."

"Please, if we are to do this, you must first remove Kaspar. Place him in a corner if you will, but not on this table."

"Very well, if you insist." Priscilla picked up Kaspar and transported him to one end of the room. He didn't seem to mind.

"Much better," Mrs. Whitedove proclaimed. "Everyone, take a seat."

Priscilla sat—Cary on one side of her, Noël on the other. Gielgud and Olivier were next to Susie and Welles. Mrs. Whitedove scowled when she noticed Welles's ever-present cigar. "Be rid of that foul thing," she ordered brusquely.

"Why would I want to do that?" asked a sanguine Welles.

"The spirits hate cigar smoke."

"The spirits have a sense of smell?" Welles remarked, amused.

"Get rid of it." Not waiting for Welles to act, Mrs. Whitedove yanked the cigar from his mouth.

"What the—" Welles's plump face twisted angrily.

Paying no attention to him, Mrs. Whitedove held the smouldering cigar out to Susie. "Take it away!" Susie plucked the cigar away from Mrs. Whitedove and, holding it daintily, hurried out of the room trailing smoke.

Welles gave Mrs. Whitedove a withering look. "I don't suppose you have any idea who I am."

"Not only do I know who you are, Mr. Orson Welles, but I have seen your future. You are trying to make a movie that you have titled, for no good reason I can understand, *The Other Side of the Wind*."

"Anyone who reads a newspaper knows that," said Welles.

"You will *never* finish your movie." Mrs. Whitedove's voice rasped with authority. "You will film it for years and years, right up to the time of your death. But because you are cursed, so is the movie. It will not be completed."

"I aim to prove you wrong," said Welles. He was trying to put on a good front, but the energy had gone out of him.

"But you *won't*, Mr. Welles."

Welles waved her away with the hand that usually held his cigar.

Susie came back and took her seat. Mrs. Whitedove reached into the big cloth bag she carried and pulled out a large board that she positioned in front of her. "Now, everyone, place your hands on the table, palms flat, with your fingers touching one another."

"At least I don't have to hold Noël's hand," said Olivier.

"I've been holding it for forty years," Gielgud said.

"Quiet, please!" demanded Mrs. Whitedove. "We must have total quiet."

Everyone complied, accompanied by a flurry of back-and-forth glances. Mrs. Whitedove opened the board to display rows of letters and numbers.

"What is that?" demanded Olivier.

"The spirit board will enable us to communicate with the spirits," Mrs. Whitedove explained.

"I thought we were ridding ourselves of a curse," put in Welles.

"The spirits will reveal the path we must take in order to do that."

She placed a plaque atop the board. "Our spirit guide," she announced. "Now we approach the most difficult part of the seance: moments when we must cross over to contact the spirit world. For this, I require silence and complete concentration."

Candlelight flickered across the board. The ominous rumble of thunder rattled the windows. Mrs. Whitedove stood suddenly, dramatically, head thrown back as she began to chant,

Dead souls in time, dead souls in rhyme.
Rise spirits rise, tell us no lies.
Rise O spirits, rise, rise, hear our cries…
Help us to know, to see through your eyes…
The truth of the curse—that's the prize!

Mrs. Whitedove's voice dropped to a guttural rasp. The candlelight played off the hard edges of her face, her head held back, eyes closed, hands on the plaque. Her incantations became a nonsensical babble. She had fallen into a trance—or seemed to have. Priscilla wasn't sure if it was real or if she was putting on an act.

The plaque began to move from one letter to the next. Priscilla followed its progress intently along with the others.

"*T*…!" Mrs. Whitedove cried out. Then: "*E!*" And after that "*M*…"

"Tempest!" blurted Gielgud.

"Hush!" cried Mrs. Whitedove.

Priscilla, mortified, saw that the plaque had in fact spelled out her name.

"What is the meaning of this?" Mrs. Whitedove called out loudly, startling everyone. "Tell us, spirits. Tell us!"

The plaque began to move again. "*D*," Mrs. Whitedove announced. Then "*E*" followed by "*A*."

"Death," shouted Mrs. Whitedove, again startling everyone. All eyes were on Priscilla.

"What has this got to do with extinguishing the curse of the Savoy?" Noël asked.

Mrs. Whitedove once more called for quiet. "The spirits have their way. They will tell us what they want us to know— nothing more!"

The plaque began moving again. "That's the number one," said Orson. The plaque then moved to the number 5, and then quickly again to 5, followed by 1 and then 7 and finally 1 again.

"155171—what does that mean?" asked Cary, mystified.

No one said anything. Mrs. Whitedove righted herself, removing her hands from the plaque. Her eyes fluttered open. Her breath came in quick gasps. "They have departed," she announced melodramatically.

"What do you mean? Gone?" Welles said in exasperation.

"The spirits have spoken, that is the end of it."

"Tempest. Death. And then these numbers. That hardly brings about an end to the curse." Noël's displeasure was evident as he and the others began to rise from the table. "Frankly, I would have expected better from you, Mrs. Whitedove."

"Do not blame me," replied Mrs. Whitedove defensively. "I can only summon the spirits. I have no control over what they tell us."

"What are we to take from this, Mrs. Whitedove?" asked Susie. "Have the spirits issued a warning to Priscilla?"

"My job is to contact the spirits. Make of the results what you will."

"Such gobbledygook," said Olivier. "Why, you are going to scare poor Priscilla to, well, death."

Cary took Priscilla's hand. "That was quite unpleasant."

"The entire exercise was a waste of time—as I suspected it would be," Priscilla spoke in a shaky voice.

"What about those numbers?" Gielgud asked. "What are they about?"

"How would I know?" retorted Mrs. Whitedove, busily closing the board, depositing it along with the plaque into her bag. "Some things I can see, others I cannot."

"Very frustrating," said Cary, "and a bit frightening."

"Well, I don't imagine we lifted any curses tonight," Gielgud said.

Mrs. Whitedove looked at her watch. "I must be off." She gave Susie a dark look. "You will pay my cab fare."

"Is that a prediction?" Welles asked acerbically.

"That is part of the *price* of doing business with me."

"I will see you out, Mrs. Whitedove," Susie said. "We'll take care of your cab, not to worry."

"I always worry," said Mrs. Whitedove. "When you can see the future, you always worry."

She stopped at the door to peer back at Priscilla. "Be vigilant," she said. "You are surrounded by evil." She then focused a glare at Welles. "And watch him. He cannot pay his bill."

"Evil indeed," observed Gielgud.

155171

Everyone, with the exception of Orson Welles, had retreated to the American Bar for badly needed drinks. The bar was quiet at this time of night, the pre-theatre crowd having departed, post-theatre patrons yet to arrive. Priscilla had already consumed one Buck's Fizz and was about to order another. Since hers was a death foretold, she decided there was no harm in throwing caution to the wind.

"What happened to Orson?" inquired Cary.

"He seems to have disappeared," Olivier said.

"Mind you, if a medium divined that I wouldn't be able to pay my hotel bill, I might disappear, too," Gielgud said.

Cary leaned into Priscilla. "You must not take this nonsense seriously."

"I'm trying not to," Priscilla said.

"*Tempest, death?* Meaningless words." Cary looked at Noël. "What do you think?"

"It's probably nothing," Noël said carefully. "Still…"

"Still?" Cary said. "What do you mean *still?*"

"I've had experiences with Mrs. Whitedove in the past, and I do believe that, as mediums go, she is honest," Noël said, fumbling for a cigarette. "It's probably a good idea to treat this evening as nothing more than a parlour game. Even so, I would advise Priscilla to be vigilant."

"And get rid of that cat," added Susie.

"I'm not so sure." Noël had found a cigarette and was now inserting it into his holder.

"Mrs. Whitedove said it herself," Susie pressed. "Kaspar is evil."

"I would argue that it's Kaspar who overrides the curse—that is, if you believe in any of this. Get rid of him and you still have the curse."

That reduced everyone to silence. Patrons had begun to line up at the entrance to the bar. The theatres were out. Drinks were needed. A rumble of conversation bubbled up around them.

"I do wonder about the numbers." Priscilla, as though speaking to herself, broke the silence.

"Yes, those numbers are quite mystifying," Cary said.

"Those six numbers the board spelled out at the end, 155171," Priscilla said. "Do they mean anything to any of you?"

"Maybe they have some dark meaning," said Susie. "You know, like 666 in the Old Testament is the number of the Beast."

"How do you know that?" Gielgud asked her.

"My parents, good Church of England folk, made me go to Sunday school," replied Susie.

"I am impressed you can remember the numbers," Olivier said to Priscilla.

"How could I not?" replied Priscilla bleakly. "They might just get me killed."

Priscilla couldn't get the numbers out of her mind when she returned to her office. What did they mean? Nothing probably. She was mad to give what had happened at the seance any thought at all. Still, she found herself with a piece of notepaper, writing down the number sequence so that she wouldn't forget it: *155171*.

Movement in the outer office drew her out of her reverie. Major Jack O'Hara appeared. He was carrying Kaspar. He didn't look happy. "Sorry to disturb you, Miss Tempest."

"It's all right, Major," Priscilla said quickly. "I see you've found Kaspar."

"He was in the Pinafore Room. No idea what he was doing there. I understood you had taken possession of him."

"Yes, I'm afraid he got left behind this evening," Priscilla said. "Thank you for bringing him back."

"You are working late, Miss Tempest," O'Hara said as he brought Kaspar over to her desk.

"As are you, Major."

"Working to track down that blighter Harry Alan Towers."

"Any luck?"

"A bit. He took a flight to Toronto. I managed to get in touch with authorities, and they detained him when his plane landed. He's pleading ignorance, claiming that an associate, Kirk Strong, was supposed to have paid his bill. Now it turns out that Scotland Yard is also looking for this Strong character. A bit of a mess, I'm afraid." He looked at Kaspar. "Where would you like me to put this fellow?"

"Just set him down," Priscilla said. She did not want the cat anywhere near her. But what choice did she have?

"Interesting," O'Hara said, his eyes fixed on her desk as he deposited Kaspar.

"What's that, Major?"

"Those numbers," O'Hara said, his forefinger tapping the paper on which they were written.

"What about them?"

"I've seen them before, but I don't imagine—"

He suddenly had Priscilla's full attention. "Where have you seen them?"

"Similar numbers can be found on every police officer's warrant card."

"Warrant card?"

"The identification card all policemen carry. Each officer is assigned a six-digit number. It's nothing, obviously. It's just that those six numbers are similar." The Major gave Kaspar one last baleful look. "Makes you feel a bit uneasy, doesn't he?" O'Hara gave a shrug. "Must be off. Good night, Miss Tempest."

O'Hara was halfway out the door when Priscilla had a thought. "Major…"

He turned to her. "Yes, Miss Tempest?"

"Kirk Strong, who was supposed to take care of Mr. Towers's bill?"

"That is what our Mr. Towers claims," the Major said.

"Any idea why the police are looking for him?"

"They tell me he's the suspected mastermind of a scheme to blackmail well-known people who should know better but can't behave themselves." O'Hara was in full authority-figure mode, very comfortable territory for him, Priscilla reflected. "A bit unusual, if you ask me. But could be that's why he associated himself with Towers. Gave him access to guests here at the Savoy. Why people such as myself have to stay constantly on our toes. Villains like that are always about, aren't they?"

"Do the police have any idea where Kirk Strong is?"

"I'm not sure, but he's probably long gone by now."

"Thank you, Major."

Major O'Hara's eyes narrowed. "Everything all right, Miss Tempest?"

"I'm like you, Major. I dislike people such as Mr. Towers and this Kirk Strong preying on our guests."

"We will bring 'em to heel, not to worry."
Priscilla was left alone. Except for Kaspar.
He refused to take his eyes off her. Damn cat.

Good Night, Dear Priscilla

Feeling miserable, Priscilla crossed the deserted Front Hall and came out onto the Savoy Court. Cary Grant, his arms folded and looking as though he just walked off a movie set—or out of a dream—leaned against a Rolls-Royce Silver Shadow. He grinned and said, "I thought you might need a ride home."

"You are far too kind, Mr. Grant."

"Not at all, Miss Tempest." He dashed around to open the passenger door. "Your carriage awaits."

As soon as she stepped into the interior full of rich leather scents, the fatigue washed over her. She found herself fighting to stay awake as Cary got behind the wheel and started the engine. She reminded herself that Cary Grant was driving her home in a Rolls-Royce. A darned good reason to do her best to stay awake and savour the moment.

The Rolls seemed to float over the Strand on air. As they passed the imposing facade of Somerset House, the majestic spire of St. Mary le Strand, lights from the odd oncoming vehicle illuminated the hood's chrome accents and cast shadows across Cary's celebrated profile. Most men, she reflected, had terrible profiles. Cary Grant most definitely was not one of those men.

It was a short drive to her Knightsbridge flat. Too short, as far as Priscilla was concerned. She directed him to a parking space in front. He turned off the engine. She put her hand on his arm. "Thank you," she said. "You're a lifesaver."

"I'm no more than a chauffeur, happy to be of service to a young lady whom I suspect is more troubled than she would like to admit."

"Nothing a good night's sleep won't cure," Priscilla said.

"I hope so," he said. He moved closer to her. "You know, in my movies Cary Grant makes certain that the women kiss him first. But tonight, Archie Leach would like to kiss Miss Priscilla Tempest. If that is all right with Miss Tempest."

"Yes, please, Mr. Leach," Priscilla said, nestling into his arms and turning her head up so that his lips could easily come down on hers. They kissed deeply. The temperature inside the Rolls intensified. Archie Leach be damned, Cary Grant was kissing her passionately. "I want you to come up," she murmured against his mouth.

He held her away with a gentle smile. "I'm going to walk you to your door."

He got out of the car and went around to open the door for her. She stepped out, and together they went up the walkway to her building. He stopped and drew her to him so that they could kiss once more. "Good night, dear Priscilla," he said. "It has been an evening I shall never forget."

"I do believe you are saying a polite no," she said.

"You need sleep more than you need me."

"That's not true. Tonight, more than anything else, I need Cary Grant."

"I'm afraid you would end up with tired old Archie Leach, and very disappointed."

"Impossible," she said.

He kissed her again. "Besides, how can I leave a rental Rolls-Royce overnight on a London street? The fates are against us, I'm afraid."

He kissed her one more time and then went back to his car, leaving her weak-kneed, out of breath and a little sad.

Priscilla fell into bed, heart pounding, mind swirling with thoughts of a spirit world that promised her death and a movie star who declined to sleep with her.

She had been rejected by Cary Grant! No wonder sleep refused to come.

She tossed and turned until the phone rang. Her heart leapt. Cary having changed his mind?

Cary hadn't.

"Priscilla, this is Mariella." A tortured voice on the edge of panic. "Mariella Novotny."

"Yes, I know who you are, Mariella," Priscilla said, sitting up in bed, grasping the receiver. "What's wrong?"

"I am so sorry to ring you so late. I am at a call box. They are after me."

"Who? Who is after you?"

"Please, please, can I come to your place?" Mariella sounded even more frantic. "You are my last hope."

She was beginning to think she must be the last hope late at night for most of the women in London. "Do you want me to call the police?"

"No!" Mariella sounded more frantic than ever. "No police. Please. I just need a place to rest for a while."

"Do you know where I am?"

"Yes, I have your address. I am nearby, in fact. A couple of minutes. Please!"

"I will meet you out front," Priscilla said.

"Thank you, thank you." Mariella's voice filled with relief. "I won't be long."

Priscilla forced herself out of bed and dressed hurriedly in a pair of pedal pushers and a T-shirt, at a loss to understand why Mariella would come to her flat at this time of night. She was halfway down the stairs before it struck her that Mariella shouldn't know where she lived.

And yet she did.

Out on the street, Mariella, a small, shadowy figure in a short leather coat hurried toward her. When she reached Priscilla, she threw herself at her, tiny face full of anguish. "I am so sorry, Priscilla. So sorry." She kissed Priscilla hard on the mouth.

Priscilla was so taken by surprise that she caught only the briefest glimpses of the black delivery van, vaguely heard the sound of an opening door, as hands grabbed at her, pulling her away enough so that a cloth could be shoved against her mouth and nose. Her nostrils filled with the awful aroma of chloroform. Struggling, she reflected that the smell was like that of nail polish. Her vision began to blur. She choked on the rag pressed hard into her face. Everything slipped away and she tumbled down a dark rabbit hole.

At the bottom of the deep hole, Kaspar the cat's bright eyes gleamed evilly out of the dimness. Kaspar was saying something Priscilla couldn't quite make out. But that wasn't possible, was it? Black cats, no matter if they were real or sculptures, couldn't talk. But this one could: *"Tempest…death…Tempest death…Tempest …death…"* On and on.

Priscilla jerked into consciousness, breathing hard. The world began to come back into focus. Mariella was an uncertain hazy shape in front of her.

"You're all right, Priscilla," Mariella was saying gently. "It's all right."

Mariella was wrong about that, wasn't she? Nothing was right.

257

Priscilla tried to take in her surroundings, get some sense of where she was, but she couldn't see beyond the fuzzy distortion of Mariella's face, pinched with concern. "You must co-operate." Mariella's voice was louder now. "Give him what he wants. He's quite desperate…"

"Wants…?" Priscilla murmured. She had no idea. "I don't know…"

"Please, co-operate with him. He will be back soon. Just tell him."

Priscilla's head had cleared enough so that she could focus on the formidable presence in a long black coat emerging from the surrounding darkness. Priscilla was impressed all over again by Kirk Strong's height and muscularity. "I tried to warn you, Priscilla." He spoke directly to her, ignoring Mariella. "I told you to stay away from this. But you wouldn't listen."

Mariella backed away to allow Strong to draw closer. He adjusted his glasses as though to satisfy himself that it really was Priscilla. He needed a shave, she couldn't help thinking. Perhaps a good night's sleep too, she thought as he trained bloodshot eyes on her.

"You have some photographs I want," he said.

"I don't have any photographs," she protested. "I've got nothing to do with—"

Strong slapped Priscilla hard across her face with the flat of his enormous right hand. The force of the blow knocked her off the chair she had been sitting on and sent her sprawling onto the floor. Mariella's scream pierced the air. One would have thought it was Mariella who got hit, Priscilla thought dimly, trying to clear away the stars exploding before her eyes.

From somewhere far away, Strong spoke in slow, clipped tones, as though otherwise she might have trouble understanding him. "I've been to your flat, Priscilla, but I couldn't find them."

"No…" Priscilla said. "No idea what you're on about…"

"That bastard Harry Towers left town with negatives and photos that I need in order to complete my arrangement with Lord Mountbatten. Harley had copies, but they weren't in his flat when I went around there after the police were finished. I know the police don't have them. That leaves you, Priscilla. You found his body. You must have taken the photos. Where are they?"

In the chaotic depths of her mind, it registered that whatever Strong was, however much the villain, he was not Harley's killer. She moved her head back and forth, seeing more stars. "I don't know…no idea…"

Strong hit her again. "Talk to me. Where are they?" His voice was hoarse with anger.

Mariella let out another scream. "You promised, Kirk. You promised no violence."

"Did I?" Strong said with a thin smile. "Then make Priscilla tell me so I don't have to hit her again."

"The police know…they're looking for you…" Priscilla managed.

"I told you, Kirk, I told you," Mariella said anxiously.

Kirk swung around and hit her. "Shut up," he said.

"You used me…" gurgled Mariella, holding the side of her face.

"Used you? How can I have used you? You are useless. All you've ever done is get in the way."

"Kirk, don't…don't say these things…"

Strong ignored her, turning to Priscilla and yanking her up off the floor. He threw her against the wall, knocking the wind out of her. She heard Mariella scream again. "Kirk, no!"

Priscilla collapsed again, and Strong towered above her, hands curled into big fists preparing to renew the attack.

That's when Mariella shot him in the leg.

Strong turned to her as though he couldn't quite believe it.

"You shouldn't say those things, Kirk...you shouldn't hit me..."

Mariella must have had the gun in her coat pocket. The gun gave the tiny figure who otherwise was lost in the overpowering shadow of Strong very much the upper hand. The power of a little gun, Priscilla thought as she attempted to regain her feet.

Strong said, "Goddamn," before he fell down, holding his thigh. His glasses fell away. He no longer looked quite so professorial, Priscilla thought. More like an average bad guy needing a shave. Mariella backed against the wall, still holding the gun, her face set with what looked to Priscilla like satisfaction. She had made the decision to use it and now she had done so.

"Get away from here—now," she said with steely calm.

Priscilla stepped past Strong, eyes fixed on Mariella. "Are you going to be all right?"

"No," Mariella said with a sorrowful smile. "But I will figure a way out. I always do. But you must leave."

"I'll get the police."

"No! Please do me this one favour, Priscilla. Do not call the police. Let me handle it. Please."

"You're sure?"

"Yes, please get out—now."

When Priscilla reached the door, Mariella called to her.

"I did, you know," she said.

"What?"

"I *did* sleep with the Kennedy brothers."

CHAPTER FORTY-ONE

His Father's House

Priscilla leapt down a set of narrow stairs that took her out into a bleak landscape filled with industrial-type brick buildings. As she ran, the silence was broken by the sound of her echoing footfalls and her heavy breathing coming in ragged gasps. She turned past a single streetlamp at the corner to be confronted by an endless street. She started along it with no idea where she was or where she was going, anxious only to get as far away as possible. It began to rain lightly. She stopped, leaning over to catch her breath. The first milky light of dawn filtered through the rain, lighting a cloud-covered sky.

Behind her, she heard a motorcar and turned to see the flash of oncoming headlights. Friend or foe? She decided to take a chance and wave the car down.

It slowed as it approached and then came abreast of her and stopped.

Oliver Brock was behind the wheel. "Priscilla, get in," he said. "Hurry."

"The information you provided me about Kirk Strong added to what we were already learning about an extortion plot against Lord Mountbatten. We've established that Mr. Strong was the group's ringleader." Oliver spoke as he navigated through streets beginning to come alive with early morning traffic.

"Obviously Strong could no longer be found at Swain's Lane," he explained, eyes fixed on the road ahead. "However, searching the house at No. 11, we found another address. I was assigned to stake it out. You can imagine my surprise when he rolled up with you in tow. I wasn't quite sure what to make of it until I heard the gunshot. Then you bolted outside." He cast a quick sideways look at her. "That's when I came after you."

"I'm so glad you did," said Priscilla with relief.

"We're not certain about the people Strong is involved with," Oliver continued. "You could still be in danger."

"Not surprising, I suppose," she said resignedly.

"That's precisely why I've been told not to take any chances as far as your safety is concerned," Oliver continued. "Right now, it's not a good idea for you to return to your flat. My father's house isn't far. I can protect you there. You look completely knackered."

"I am that," Priscilla admitted.

"Let's get you some sleep. I'll keep an eye out. Once you're rested, we can figure out next steps."

The exhaustion was a wave suddenly washing through her body. She could barely keep her eyes open. She nodded assent. "Yes, thank you, Oliver—thank you for rescuing me."

"I do believe you rescued yourself, Priscilla. I merely picked you up off the street."

"It was Mariella Novotny, actually. She saved me from Strong. She shot him. I hope she's all right."

"My colleagues are on their way to take care of the scene and arrest Kirk Strong. They will also deal with Mariella Novotny."

"And your father, the great Tommy Brock, who doesn't think you and I should be together, he won't mind me showing up on his doorstep?"

"I didn't say anything to you earlier, but Dad's had a rough time with his health these past few years. He's largely bedridden, confined mostly to the third floor of our house. He won't even know you are there."

"I'm sorry he's not well."

"By now I'm used to it. Part of life, I suppose. He was a remarkable police officer in his day. Like I told you before, a strong influence on me. Maybe too much."

"I imagine you joined the force because of him."

"Didn't have a lot of choice. It was in his blood, and therefore it was a given that it would be in his only son's as well. He was a very different police officer than me—very conservative, like most of his contemporaries. He believed in the status quo. His job, as he saw it, was to protect the ruling classes from the criminal classes. It was all very simple as far as he was concerned."

"Not what you believe, obviously."

"Not at all," Oliver said. "I think the establishment and its self-serving practices are destroying this country."

"Whatever you believe, I'm just terribly glad you're here," she whispered.

"I'm here for you, Priscilla," Oliver said gently. "Not to worry."

The half-timbered facade of a Tudor-style house with a steeply pitched roof and decorative chimneys stood against a threatening sky. Oliver parked in the wide drive beside the house. He led Priscilla through a side entrance, up a short flight of stairs and into a long hall. Further along the hall, a staircase stood adjacent to a large sitting room cast in gloom, full of dark wood furniture. The house struck her as rather old-fashioned and forbidding, but it was a safe place, and right now that's all that mattered. That, and a bed.

Oliver led her up to the second floor. "The guest room is on the right," Oliver instructed. "I'll be downstairs. There are a few phone calls I should make."

"I'm so tired," she said by way of explaining that for now sleep was all that interested her.

"I understand," he said.

She leaned to give him a quick kiss. "Thank you, again."

The bedroom contained a dressing table with an oval-shaped mirror, a large wardrobe and a high queen-sized bed in a mahogany frame. An ensuite bathroom with a large tub tempted her, but no, she was too tired for anything but that big, welcoming bed. She flopped onto it.

And promptly fell asleep.

CHAPTER FORTY-TWO

Father and Son

Priscilla had no idea how long she slept or what time of day it was when she awoke. She sat up, still feeling groggy, listening for sounds of movement. There were none. She could, however, hear noises coming from outside. She got up and padded barefoot over to the window. Below, in a small yard, Oliver was trimming the overgrown privet using a pair of garden shears. He wore jeans and a pullover. Watching Oliver at work, she took satisfaction in knowing that there was more to him than simply the copper in a suit. Although until now she hadn't thought a lot about the need for a gardener in her life.

She turned from the window thinking that she had better find a phone and call Susie, who undoubtedly would be starting up her usual panic.

As a policeman, Oliver almost certainly would have a phone in his bedroom. A good excuse for a little snooping, Priscilla thought. She went out into the hall. There was an open bedroom door on the other side. Oliver's bedroom? She slipped across and entered the room. The interior was much like her guest bedroom, except for the deep blue floral wallpaper. That would have to go, she thought. In fact, the whole house...well, the best thing would be to gut the interior and start from scratch. But perhaps she was getting ahead of herself. Otherwise, his room was everything she might have imagined: neat and tidy, no clothes lying about. She wondered how he felt about being involved with—honestly, she wasn't a slob, as such, although she might easily be mistaken for one. A touch messy perhaps.

The phone was on a side table adjacent to the bed. A Beretta pistol lay next to Oliver's identification card. Did he sleep with a gun beside him? Yes, he was a detective, but even so, she wasn't quite sure how she felt about the presence of a gun in their lives. *In their lives? Redo the interior?* Whoa, hold on a minute, she cautioned herself. There was the problem of his father. She would have to win over Tommy Brock. But she was such a charmer, she told herself, that couldn't be so hard.

She picked up the warrant card. The postage stamp photo showed a glum, humourless Oliver. It took her a moment to register the ID number next to the photo, the unique set of digits all police officers were assigned—*155171*.

Tempest. Death. 155171…

No, this couldn't be, she thought, throwing down the warrant card as though it were infected—which, in a way, it had become. The seance had been meaningless, a silly parlour game. Yet she was not mistaken about the number—it was burned into her brain—the same number that was on Oliver's warrant card. No getting around that.

Was this simply a dreadful coincidence? Or was she suddenly in the very danger Oliver was supposedly protecting her from? She backed out of the bedroom and into the hallway. What had initially seemed like Oliver arriving in the nick of time had now become questionable. Why had he not taken her to a police station? Why had he brought her to his father's house? She had been so relieved and tired when he arrived that those questions never occurred to her. But then if he planned to do her harm, why would he bring her to where his father lived? A former police inspector presumably wouldn't want his son murdering women in his house, even if he did deem her morals to be questionable.

Would he?

Maybe the best thing was to introduce herself to Tommy Brock and satisfy herself that she was imagining the worst. He would be the reassurance that she had become much too caught up in all the curse nonsense.

She started up the stairs to the third floor. At the top there was another landing and a door. The air hung hot and stuffy. She went to the door and knocked. "Mr. Brock, hello? May I come in?"

There was no response.

She knocked again and still there was nothing. Perhaps he was asleep, she thought. He had been in ill health lately, according to his son. Could something have happened to him? With an old man, anything was possible. It wouldn't hurt to check on him.

She tried the latch and the door opened. She stepped into a shadowy room with a slanted ceiling. The smell was of someone old and sick. She didn't quite shriek when she saw what was laid out on the bed—her hand shooting to her mouth stifled that.

The corpse on the bed wore a faded blue suit. Skin like dried brown leather clung grotesquely to the skull, emphasizing the black hollows of the eyes. Priscilla kept her hand clamped over her mouth to muffle further screams. She stared at the corpse with a combination of horror and shock. This couldn't be real. But lying before her had to be the much-adored Inspector Tommy Brock. Or what was left of him.

"Dad so admires Lord Mountbatten." Priscilla jumped in surprise, whirled around to find Oliver in the doorway. His face was sweaty and streaked with dirt from his work in the yard. He held the garden shears in his right hand.

"Oliver—" Priscilla began, numb with shock.

"He served with Mountbatten during the war. Loved the man. He would do anything for him. When he was told that a criminal group threatened to blackmail His Lordship, my father was determined to discover the culprits and put a stop to the plot."

Priscilla gathered enough strength to ask, "Determined enough to kill?"

"If it came to that, unfortunately, yes. I have tried many times to convince him otherwise, but he won't listen to me. He is very much his own man—a legend on the force back in the day.

"I've done my best, but I believe I have disappointed him in my career. I've worked to make him proud but without success. I'm weak when it comes to upholding law and order, according to him. I should be much tougher, much more of a man."

Priscilla fought to keep at bay the wave of fear beginning to wash over her. "Did you try to talk him out of killing James Harley?"

"Yes, I most certainly did." Oliver nodded eagerly. "But Harley was deeply involved in the blackmail, feeding scandalous information gained by the group to Jack Cogan, who had just taken over his father's failing news empire. He was desperate for the sort of salacious information this group could provide, to boost circulation—and he would pay well for it."

"Then it must have been your father I saw leaving Harley's apartment," Priscilla suggested. "I must tell you, he left some incriminating photographs behind. Very careless of him."

For an instant, Oliver's impassive face filled with confusion. "My father didn't make mistakes," he maintained defensively. Oliver paused to regain his composure. "All I can think is that the sound of the doorbell you rang interrupted him. He must have thought it was best to get out of there."

"Even so, as good as you say he was, as efficient, your father couldn't have acted alone. He must have had help identifying Lord Mountbatten's enemies," Priscilla said, trying to make sense of what Oliver was telling her. Did he truly believe that his father was the killer and not him? Apparently he did.

"Lord Mountbatten's man, Colonel Wolfe, was most co-operative in identifying those responsible for the extortion," Oliver explained, moving slowly, she noticed, but coming inexorably closer in a room that seemed to grow smaller and more claustrophobic each moment. "Particularly as the Queen's dinner approached. He was as determined as my father to make certain that no attempt at blackmail involving Lord Mountbatten would succeed."

"But what about Ethel Cambridge?" Priscilla asked, anxious to buy some time. "How was she a threat?"

"Mrs. Cambridge was making threats she should not have been making. Dad was forced to take an action he regretted but that he felt was necessary. Luckily, I was able to inject myself into the subsequent investigation and cover for him."

"That's when you met me." As she spoke, Priscilla eyed the bedroom doorway, figuring out the possibilities for getting past Oliver. Those possibilities did not look good.

"So wonderful on the one hand and yet unfortunate." There was a hint of sadness in Oliver's voice.

"What do you mean?" Priscilla did not like the sound of that word.

"As I told you previously, my father was critical of what he viewed as your rather...questionable reputation. I've tried to assure him that the two of us are in love and you hold no threat, particularly if we marry."

Marry? The murderous Oliver Brock? Priscilla shuddered. God help her...and with *that* wallpaper...

"However," Oliver went on, "I'm afraid he is not convinced."
Which sounded even worse.

"What do *you* want, Oliver? You don't want to hurt me, do you?" Her mind was racing, dreading he would do exactly that.

"It's not up to me, Priscilla," Oliver said reasonably. "My father decides these things."

"Your father decides nothing," Priscilla argued. "You are your own person. You say you care about me, love me; that means *you* can decide not to hurt me. You can do that. The way you feel about me, the way"—and here she nearly choked on the words—"I am feeling about you..."

"Then you *do* love me," Oliver said excitedly.

Priscilla had to force herself to say, "You know that. You know how I feel."

"Yes, yes, I do." Oliver sounded like a happy schoolboy hearing words of love from his first girlfriend.

She stepped away from him, trying to hold on to an expression she hoped would be mistaken for undying love. Her leg hit the edge of the bed. She could retreat no further. Oliver moved closer, blank-faced, the shears in his hand.

"My love," he said gently.

"Oliver," she said imploringly, pressed against the bed. His expression was softly loving. If she didn't know better, she would have thought he was about to kiss her.

But he wasn't.

"Please...you *know* this isn't your father. It's you, you're the one who's going to do this..."

"Get away from him," Oliver ordered. The loving voice was cut off.

In desperation, Priscilla turned and yanked at the bedsheet beneath the corpse, sending it flying into the air. The remains of Tommy Brock hit the floor, his parchment-like body coming apart as it did.

Oliver's face flooded with horror. "Father!" he cried, leaping toward the bed. In his haste, Oliver tripped. He landed hard on his father's corpse. That gave Priscilla the moment she needed to dash for the door. She made it out and started down the stairs, Oliver's plaintive cries coming from the bedroom.

Then, as she got to the second floor, the cries ceased abruptly. She heard Oliver's footsteps descending. Sprinting into the bedroom, she spotted his pistol on the nightstand. She managed to grab it as he crashed into the room.

Priscilla turned, fumbling for the safety, as Oliver sprang at her with the shears. She fired point blank, hitting him in the chest, but too late to stop the blades from thrusting into her side. She cried out in pain, lurching away, then reeled past him, out of the bedroom. She was already weak, with blood from the wound running down her T-shirt and onto her leg.

By the time she reached the vestibule, the pain had become so intense she almost blacked out. She dropped the gun and collapsed to the floor. There was time enough to think in her wildest imagining that she might actually have gotten away, that she was going to live. But soon enough she realized that was no more than wishful thinking. It had nothing to do with reality. Reality was Oliver, somehow very much alive, suddenly on the landing above. His expression was a mixture of hate and regret as he swayed uncertainly for a moment, then fell forward and toppled down the stairs.

Priscilla managed to rise to her feet. She started backing toward the door, watching him, willing him not to move.

But then he moved. Bleeding from his chest, blood streaming down his face from where he had landed and broken his nose, Oliver, against all odds, lifted himself to his feet, uttering a primal howl of rage.

Before Priscilla could get away, he threw himself against her. Then the small reservoir of strength Oliver had been able to summon gave out. He uttered a final, angry cry before letting her go, and she burst out the door.

A passerby walking a small white dog reacted in alarm as Priscilla stumbled down the walk toward him. "Help," she called out to him. "Help me…"

The dog began to bark.

CHAPTER FORTY-THREE

Recovery

The crisply uniformed nurses manning Priscilla's drab grey ward in the grand Victorian pile that was St. Bartholomew's, Britain's oldest hospital, made no pretense of hiding their excitement when Cary Grant strode in. He was dressed casually in a brown corduroy sports jacket. He carried a huge bouquet of flowers.

As he neared the entrance to Priscilla's room, done in the same grey tones as the rest of the ward, the nurses gathered agog at their station. Cary took all the rapt attention in stride. Once the movie star, always the movie star, Priscilla concluded as he came into her room. If anything could draw her out of her funk in the aftermath of shooting the lover who used a pair of garden shears to attempt to kill her, it was Cary Grant with flowers.

She sat up in the white-frame hospital bed, thrilled to see him but at the same time wishing that she had thought to put on at least a smidgen of makeup.

"As you can plainly see, I have brought you flowers," he announced.

"You didn't have to," Priscilla said, delighted nonetheless— and there was the added benefit of him being the first visitor in the past three days who wasn't dour-faced, asking a lot of questions that were either threatening or demanding or a combination of both.

"Nonsense," Cary said, all but lost behind the bouquet. "I cannot tell you how many of my co-stars I've had to bring flowers to over the years. Deborah Kerr in *An Affair to Remember* comes to mind." He gave the flowers a stern look. "What we need is a vase of some sort."

"Put them down on that table over there, and I'll get someone to bring a vase," Priscilla ordered.

Cary did as he was told, happy to be rid of them. He bounced over to sit beside her, taking her hand. "Actually, I should not forgive you."

"Why is that? What have I done?"

"You embarked on another adventure that, from what I can understand, almost got you killed. I don't like you dead, Priscilla. I much prefer you alive."

"Well, much to my amazement, I've managed it, more or less," Priscilla conceded.

Cary held her hand tighter. "Look, I don't know the details, but I do know you've had a tough time of it. You're a courageous young woman and you don't stop, but that doesn't mean you're not suffering. I hope you're going to be all right."

Priscilla hoped so too, not feeling particularly courageous, definitely suffering and wanting nothing more than to bring everything to a stop and disappear into the clouds. But for Cary she rallied a brave smile. "Cary Grant is holding my hand. I'm going to be okay."

"You should know that the Queen has cancelled her dinner for Lord Mountbatten, to avoid any potential scandal. I'm not sure what it's all about, but they have arrested Louis's assistant, one Colonel Wolfe. All sorts of rumours are flying around."

"I suppose I'm not surprised," Priscilla allowed. "What with Colonel Wolfe's arrest, it's probably not a good idea for the Queen to be celebrating her cousin."

"It sounds like Louis has been a very bad boy, or he has allowed himself to be associated with bad boys. He assures me he's the innocent victim of an extortion plot. Louis is always the innocent in these matters." He gave Priscilla another severe look. "Or do you know things I don't?"

She did, but Cary didn't have to know. She wasn't sure if she had sorted everything out herself.

"The way I'm feeling, I don't know much of anything," Priscilla said aloud.

"I'm not here to quiz you, dear Priscilla. I'm on my way to the airport but wanted to see you and say goodbye."

"I'm sad that you're leaving." And she was. The good men always seemed to be exiting, she thought. The crazy ones stuck around and tried to kill her.

"Back to L.A. and business." He stood and then bent to buss her on the forehead. "I will miss you."

"Miss you, too," she said, tugging him gently by the tie so that she could bring him into lip-kissing range. "That's much better," she murmured. "A proper goodbye."

Cary was flushed as he straightened and then presented her with one last crinkly Cary Grant smile, the one that he saved for the women in his life—Katharine Hepburn, Sophia Loren, Deborah Kerr, Grace Kelly, Audrey Hepburn and now Priscilla Tempest. "Make sure you get those flowers into a vase," he advised in a voice that was full of emotion.

And then he strolled away, leaving a trail of awestruck nurses in his wake, seeming to take the air with him out of the room. She felt empty, even more alone and dejected than ever. The nurses slipped away. The ordinary hum of hospital life resumed. She lay back in the bed, brushing away the damnable tears that seemed to spring from nowhere this last while. There was so much else to consider other than Cary Grant. He was fading myth; the reality of what had happened now reasserted itself.

The questions from police had been relentless. Inspector Lightfoot, in particular, appeared to struggle with the notion that his straight-arrow, anti-establishment subordinate could have killed three people he deemed to be a threat to the very ruling classes he railed against.

Priscilla, as patiently as she could, repeated time and again that it wasn't Oliver doing the killing; in his mind, it was his father—the great Tommy Brock, the copper's copper who admired Lord Mountbatten and was a true believer in, and protector of, the status quo.

"Our investigation is ongoing," admitted Inspector Lightfoot grudgingly, "but right now we suspect DC Brock was able to engage the services of a former pathologist he had previously arrested on drug charges. We think the pathologist was paid to mummify the remains of Tommy Brock. The son truly is a sick blighter, I must say."

What Oliver, the sick blighter in question, would have to say about all this remained a mystery since, according to what the nurses were telling her, he had yet to regain consciousness. He had been rushed to the same hospital as Priscilla. She'd had nightmares about him regaining consciousness and then turning up in her room and smothering the life out of her with a pillow.

There was no curse, Priscilla told herself yet again. Kaspar was a cat sculpture, nothing more. There was a very disturbed man killing people because he thought that's what his father wanted. There was the pain from the wound in her side, which would eventually go away. The pain in her cracked and betrayed heart? That would take much longer to heal.

She must have dozed off because the next thing she knew Susie was beside her bed, holding an ugly green cut-glass vase.

"Mr. Grant phoned from the airport," she said. "He asked me to find a vase." She held up the green thing as evidence.

"Much appreciated, Susie."

"Plus, I couldn't wait to get here to tell you the news."

"About what? Have I been promoted to assistant manager at the Savoy?"

Susie let out a burst of laughter. "You must be joking. However, it is a good thing that Mr. Banville has been asking about you."

"That is not necessarily good," Priscilla said.

"Actually, he seems quite concerned. But that's not what I want to tell you."

"What?" asked Priscilla impatiently.

"The Queen!" exclaimed Susie.

"What about the Queen?"

"She wants to see you—*again!*"

CHAPTER FORTY-FOUR

The Queen's Own

Perhaps because her second audience with the Queen had elevated Priscilla's status, or maybe due to the fact that she had been wounded in action, whatever the reason, a maroon-coloured Bentley saloon car was sent for her, accompanied by a crisply uniformed chauffeur.

This time, the car barely slowed for security as it swept through the gates of Buckingham Palace. This time, she was not left alone to fend for herself. A red-coated footman escorted her through the palace to the Green Tea Room—slowly, given the pain in her side that had forced her, at least temporarily, to walk with the aid of a cane. "Her Majesty is running a bit late, ma'am. Perhaps you wouldn't mind waiting in here," said the footman, diverting her through a side door.

Priscilla found herself in a drawing room, the coffered ceiling obscured by two great chandeliers. A seated royal personage in a gilt frame glared down at her from his perch above the elegant fireplace, not happy to have been left alone with a mere commoner.

Commander Peter Trueblood, head of the secret organization known as the Walsinghams, came through a doorway at the far end of the room. He was an all-too-familiar bloodless wraith-like figure against the royal red of the carpet as he crossed to her.

"Miss Tempest, we meet again." He might have added *unfortunately*. "How are you feeling?" He had taken note of her cane.

The question contained all the compassion of an elevator announcing the floor number.

"Rather confused, Commander." Not to mention peeved at being ambushed by the man who might well be as dangerous as Oliver Brock. The Walsinghams were known to use extreme methods in order to protect the royal family. "I believe I have been summoned by the Queen."

"You will not be seeing Her Majesty today," said Trueblood brusquely. "There has been a misunderstanding."

"Whenever I encounter you, Commander, there always seems to be a misunderstanding."

"There are a number of things of which you should be aware," Trueblood said. "I wanted to take a few moments to brief you."

"And what things would those be?" asked Priscilla, certain the worst was soon to come.

"Scotland Yard has charged DC Oliver Brock with the murders of James Harley and Jack Cogan. Charges are also expected soon in connection with the death of Mrs. Ethel Cambridge. DC Brock is in serious condition as a result of the gunshot wound he suffered, but I am told he is expected to recover."

"I'm relieved to hear that," Priscilla said, thinking that no matter what, she did not wish to be responsible for someone's death. "He is a very sick man who needs help."

"I don't know about that," Trueblood said distastefully. "He certainly needs to be in prison for the rest of his life."

"What about attempted murder charges?"

Trueblood looked puzzled. "Who did he attempt to murder?"

"Me," Priscilla blurted. "He tried to kill me with a pair of garden shears."

"Yes, well, that investigation is ongoing."

"Ongoing? How can it be ongoing?"

Trueblood hesitated, as though gathering his thoughts around what he was about to say. "There is little doubt in the minds of everyone at Buckingham Palace that there has been an extortion attempt against Lord Mountbatten. The extortion was planned and executed by a criminal group specializing in such things, led by an American, Kirk Strong. Along with my partners at MI5, we have learned that Strong and his associates set up Lord Mountbatten with a former inmate of the Borstal prisons. Had that indiscretion been revealed and photographs of the two made public, it might very well have ruined an exemplary life and a stellar career."

"Or perhaps it would have brought some much-needed scrutiny into his dealings," interrupted Priscilla.

"Which go beyond this investigation's purview. Let me remind you that His Lordship was the victim of an extortion plot, based on his personal activities—ones that are no longer illegal in this country, I might add. That plot, I am relieved to say, has failed. Kirk Strong is currently being held pending his deportation to America, where he is wanted on a number of outstanding fraud charges. On his arrival in New York, he is to be taken into custody by agents of the Federal Bureau of Investigation."

"Then he won't be charged here?"

"The FBI has requested that he be turned over to them."

"How convenient for you," Priscilla said accusingly. "This way, you avoid having to deal with Kirk Strong—but you will still have to face the fact DC Brock killed three people, encouraged and guided by Colonel Wolfe."

"Colonel Wolfe did what he felt was necessary to protect a member of the royal family from ruination."

"And what is to happen to Colonel Wolfe?"

"As a result of accusations that have been made against Colonel Wolfe, although they are unfounded—"

"You know as well as I do that Colonel Wolfe is behind DC Brock's actions."

"I know no such thing," Trueblood maintained. "DC Brock acted alone, driven by whatever demons swirl inside that sick head of his." Trueblood drew a deep breath. "However, given the circumstances, Colonel Wolfe thought it best to offer his resignation. Lord Mountbatten has accepted it."

"And what about Mariella Novotny, who probably saved my life?"

"I believe for the time being Scotland Yard is questioning her," Trueblood said. "No decisions as to her future have been made, although I understand she is being co-operative—demanding but co-operative."

The demanding part certainly sounded like Mariella, thought Priscilla. Good for her.

"In the meantime," Trueblood continued, "I am told that should DC Brock survive and go to trial for his crimes, there is enough evidence gathered at his father's residence so that it will not be necessary for you to testify. Nor will it be necessary for your involvement to be made public. There is, however, the matter of missing photographs."

"Photographs?" Priscilla adopted the look of innocence she always hoped would work with Clive Banville but never seemed to. Perhaps it would work better here.

"Mariella Novotny has told the detectives questioning her that the reason Kirk Strong abducted you is because he believed you had in your possession certain photographs that could be used against Lord Mountbatten."

"I understand what Mr. Strong thought," Priscilla said, "but I know of no such photos."

"You don't have them?"

"How could I possibly have them?"

Priscilla wasn't sure where he emerged from, but suddenly there was Lord Mountbatten, coming toward her out of the gloom at the far end of the room. He wore a double-breasted grey business suit. His craggy face was without humour, set severely.

"Admiral, I wasn't expecting you to be present," a stunned Trueblood said.

"I thought I'd better reacquaint myself with this young woman who seems to believe I am such a terrible person," Mountbatten stated with a dour smile. "Try to convince her I am the victim of events, not the instigator of them."

"Commander Trueblood has been doing his best to make me aware of that," Priscilla said.

"And has he convinced you?"

"I don't know. Does it make any difference?"

"It makes a great deal of difference," maintained Mountbatten. "I have spoken to your boss, Clive Banville, and Noël Coward is a friend. I am working very hard to ensure that he receives the knighthood long overdue to him. One of the problems has to do with Noël's lifestyle. This is an obstacle that can be overcome, but it is a reminder that we all have secrets, parts of our lives that we keep to ourselves. Unfortunately, there are unscrupulous men who would take advantage. That is what has happened to me. Thankfully, these people have been stopped in their tracks."

"By means of murder," put in Priscilla.

"That's quite enough," ordered Trueblood.

"I have given a lifetime of service to Queen and country," Mountbatten declared. "The Savoy equally has been a bulwark since what? 1889? Maintaining the highest standards and the finest repute. When all of that is threatened, it is up to all of us to overcome those threats. Whether you like it or not, Priscilla, you are part of this, and one of us. You must behave accordingly."

"Is that an order, Lord Mountbatten?"

"That is a suggestion," replied Mountbatten dispassionately.

"There we have it," Trueblood said, turning to Priscilla. "Thank you, Miss Tempest. A footman will see you out."

"That's it?" demanded Priscilla. "That's the end of it? I am summarily dismissed?"

"With our gratitude," said Mountbatten. "Now, I must be off as well."

He was starting away when the same door Trueblood had come through opened.

"There you are, Priscilla," said the Queen of England. She was dressed in pale blue today, a pearl necklace at her throat, a grave expression on her wan face. "I was wondering what had happened to you."

The Queen delivered a hard, angry glare in Mountbatten's direction. "Please understand, Dickie, I remain most upset with you."

"Ma'am?" Mountbatten actually seemed taken aback. Apparently he had already suffered the Queen's ire. Now here she was back to provide more.

"Don't think for a moment I'm unaware of what's gone on here. Cancelling your dinner is not the end of it by any means. Do you understand?"

"I'm sorry you feel that way, ma'am. I assure you that I have—"

"Stop it!" The Queen interrupted angrily. "I don't want to hear your excuses. You have dishonoured the family you are sworn to serve. I suspect if it were not for Priscilla, you would be in a great deal of trouble—perhaps on your way to prison, from what I have been told. And what a dreadful fool I would look for seeming to support you."

Mountbatten lowered his eyes but said nothing. Commander Trueblood looked nervous, as though he might be next in line for the Queen's wrath.

Instead, she turned from the two of them. "Come along, Priscilla. Our tea will be getting cold."

CHAPTER FORTY-FIVE

Pals

"Are you still in a great deal of pain, my dear?" the Queen asked, watching Priscilla use her cane to ease cautiously into a chair at the little table where Queen Victoria's tea set was laid out. Getting away from her cousin appeared to have calmed her considerably.

"Only when I have to deal with men like Commander Trueblood."

"The commander is an acquired taste," the Queen acknowledged.

"It is one I have yet to acquire, certainly." Priscilla looked at the Queen with concern. "Is everything all right, ma'am?"

"I am very angry with Dickie, but not at all sure what to do about him without creating questions and perhaps bringing about the scandal that his people have been doing everything in their power to avoid."

"I understand, ma'am," Priscilla said.

The Queen lifted Victoria's teapot and poured into Priscilla's cup. "You may observe that once again I am serving the Earl Grey." She gave Priscilla a questioning look.

"Delightful," Priscilla hurried to agree.

When she finished, the Queen inquired sympathetically, "Did they give you a rough time?"

"A bit of one, yes." Priscilla admitted. She was daintily holding her tea cup.

"What did they want from you?"

Priscilla reached down to where she had dropped her shoulder bag. She extracted a manila envelope and placed it on the table beside the tea set.

"What's in there?" the Queen asked, eyeing the envelope.

"Photographs."

The Queen hesitated before she said, "And that's what they were after?"

"Yes." That was a very nervous yes. Priscilla was deep in unknown territory, totally uncertain as to how the Queen would react.

"But you didn't hand them over."

"I believe it would be better if you had them," Priscilla said. She felt her stomach tighten. Never a good sign.

"What would you like me to do with them?"

"What you will, ma'am," Priscilla answered hesitantly. "I'm afraid I don't trust anyone else."

"I'm banishing Dickie to Ireland," the Queen said in a strong voice. She took her gaze off the envelope. "Out of harm's way. That's about as far as I can go for the time being. I will also inform Commander Trueblood that you are not to be bothered further."

"I very much appreciate that," Priscilla said, thinking it would be much easier to get back to her job without the threat of Commander Trueblood hanging over her.

"As for whatever is contained in this envelope..." Picking it up, she rose from her chair and walked across the room to where a fire burned in the hearth. She hesitated a moment and then dropped the envelope onto the fire. Flames quickly curled around it.

Wordlessly the Queen returned to the table. She straightened as she took her tea cup and sipped its contents. Then she set the cup down and turned gentle eyes on Priscilla.

"I like you, Priscilla," the Queen said decisively, as if that would be the end of any discussion of the matter. "I know a great deal more about recent events than I am letting on. In fact, I have found over the years that it is helpful to know much more than I let on."

"I'm sure," Priscilla said.

"I've taken the liberty to let your general manager know that I am most impressed with the actions you have undertaken to protect the Savoy's good name and also what you have done for the monarchy. In the future, should you need help, you are to contact me. I'm not sure I will always be able to do much, but I believe I can at least lend a sympathetic ear amid the loud noise from men who don't pay much attention to the likes of us."

"I—I hardly know what to say, ma'am." And she didn't. The Queen of England as her new pal. Who could possibly imagine? "I am most appreciative."

"However, I do have one caveat."

Uh-oh, Priscilla thought. Aloud she said, "I suppose I must keep my mouth shut."

"No, no, I want you out there talking, being contrary. Your inability to follow orders, to plough through and find your own way, those are characteristics of yours I admire tremendously."

"Then what?'

"A royal decree, in force when you are with the Queen…"

"Yes?"

"You must drink tea."

"I will consider your proposal," Priscilla said.

They laughed together, raising their tea cups, Priscilla and her new best pal, the Queen of England.

A Confession

Given the early evening hour, when things ordinarily quietened down, the Front Hall was unusually busy. It took Priscilla a moment to spot the formidable figure of Orson Welles at reception. Two porters were stationed beside a cart piled high with his luggage.

"Ah, there you are, Miss Tempest." The cunning gleam was firmly set in Welles's eyes. He wore a mink coat that had the effect of enhancing his immensity. A Swiss Alpine hat, complete with feather, topped his head. "Come to make sure I haven't absconded with the towels?"

"Not at all, Mr. Welles," Priscilla replied.

"But relieved that I have paid the bill and am not slinking away in the dead of night."

"It never crossed my mind," Priscilla said. Although it had.

"Fortunes change," Welles said. "The vagabond's life. One moment I'm destitute, the next the gods are smiling on me and I'm off to Romania, first class, to play an emperor for the Germans. I'm rather at home playing emperors."

"What about Mariella? Will she accompany you?"

"Alas, Mariella, as I'm sure you know, has been detained by the authorities." Orson arranged an expression of sadness that, to Priscilla, didn't seem quite authentic. "Trouble seems to follow that woman wherever she goes. Not that I'm particularly upset. I believe she mistook me for someone with money, a failure of perception I found breathtaking. Worse, she kept comparing me to the Kennedy brothers. I'm afraid I suffered by comparison."

"I'm sure that's not the case," Priscilla said tactfully.

"I do have to say, it's been a time, Miss Tempest," Welles replied merrily.

"It certainly has, Mr. Welles. I hope you return soon."

"As soon as I can find another producer with money, I'll be back," Welles said.

He started away but then paused and turned around. "Oh, and by the way, see what you can do about that curse by the time I return, will you?"

"I'll do my best," Priscilla said with a grin.

And off he went, followed by the porters and his luggage, a furry mastodon parting the throngs. When Welles was out the door, Priscilla turned to find Noël Coward coming off the lift. "You just missed Orson Welles," she said to him.

"Life is full of unexpected little blessings," Noël said with a smile.

"Thank you again," Priscilla said. "I'm not sure what would have happened to Mr. Welles if you hadn't settled his bill."

"Quite selfish of me," said Noël. "This way the Great Orson can continue to be the Great Orson, and I can continue to know better."

She kissed him on the cheek. "Be careful, Priscilla," Noël said cheerfully, "I do believe employees kissing guests is strictly forbidden at the Savoy."

"As you keep telling me, I'm a bit of a gadfly around here," Priscilla said.

"You certainly are, my dear, and thank goodness for it. Where are you off to?"

"I'm about to end a curse."

"My goodness," exclaimed Noël. "End the curse of the Savoy? Never! It's too good a story."

"I was ready to leave," Mrs. Whitedove said huffily as soon as Priscilla entered the outer office at 205. She was smoking a cigarette and wearing a purple-and-gold scarf around her head, as though to remind Priscilla that she was indeed the spiritualist she claimed.

"I was having tea," Priscilla said.

"I do not like to be kept waiting," Mrs. Whitedove said. "Evil continues to permeate this place, and yet I sense you still do not believe."

"You sense correctly, Mrs. Whitedove. However, I do firmly believe you are a bit of a charlatan."

Mrs. Whitedove stiffened. "If you called me here to insult me—"

"I called you here because I want to know."

"Depends on what you want to know," Mrs. Whitedove said noncommittally, inhaling languidly on her cigarette.

"A number, that's all—*155171*."

Mrs. Whitedove seemed caught by surprise. "Why would you want to know about that?"

"I can imagine announcing 'Tempest. Death.' That came easily enough in light of why Susie called you. But what about 155171? The spirits certainly didn't send those numbers to you."

"Do not underestimate the power of the spirits." Mrs. Whitedove extinguished her cigarette in the ashtray on Susie's desk.

"I do not underestimate your duplicity, Mrs. Whitedove. You are clever enough, I will give you that. Using those numbers adds mystery to your performance, and therefore a veracity that might otherwise be missing."

"As I keep telling you, it is the spirits who provide this information," said Mrs. Whitedove airily. "I am merely the conduit through which it is delivered."

"Mrs. Whitedove, here is the thing: I have yet to approve your invoice. I will do so and add one hundred pounds, but you must tell me how you came up with 155171—and do not insult my intelligence continuing to insist that spirits had anything to do with it. We both know that is not true."

Mrs. Whitedove was rummaging inside the leather bag slung around her shoulder.

"One hundred pounds you say?" Her worn and lined face took on a gambler's slyness.

"That's what I said."

"One hundred and fifty."

"One hundred. You talk, or the invoice never gets paid and we can go to court after I have a word with my friends at Scotland Yard."

"The evil of Kaspar has possessed you," breathed Mrs. Whitedove peevishly..

"Tell me," said Priscilla insistently.

Mrs. Whitedove hesitated, as though looking for one last line of defence. Finding none, she exhaled loudly and said, "There was some trouble last year with Scotland Yard."

"What kind of trouble?"

"There was no merit to the charges. They were entirely fabricated by the police." Mrs. Whitedove managed to summon dismay at the thought of anyone having the audacity to make allegations against her. "They accused me and several associates of, well, the term they chose to erroneously employ was *fraud*. Nothing to it." She gestured with a bony, dismissive hand to emphasize the point. "One of the detectives involved in the case became obsessive about bringing me and my friends to what he called *justice*. Ha! There is no *justice*. I was being harassed because of who I am."

"How does any of this explain the numbers?" Although Priscilla was beginning to reckon she knew the answer.

"When the detective questioned me, I demanded to see his identification. He showed me what he called his warrant card."

"DC Brock had the identification number 155171."

That certainly got Mrs. Whitedove's attention. "How do you know that?"

"Go on, Mrs. Whitedove."

"I now use DC Brock's ID number in all my seances. It lends them a certain…authenticity, as you say. Small revenge for what DC Brock has done to me—although I don't suppose it affects him one way or the other."

Mrs. Whitedove would never know just how much effect it had, Priscilla thought.

"Then when you used that number during our seance, it was chosen randomly, simply because you dislike DC Brock?"

"The spirits," Mrs. Whitedove maintained adamantly. "They tell me to use the numbers. I listen to them. They guide me. Why does this interest you so much?"

"Something that needed clearing up," Priscilla said. "And now it has been, that's all."

"When do I get paid?" Mrs. Whitedove was on her feet, adjusting her shoulder bag.

"I will write you a cheque," Priscilla said, rising and going into her office. Mrs. Whitedove followed closely, as though to ensure Priscilla didn't make a run for it.

She came to a stop when she saw Kaspar on the end table. "He is *still* with you," she croaked. "I was right. The curse fills the air. It has not gone away."

Priscilla could not be bothered to respond. She withdrew her chequebook from a bottom drawer.

"Say what you will, Miss Tempest," Mrs. Whitedove prattled on fiercely. "Deny the curse at your peril. That number means something to you. I'm not sure what, but it is part of what has happened to you as a result of the curse."

"You are mistaken, Mrs. Whitedove. You have simply led me back to the place where all this began—there is no curse, and you are a fraud." That's what she would always maintain, for public consumption anyway. The thought she couldn't shake off? Perhaps that was something else...

Priscilla finished writing the cheque and handed it to Mrs. Whitedove. The medium inspected it carefully before folding it in two and sticking it into her bag. She gave Priscilla a piercing look. "I will need my cab fare."

"I'm afraid you're going to have to pay for your own cab," Priscilla said.

"I always get cab fare," persisted Mrs. Whitedove.

"Not tonight," said Priscilla.

"Then a curse be on you!" Delivering one last wild-eyed glare, Mrs. Whitedove flounced away.

Priscilla, in the dim light of her office, became overwhelmed suddenly by emotion. Those couldn't be tears. Impossible. She found a tissue that she used to dab quickly at her eyes, her gaze falling inescapably on Kaspar gleaming malevolence in the dimness.

His almond-shaped eyes were aglow. And that cat smile...he *was* smiling wickedly, knowingly, she was sure of it...

Or was it her imagination? That's it, she decided. That's what it had to be. After all, there was no such thing as a curse.

Guests of the Savoy

Mr. Orson Welles continued the mad business of putting together, partially filming and then discarding various movie projects. To make ends meet, he acted in other people's productions, working across the globe for just about anyone who would hire him. Toward the end of his life, Mr. Welles lived in Los Angeles, where he could be found lunching almost daily at Ma Maison, at the time the most popular meeting place for Hollywood's cognoscenti. Mr. Welles occupied a table, usually alone, in the midst of the restaurant, where he could see and be seen, an immense presence scowling at the passing famous and powerful. They would often stop to pay homage to the wunderkind who, at the age of twenty-five, had made what is regarded as the greatest American film, *Citizen Kane*. As Mr. Welles often pointed out: sadly, everyone wanted to meet him but no one wanted to hire him to direct a movie. As prophesied by Mrs. Whitedove, Mr. Welles never completed *The Other Side of the Wind*, the movie he announced at the Savoy. A version of the film was finally pieced together, but not until many years after his death. Welles died of a heart attack in 1985 at the age of just seventy.

At the time Cary Grant turned down Mr. Alfred Hitchcock, the legendary star had been retired for two years, after acting in over seventy motion pictures. Although he received many offers, Mr. Grant stuck to his guns and never made another film. At the end of his life, he toured the country doing one-man shows titled *A Conversation with Cary Grant*. He had a massive stroke while on tour in 1986 and died in Davenport, Iowa, at the age of eighty-two.

Arguably, no director in the history of cinema has been more influential than Mr. Alfred Hitchcock (sorry, Mr. Welles). That said, *Topaz*, the movie he went off to France to make, was neither a critical nor a commercial success. Frederick Stafford, the Czech-born actor who played the lead, was certainly no Cary Grant. After *Topaz* bombed, Hitchcock quickly disowned it. He made only two more films, *Frenzy* and *Family Plot*, before his death in 1980 at the age of eighty.

Mr. Norman Mailer actually did stab his wife, Adele Morales, with a rusty penknife during a drunken party in 1960. Ms. Morales was rushed to hospital in critical condition. Meanwhile, Mr. Mailer appeared on a talk show without mentioning anything about the assault. He was finally arrested, but his wife refused to press charges. They divorced in 1962. According to one of his biographers, Richard Bradford, Mr. Mailer was an egotistical brawler, boozer and relentless fornicator who married six times and sired eight children (he adopted a ninth). On a quest to write the Great American Novel, he churned out a wide range of fiction, non-fiction, plays, essays and even movies, including the widely distributed *Tough Guys Don't Dance*. Whether he succeeded in his quest is a matter of debate, leaning to, no, he didn't. Mr. Mailer mellowed considerably in his later years and died in 2007 at the age of eighty-four.

With the passage of time, Miss Christine Keeler, the so-called party girl who dominated tabloid headlines in the early 1960s has evolved into a victim in the scandal that blew up in the wake of revelations about her affair with Conservative cabinet minister John Profumo. Miss Keeler argued that in a world of lies, she was the only person who went to jail for lying. Miss Keeler claimed in her autobiography that she had been made pregnant by John Profumo (and had an abortion as a result). She also accused Stephen Ward, the osteopath who introduced her to Profumo and later committed suicide, of being "a spymaster" for Soviet intelligence. There was no evidence that was the case. Suffering from chronic obstructive pulmonary disease, she died pretty much penniless in 2017 at the age of seventy-five.

Whispers about Lord Louis Mountbatten kept London's gossip mills—and various intelligence agencies—busy throughout his life. Lord Mountbatten himself admitted that both he and his wife, Edwina, had trouble keeping to their own beds. After his death in 1979—caused by a bomb planted by the Irish Republican Army—a biography of Lord Mountbatten by British historian Andrew Lownie revealed intelligence reports, going back as far as 1944, detailing his "lusting" for young men. An FBI report described the Mountbattens as "persons of extremely low morals." Mountbatten's sexual activities while in Ireland was one of the reasons the IRA gave for assassinating him.

Miss Mariella Novotny really did claim to have slept with both John and Robert Kennedy. London's *Daily Mirror* described Stella Capes—Miss Novotny's real name—variously as a "blonde bombshell" and "a sex queen" who hosted orgies, armed with a whip and wearing a black mask. Miss Novotny claimed she had been enlisted by Scotland Yard as an undercover informant, exposing corrupt police officers paid off by London gangsters—so-called "bent coppers." A friend of Christine Keeler, she played at the outer edges of the Profumo scandal. It was a producer, Mr. Harry Alan Towers, who flew Miss Novotny to the United States, promising to make her a star. She met actor Peter Lawford, who introduced her to president-elect John Kennedy. Their affair attracted the attention of the FBI. Towers was arrested for what is now called sex trafficking (white slave trafficking back then). As a result of those charges, Miss Novotny was deported back to Britain. She died of a drug overdose in 1983. However, her biographer, Lilian Pizzichini, disputed the cause of death, suggesting the possibility that Miss Novotny was murdered by men in high places who wished to keep her quiet.

Not that it did Mr. Orson Welles much good, but in his lifetime Mr. Harry Alan Towers actually produced from eighty to 100 movies, most of them low-budget exploitation and action pictures. However, it was the darker side of Mr. Towers's career that was more fascinating than any movie he ever produced. Something of a man of mystery, Mr. Towers appeared to lead a double life. In New York, he was arrested for running what was referred to as a call-girl business. His girlfriend at the time, Miss Mariella Novotny, told the FBI that he was a Russian agent using his business to compromise important American men. Mr. Towers contended he had been set up, jumped bail and fled to Europe, where he supposedly concentrated on movies, although where Mr. Towers was concerned, nobody could ever be quite certain. He died in 2009 at the age of eighty-eight.

Her Majesty Queen Elizabeth II, Britain's longest-serving monarch, died at Balmoral Castle on September 8, 2022, aged ninety-six. Undoubtedly, she took a great many secrets to her grave. Countless news stories, books, movies and television shows have dealt with how she weathered a multitude of controversies over the seventy years of her reign. At the time Miss

Tempest met her, the Queen was forty-two years old and had been on the throne a scant sixteen years. She had recently dealt with her cousin Lord Mountbatten's suspected involvement in a plot to overthrow the Labour government of Harold Wilson. His sexual proclivities, and reports that American intelligence had in fact been keeping an eye on him, did not help matters. That Mountbatten's behaviour at the time, both politically and privately, was mostly kept quiet says a great deal about the Queen's influence.

Miss Priscilla Tempest continues to head the press office at the Savoy Hotel. As to her future employment, well, that is always up in the air, is it not? We shall have to see…

But what about Kaspar?

Yes, there really is a Kaspar, and he is very much a part of the Savoy. The origins of the curse described in our story are, for the most part, factual so far as can be ascertained. Does the curse still haunt the Pinafore Room? That depends on one's belief in superstition. However, should there be thirteen for dinner, it is strongly suggested that Kaspar be added—just in case. He will require a white napkin to be placed around his neck, and, of course, he expects to be served the same dinner as the other guests.

Acknowledgements

Arriving back in Canada after six weeks in the South of France, I telephoned co-author Prudence Emery to discuss the editing of our fourth novel. It was afternoon in Victoria, BC, where she lived, and so I didn't think too much about it when I couldn't get hold of her. She would call me back later.

Only this time she didn't.

Later that night, I received an email from a friend of hers. Pru had died that afternoon.

She had been in deteriorating health for the past year after being diagnosed with a rare condition called multiple system atrophy, a Parkinson's disease-like degenerative neurological disorder that affects motor control. There is no cure for MSA, and though it does lead to death, it can be managed for years.

When we'd last spoken, Pru had seemed to be doing better and was very much involved in the writing of this novel. The news of her death, so unexpected, was devastating.

We had met in 1974 on the set of a horror movie, *Black Christmas*. She was the film's unit publicist, and I was the freelance writer doing a story about it. Pru would go on to do the on-set publicity for 120 movies over the following years. Every so often she would phone and say something like, "Basie-kins"—I was always Basie-kins—"come to Israel to interview Tony Curtis." The next thing I knew, I was interviewing Tony and, more enjoyably, snorkelling with Pru in the Red Sea.

We were together in a snowbank in remote Barkerville, BC, with the American actor Rod Steiger. We drank champagne with the legendary British playwright John Osborne in Montreal. She used her wiles to get the English actor Oliver Reed to drink with me (not so hard!) and the actress Ann-Margret to kiss me (long story!).

Along the way we became great friends, often—too often perhaps—hearing the chimes at midnight and turning the moon to blood.

I knew that in an earlier life Pru had worked in the press office at London's iconic Savoy Hotel, but I had no idea of the kind of glamorous existence she had led while there until she published her memoir, *Nanaimo Girl*.

In the five years she was at the Savoy, Pru rubbed shoulders with just about everyone who was anyone. Playwright Noël Coward was a friend (she organized his seventieth birthday party at the hotel). She dined with the legendary director John Huston; got to know another legend, musician Louis Armstrong; kept still another legend, actress Elaine Stritch, company late into the night. Canadian Prime Minister Pierre Trudeau crossed her path, and so did Beatle Paul McCartney.

Pru lived the high life. Champagne arrived at the press of what became known as the "waiter button" on her desk. Not surprisingly, that button made her very popular not only with visiting celebrities but also with the Fleet Street reporters who chased them. There was first-class travel on the Continent, various affairs and lovers, but eventually, even for Pru, that life became too much. She retreated to her native Canada and began a new career as a publicist.

Reading about her years at the Savoy, I was struck with the notion that they might form the basis for a novel: a plucky young heroine at a grand hotel in Swinging London transformed into an amateur sleuth solving a mystery or two. I telephoned Pru and ran the idea by her. "I've never written a mystery," she said. "Well, I have never stayed at the Savoy," I countered. "Together we make the perfect combination."

And we did. If nothing else, I thought as we started out, our fledgling collaboration would be a good excuse to rekindle a long-ago friendship. We talked on the phone for hours about old times, people who had come and gone in our lives. Once in a while we even discussed our book.

I've often been asked what it was like collaborating with another writer after a lifetime of going it alone. With Pru it was a joy. I would write a couple of chapters in Milton, Ontario, and then send them off to Pru in Victoria. Pru came up with our heroine's first name, Priscilla. I added her surname, Tempest. Thus was Priscilla Tempest born. It was that kind of easy collaboration. If I needed inspiration for Priscilla, I didn't have to look much further than Prudence.

We wrote what became *Death at the Savoy* more or less as a lark, with no particular expectation on the part of either of us. Due to the efforts of our agent, Bill Hanna, publishers were found in Canada and France. The film rights were optioned. An audio book deal was made. Prudence and I found ourselves writing not one Priscilla Tempest mystery but four of them. No one was more amazed by this turn of events than the two of us.

Curse of the Savoy was completed with a heavy heart, but completed it was, aided by the remarkable group that has worked on all four of these novels. My wonderful wife, Kathy Lenhoff, was back in her role as first reader. Editors James Bryan Simpson and Ray Bennett have worked with me for years. Editor Pam Robertson has overseen all four novels and once again smoothed out a plot thicket or two—or three! Much appreciation goes to to copy editors Lucy Kenward and Noel Hudson and to everyone at Douglas & McIntyre in Canada, as well as at Éditions de La Martinière, our French publisher. Once again, a special shout-out to our agent, Bill Hanna.

Linda Scallion provided insights into the world of spiritualism, and Kim Hunter was the expert to talk to when you need information on mummifying a relative.

At the end of it all, there is Prudence, larger than life, so full of laughter and mischief, so dearly missed. Thank you, my dear Prudencia. None of this amazing adventure would have been possible without you.

About the Authors

RON BASE is a former newspaper and magazine journalist and movie critic. His works include twenty novels, two novellas and four non-fiction books. Base lives in Milton, ON.

PRUDENCE EMERY worked as the press and public relations officer at the Savoy Hotel, and later as a publicist on more than a hundred film productions. She is also the author of the best-selling memoir *Nanaimo Girl* (Cormorant Books, 2020).

Both Prudence and the fictional protagonist, Priscilla Tempest, held the job as press secretary at the Savoy. When asked just how much they had in common, Prudence would answer, with a twinkle in her eye, that "there are things that Priscilla does that I would never do... and there are things I have done that Priscilla would never do. I will not say anything else."

Emery died in Victoria, BC, on April 14, 2024, at the age of 88.

A PRISCILLA TEMPEST MURDER MYSTERY NIGHT

Inspired by the elegance and drama of the Priscilla Tempest Murder Mysteries and featuring some familiar characters, this downloadable kit has everything needed to host an exciting murder mystery party (except the gin). Includes a Hosting Guide, party invitation, cocktail recipe and character bios and booklets for 6 to 8 players.

https://bit.ly/3ByFAtx